A DC KENDRA MARCH CRIME THRILLER

AN EYE
FOR
AN EYE

Book 1 of the 'Summary Justice' series

Theo Harris

ALEMAR
PUBLICATIONS

An Eye for an Eye
Book 1 of the 'Summary Justice' series

Copyright © 2022 by Theo Harris
All rights reserved.

ISBN: 979-8-843874-85-8 paperback
ISBN: 979-8-352491-16-4 hardback

Second Edition, © 2024

PRAISE FOR THEO HARRIS

'Couldn't put the book down. Loved it.'

'The pacing of the book was impeccable, with each chapter leaving me hungry for more.'

'WOW! I was not expecting much but totally surprised.'

'One of my favourite reads of the year, waiting for the rest of the series!'

'Really gripping storytelling that is clearly well researched and engaging.'

Cool gritty romp... Excellent lead character and plot - really enjoyed the story.'

Before AN EYE FROM AN EYE...
There was

TRIAL RUN

An exclusive Prequel to the **'Summary Justice'** series,
free to anyone who subscribes to the Theo Harris
monthly newsletter.

Find out what brought the team together and the
reasons behind what they do... and why.

Go to **theoharris.co.uk**
or join at:
https://dl.bookfunnel.com/7oh5ceuxyw

ALEMAR
PUBLICATIONS

———

Think you've gotten away with it? Think again!

CONTENTS

PROLOGUE

KENDRA MARCH STOOD PROUDLY TO ATTENTION, FINDING IT difficult to stop herself from smiling, as the commissioner of the Metropolitan Police approached with the highly polished and much coveted Baton of Honour. The greatly prized award was given to the student that met the highest standard of leadership and achievement and exemplified the values that the world's most revered police service strove to impress upon their staff.

'Well done, Miss March, you should be very proud of this achievement,' said the commissioner, handing over the award. 'I hope that you achieve everything you wish for; you have a very exciting future ahead of you, and I will be keeping a close eye on your progress.'

'Thank you, ma'am,' replied Kendra, beaming with pride.

She looked over at her grandparents, who had raised her from a very young age, and saw them both grinning from ear to ear, her grandmother dabbing away a tear.

There was so much for her to look forward to, and she couldn't wait.

1

CAPTURED

IT'S FUNNY WHAT YOU THINK ABOUT WHEN YOUR WORLD TURNS upside down and you realise it wasn't what you'd always thought it to be. Kendra was having one of those thoughts, a flashback to innocent days when everything had looked rosy and the world was her oyster. Now, looking out of the hospital window as the driving rain lashed against it, her thoughts were filled with pain, anger, frustration, and a sense of loss that she had always hoped to avoid.

But mostly pain.

At least he is still alive, she thought, hoping it would help. It didn't.

Her partner was lying in a bed in intensive care, on a different floor not too far from her, fighting for his life. There were tubes and wires attached to almost every part of his body, as his vitals were constantly monitored and checked for changes. He had lost a lot of blood, and doctors could not guarantee his survival.

Everyone at the station wanted to be Andy Pike's partner when his previous one had left on promotion, but it was

Kendra who had won that lottery. Pike had personally requested her as his new partner, having seen how diligent and dedicated she had been in performing her duties, however menial, when she had transferred to the Serious Crimes Unit as a fully-fledged detective.

'You just need to loosen up a little,' he had told her, 'don't be afraid to screw up and try and enjoy some of this crap, otherwise you'll go stir-crazy.'

And now he was at death's door with terrifying injuries, missing an eye and unable to walk, and she was in a wheelchair, with two badly broken legs.

'At least he is still alive,' she said out loud.

———

THEIR PARTNERSHIP HAD BEEN a spectacular triumph from their very first case. The combination of Pike's natural intuitiveness, bravado, and skilled trade craft, coupled with Kendra's meticulous attention to detail, knowledge of the law, and her now-famous talent with computers, made them an instant success. Their drive and enthusiasm in bringing criminals to justice was both refreshing and nauseating, depending on which side of the fence you were on.

Until that fateful day when they unwittingly volunteered to take on a tough new case involving the infamous Qupi gang. The Qupis, originating from Albania and led by their evil, one-eyed boss, Guran, had firmly established themselves in the East End of London as 'logistics experts.' They had mastered the art of moving weapons, drugs, cars, machinery, —and more recently, people—in and out of the East End. They controlled everything east of Ilford and had no interest in expanding further; their territory was more than adequate and extremely lucrative.

If you wanted anything brought in or taken out, then Guran Qupi was the man who controlled the operation - he was the man you needed to negotiate with. He was beyond vicious and took great pleasure in punishing those who let him down in any way. His party piece was to remove an eye, aping his own deficiency, which had been a result of the brutal fight that had brought him control of his successful empire.

He thrived on that reputation, it kept people in check.

The knife in the eye had proven worth it, however painful it was, as he was now king of the east and nobody could touch him. Despite his calling card and the sure-fire police knowledge that he was responsible, including repeated intelligence provided by trusted informants, there was not a jot of usable evidence that would help towards an arrest, let alone a conviction, and nothing was ever expected. He ruled with an iron fist and made sure that everybody knew it.

'NOBODY IS UNTOUCHABLE,' Pike had smirked at a briefing on Qupi's lucrative people-smuggling ring, 'give me a couple of weeks and I'll have all the evidence we need to put them away for life.'

Such was his confidence. He looked over at Kendra and winked, to which she rolled her eyes. His confidence was infectious - how could anyone doubt him?

The team – professionally known as the Serious Crimes Unit – or the 'dream machine' to the team itself, had gathered for their briefing, deep in the bowels of the police station. It was where they celebrated their frequent successes with tea and doughnuts, usually bought by the newest member of the team or by someone who'd screwed up in some amusing way. Today it had been Wilf Baker's turn, after inadvertently leaving the station with his ID still showing around his neck as he walked down the street, completely oblivious, much to the amusement of his partner, Nick McGuinness, who had stifled a laugh for a hundred yards before reaching over and hiding the ID.

'That's gonna cost you doughnuts, mate,' McGuinness had laughed.

The team was led by the long-serving Detective Sergeant Rick Watts, a powerfully-built man who had seen service in many specialist teams and whose icy stare had once worried Kendra. Watts had a reputation as a firm but fair supervisor, someone you did not want to cross by abusing his fair nature. His uncompromising attitude was typical of a battle-scarred, long-serving, 'old-school' officer, who everyone respected greatly. He knew how to look after his team, and he did it efficiently and effectively. Kendra had not taken long to warm to him as she quickly saw he was the type of leader they needed, someone who gave them space but quickly put them in their place if they crossed the line - which wasn't often, thankfully.

The team were close. There were only ten of them, but they worked well together, trusted each other implicitly, and had each other's backs.

It was a great posting for Kendra. She looked around at her team-mates, all clearly comfortable and confident in themselves and their work. She was proud and happy to be a part of it, despite having earned the nickname of 'Aunt Kim,' after the famous cleaning lady, for being whiter-than-white in her dealings. Meticulous in everything she did, God help anyone who tried to take shortcuts or bend the law in her presence. She had been that way since day one and could see no other way of doing her job.

'Here you go then, smart arse,' said Watts, as he handed over the case folder to the fist-pumping Pike. 'Show us all how it's done.'

'Get the cells warmed up, Sarge, we'll be done with this in no time!'

'Just don't screw up!' replied Watts.

Fate has a way of kicking you where it hurts.

2

RECOVERY

FIVE WEEKS LATER AND THERE THEY WERE, BOTH HANDCUFFED and strung up like two sides of beef in the cold Tilbury warehouse, bloodied and bruised from the pounding they had received at the hands of Qupi's cruel goons, who were enjoying their handiwork immensely. The surveillance operation they'd set up had been going well and they had made some progress, until they had stupidly given their position away, resulting in their being spotted and hauled out of their observation post from the back of their specially-adapted van. Now they were strung up and waiting to die. The goons howled like a pack of hyenas waiting to take the first and juiciest bite from their freshly stolen carcass.

They quickly fell quiet as Guran Qupi walked in. He looked at them both hanging there and took a long drag on his gold-plated vape pen.

'This is nice,' he said, blowing the sweet-smelling smoke into his captives' faces. Despite their precarious situation, Kendra could not help but notice his accent as Central Gheg -

as spoken in the capital Tirana and its surrounding regions, confirming Qupi's Albanian heritage.

He looked at the two warrant cards that were handed to him. 'So what does the Metropolitan Police want with such a small outfit as ours?' he said, grinning as he stared at them. Even his smile implied imminent violence.

'We're thinking of giving you a good citizens award for all the help you've given the local community,' said Pike, as blood dripped from the side of his freshly-cut, swollen mouth. 'And this isn't helping your cause, is it? Now, be a good chap and let us go so that we can get you a nice shiny plaque.'

Qupi laughed out loud and looked around at his men, prompting a round of booming laughter. He handed back the warrant cards to one of his men and took out a stiletto knife that he immediately flicked open. He looked very comfortable and content to be holding the weapon, like a child holding their favourite toy. It was no toy, though. Qupi had been using this very knife since the age of twelve and had killed his first victim just a few weeks later. He had joked amongst his peers that when it was his time to die, he wished that the blade would be buried with him, preferably not sticking out of his back. At the time it had prompted nervous laughter.

'Well, maybe I can persuade you to change your mind, as I would very much like to collect that award,' he said sarcastically, as he brought the knife up to Pike's face and without hesitation, thrust the sharp point into the left eyeball in one devastatingly rapid move.

Pike screamed as the knife entered and was then swiftly removed from the ruined eyeball. A thick dark fluid ran slowly down his cheek, and he quickly passed out, his head slumping forward as his wrists took the weight of his whole body. Blood dripped slowly to the floor, splashing and leaving strangely mesmeric star-like patterns where it fell from his still-rotating body.

Kendra had watched the horrifying attack in shock and stifled her response, not wanting to antagonise the lunatic gangster. She suddenly felt a fear unlike anything in her life, accompanied by a horrible gut-wrenching feeling.

'Do you have any smart words for me, Miss police lady?' Qupi snarled as he turned towards her and stared at her trembling face.

She shook her head, still in shock.

'That's good,' he replied, revelling in his beloved role as the renowned torturer. He moved up close and looked her in the eyes. As she swayed slightly, he stood stock-still and followed her with his eyes, as if watching a hypnotist at work. Kendra could sense malevolence in the man and knew she was in deep trouble.

'Now, be a good girl and tell me why the Metropolitan Police are looking at my small operation, and I will let you live, okay?'

'I doubt that very much,' Kendra said, attempting to be brave but resigning to her fate. She stared back into those eyes and saw no change at all, almost as if he was not disappointed in any way.

'Well that is a shame, it really is. Such a pretty girl. With such a good future if you helped us out a little, don't you think?'

Kendra kept quiet, hoping and praying that somehow, he would leave her alone.

When she didn't reply, Qupi walked back to the limp

figure of Pike. He turned back to Kendra and said, 'You like this man? Your lover?'

He could sense the change in Kendra, saw the fear in her eyes as he mocked her. Before she could reply, he jabbed the stiletto knife violently into Pike's left foot. The razor-sharp knife went straight through tendon and bones as if through butter, with just a little blood flowing through the hole in the sole of Pike's trainer, dripping slowly from the tip of the knife that Qupi had left in situ. Pike swayed slightly, still unconscious and unaware of the weapon jutting from his foot.

'Why so afraid? He didn't feel a thing! See?'

Qupi withdrew the knife and stabbed down again, just as violently. And again, three more times. Pike's trainer turned red from the blood, now pooling on the floor beneath him, spoiling the pattern he had made before. His foot had been destroyed and he had no clue.

The gangster walked over to Kendra, an evil smile playing on his lips, leaning forward as if to taunt her.

'You have such lovely feet; it would be a shame to hurt them like that.'

He looked at his cohorts and laughed out loudly, before saying something in Albanian that was just as amusing to the gangsters.

'We don't want to hurt you; we just want to know why you are here. Is that too much to ask?'

'You're an animal,' Kendra whispered, 'and you won't get away with this.'

'Maybe I will, maybe I won't.' He continued to smirk, before leaning in close. 'I think I will.'

He reached out his hand without looking back, knowing exactly what one of his lieutenants was going to put in it. The wooden bat was old and scarred, it had seen much use, none of it involving baseballs.

'Are you sure, you won't tell me?' He regarded at the bat lovingly, tapping it into his left hand.

Kendra looked him in the eye. She knew where this was going and there was nothing she could do or say to change it.

'Go fuck yourself,' she said, a determined look settling on her bleeding, battered face, tears streaming down her filthy cheeks.

She closed her eyes and prepared for death, with visions of her childhood appearing in her head: her wonderful and loving grandparents, the father she had not seen enough of, and the recent but fleeting lust-filled moment she had shared with Pike in the back of the van, taking their eye off the targets and onto each other – and which had led to their discovery.

She heard the crack of bone an instant before the excruciating pain that came from her now-shattered leg. With an ear-shattering scream, her world started spinning. A mixture of stars and distorted shapes mingled with sweat and tears and dirt, none of it helping with the pain.

'Are you sure?' he asked again. He beamed in contentment, loving every second, staring at the shattered limb as it continued to sway.

'Fuck you!' she was loud and angry, but her bravery was waning.

Tears, snot and saliva splattered the floor as she glared at him in defiance, wishing him dead.

He swung at the other leg, with the same devastating results. It was her turn to pass out. Weirdly, she could hear the raucous laughter and the harsh language of the gangsters echoing in the background as if she were at a theatre.

She felt herself being lifted, the pain on her wrists easing a little just as the pain in her shattered legs intensified when they threw her roughly to the ground. She heard a thud and then a moan as Pike was similarly dumped, unceremoniously, to the cold hard floor.

Well, that could have turned out better, she thought as the laughter faded and everything started to turn black.

Just as she was about to lose consciousness completely, she heard a deafening crash and the gangsters' tone became deadly serious. They were screaming instructions to each other in their native tongue.

Kendra felt herself being roughly manhandled onto someone's shoulder and carried at speed by a powerfully built man who stank of cigarettes and dreadful body odour. She bounced on his muscular shoulder as he strode purposely towards a nearby doorway, the motion causing her badly broken legs to bounce against his lower back, worsening the pain. The shouting and the chaos seemed to slow everything down as she tried desperately to deal with the agony.

She felt the cold rush of air as they exited the building. The commotion continued and she heard what sounded like thunderclaps. An acrid smell filled her nose, reminding her of the smell of fireworks on bonfire night. Gunfire, lots of it.

The pain in her legs intensified as the bouncing increased. And as rapidly as the bouncing increased, she was flying through the air, weightless and helpless, for what felt like an age. As she was still groggy and not fully alert, it all seemed to happen in slow motion, surreal and almost magical. The stars were still there, albeit faintly, and weird patterns and shapes continued to pass by.

The sudden impact of hitting freezing cold water drove

the wind from her lungs and shocked her into consciousness. In agony, she tried and failed to kick her way to the surface. She stopped kicking and relied on her strokes, staying calm as she remembered her swimming prowess. Thankfully, it didn't take long to surface. She looked up just in time to see another body land a few feet from where she was, realising quickly that it was Pike. And he was still unconscious.

Kendra turned to move towards him, trying her best not to move her crushed legs and use only her arms. She felt helpless that she was unable to dive after him, it was impossible in her condition. She screamed out his name as loudly as she could, to no avail.

Above her, on the banks of what was clearly the Thames, she could hear more gunfire, doors slamming shut, cars revving and squealing in their haste to get away, it was just like the movies. The movies where viewers would shout 'That doesn't happen in real life!'

She looked around for Pike and for something to help him with, again with no luck. She started to feel panic at the thought of Pike losing his life because of her, despite being so close.

A loud splash next to her took her by surprise, as another body dove into the water. A few agonising seconds later the mystery man surfaced - it was the wily Rick Watts, pulling Andy Pike up with him.

'Are you okay, March?' he shouted, as he swam powerfully on his back towards the bank with a limp Pike in tow.

'My legs... the bastard broke my legs, Sarge! I'm alright for now but I... I'm gonna need some help getting out,' she replied, thankful that Pike was saved. Her arms were getting tired, but she had enough strength to stay afloat for now.

As she hung in the water, keeping her exertions to a minimum, she thought back and realised just how lucky they had both been, despite their dreadful injuries.

Very lucky, she thought grimly.

If it hadn't been for her mobile phone, tucked in the back pocket of those super-tight jeans, they would never have been found and would not had survived that meeting.

It had been a close call. A very close call indeed.

———

It was two days later, as she lay in her hospital bed, still woozy from the cocktail of painkillers pumped into her body, that the first visitor from the police arrived.

She had managed to give Rick Watts a comprehensive statement in the ambulance on the way to the hospital, despite gritting her teeth in agony. She wanted her colleagues to know exactly what had happened, who was involved, and everything they'd need to start their investigation. Professional in every sense, despite the trauma.

Except, perhaps, for how the gangsters had caught them.

Watts appeared, announcing himself with a rap on the door frame. He looked at Kendra as she lay there, thinking back to when he had first met this vibrant, intelligent young woman. Her copper curls, usually bright and shimmering in the light, lay damp and drab against her forehead, the thin sheen of sweat masking her normally flawless skin, giving her a tired, pasty look.

Kendra's strict training regimen had blessed her with an athletic, muscular build. Now, she lay in a stark hospital room, with tubes attached to her arm and with a face that showed that she was suffering despite the medication. Her legs were both raised, casts from the knees down. The doctors had worked for hours setting the shattered bones, and were confident the surgery had been successful, but her legs would now be endowed with scars, a permanent reminder of what she and Pike had endured. Despite this, Watts knew she had been lucky. He looked around the small unadorned room, taking in the familiar smell of hospital cleaning products that masked the suffering and the death that was ever-present. Kendra's monitor continued to give reassuring beeps every thirty seconds.

'How are you doing, K?'

'I've been better, Sarge.' She smiled weakly, trying not to acknowledge her current condition. 'Any news on the Albanians?'

'Nothing yet. We thought one of the wounded would help but he copped it last night and the rest have completely vanished off the face of the Earth.'

'How many did you get when you found us?'

'Three, with the one from last night. They put up a hell of a fight, which gave enough time for the ringleaders to get away. Two of ours were hurt, Rula and Norm. I'm not a happy man,' he said, grim-faced.

'How's Andy?' she asked, almost in a whisper. She hadn't been able to stop thinking about him, from the minute the drugs had started wearing off.

'He's not great, K.' Watts looked away. 'He's lost an eye, and his foot is pretty much useless, the nerves were severed in multiple places. Not sure if he's coming back to us, Kendra, he's likely to be medically discharged.'

A tear worked itself free and ran slowly down her cheek. She was devastated for Pike and felt utterly responsible.

'I didn't come here to point fingers or apportion blame, but damn it, Kendra, you should have been more careful –

both of you! If we hadn't pinged your phone, we'd never have found you. What the fuck happened? We were all in position and could have been there in a couple of minutes, what the fuck was going on that you couldn't call us and warn us that they'd seen you? That they'd stormed the van? What?'

Kendra turned her face away in shame.

'I – I can't remember, Sarge, it happened so quickly.'

'You know they're not going to drop it until they find out, don't you?' he said, referring to the Directorate of Professional Standards, the DPS, the dreaded unit that investigated police officers and their conduct.

'Let them try their best, I don't give a shit.' Her main concern was Andy, she didn't have time to think about herself and the prospect of getting into trouble.

She wanted to help Andy.

She wanted to get the bastards that had done this.

***

A few minutes after Watts had left, Kendra received a surprise visit.

'Hello, love.' The man spoke quietly as he entered her room while she was looking out of the window. She turned, her eyes widening in surprise.

'Hello, Dad.'

The infamous Trevor Giddings was rarely seen nowadays, for reasons that few people were aware of. He kept his business dealings very close to his chest: the fewer people that knew about him, the better.

'I heard you'd got yourself in a spot of bother,' he said, 'so I thought I'd pop over and cheer you up. I brought you some flowers.' He handed over a small bouquet of roses, which

Kendra smelled – more from habit than anything, before laying them down on the bedside cabinet.

'Thank you,' she said, avoiding his searching eyes.

'So, what happened, love?'

She finally looked up at him, with a steely determination borne from many an argument with him. 'Nothing to concern yourself about, Dad, just another day at the office. Thanks for the flowers.'

He was a tall, powerfully-built man, still keen on his fitness from his time as a successful amateur boxer, still handsome despite the broken nose. He kept his fitness levels high whilst training youngsters, keeping them off the street for a few hours. It was only later that he helped them with other things, grown-up things, including introductions to his criminal contacts. Just one of the many reasons Kendra had argued fiercely with him before she showed him the ultimate face-palm – by joining the police.

Giddings had, in return, stayed clear. Not because she was likely to cause him trouble as a police officer, but more because he wanted her to have a 'cleaner' life by staying away from her. It was his way of showing he cared.

He stared wistfully out of the window. He seemed conflicted.

'How's the gym?' she asked, trying to change the subject.

'Actually, it's going very well indeed. We may have found the next heavyweight champion of England.' He looked and felt very proud, especially as it was the one decent thing that he was doing – training youngsters and hoping they did not take the wrong path. The fact that he helped the strays, which Kendra described as immoral, disgusting, and shameful – well, that was her opinion. Giddings wasn't proud that he'd introduced some of the kids to his gangland connections, but in his defence, he'd done so knowing they would have become a part of that fraternity anyway at some point, and probably by a more dangerous route. He just missed the middle part out and got them in, all in one piece. What happened after that was not his business.

'That's good,' Kendra replied.

'I went to the cemetery this morning, before I came here,' he said, his eyes glistening. 'I tidied the border and left some fresh flowers; it looks nice again.'

Kendra had been a toddler when her mother Amy had died, so she felt more for the pain her father was feeling than for her own loss. There were no memories of her at all, no glimpses, only some old, worn photographs. She had seen some on the wall in her grandfather's house — Ron March was a widower when Amy died and was in no fit state to look after a toddler, so Trevor had been pleased that his parents would be raising her.

'Maybe I can come by the gym and sort my fitness out,' Kendra said, 'I'm going to need some help to get back to full strength.'

Kendra noticed the surprise on her father's face and smiled. 'Don't worry, Dad, I won't tell anyone.'

'Of course you can, K, I'll set up a corner for you so that you can do whatever you like, at your own pace.'

Maybe this was how they would bond a little more. It was about time.

3

REASSIGNED

THE DPS SPOKE TO KENDRA SEVERAL TIMES ABOUT THAT fateful night, and she retold her story exactly as she had to Watts, again leaving out the tryst with Pike in the back of the van. She didn't care about the consequences and had simply repeated, 'I don't remember,' when asked why she hadn't called for assistance. According to Watts, Pike had all but thrown the investigators out of his hospital room. He was savvy enough to keep their secret and protect Kendra, at least, from any punishment. They had both suffered enough.

There wasn't much the DPS could do, and they had little choice but to drop their investigations of misconduct.

It was weeks before she was able to leave the hospital, having convinced the doctors she would be able to manage just fine, despite doing it from a wheelchair. It would be months before she was able to walk properly again, after some intensive physiotherapy and counselling sessions and enough time to heal. Only then would she be able to return to work in a limited capacity, until she was back to full fitness.

Pike, however, did not have the luxury of returning to

work—at any time. He would not be able to walk unaided, and therefore would never be fit for normal police duties.

'He's a very angry man, don't expect to see him around again,' DI Dunne had told them all.

'Get your team back to work but keep it to simple jobs, have them get back to normal gradually, it's going to take them some time to get over any guilt that they have, okay? The DI had told Watts.

'No worries, guv, but I can tell you that they won't like it much. They want to get stuck in again quickly,' Watts had replied.

'Well, they can't, not until the boss upstairs decides otherwise,' Dunne said.

After a month or so, as he was reviewing the Qupi file, one of the team went to see Watts in his office.

'When are we getting some proper cases, boss?' asked Pablo Rothwell, a brawny northerner who, because he was coming up to retirement, was not shy about speaking his mind. Watts had personally recruited him for exactly this reason; Rothwell didn't give a wet fart about what people thought of him, so long as the job was done properly.

'We're getting pissed off with investigating crappy theft and burglary calls, it's not what we're here for.'

Watts nodded. 'Go and get the rest of the team,' he said. 'I'll give you all an update.'

Minutes later the rest of the team were crammed into the small, stuffy office. Watts could sense the tension and would have to handle things delicately.

'Look, as you are well aware, this has been a very tough month, but we have to be patient and we have to do things by the book. What happened to Pike and March has affected more than just this team, and I don't want us to rush into another shit-pile unprepared, okay? I'm not risking any of you just for the sake of getting our own back. We do things properly or we don't do anything, got it?'

'How is Kendra, Sarge?' asked Jillian Petrou, another experienced and well-respected detective who had joined the team from a homicide squad when she heard Watts was in charge.

'She seems different when I've visited, like she's with-drawn. She's mainly upset about Pike, to be honest. Her legs are both fucked but with physio and time she'll be just fine. I think she just feels guilty that she got off lightly compared to him.'

'Pike won't let any of us see him, boss,' Rothwell said. 'He's properly pissed off at everyone at the moment.'

'Yeah, I know. I did speak with him briefly and it's going to take some time —and a bloody good counsellor— to get through to him. He hates the whole world at the moment.'

They watched him intently, waiting for the word, waiting for the order to go out and find Qupi and his gang and kick the crap out of the lot of them.

'We've been warned off the case. The chief told me we're too personally involved to be able to investigate impartially and thinks we might get ourselves into more trouble.'

'That's bollocks!' shouted McGuinness, furiously. 'That's absolute bollocks, boss, he's basically given them a free pass and they've got away with it!'

'That wanker upstairs hasn't got a bloody clue!' added Baker, 'he's nothing but a pencil-pushing tosser who's never got his hands dirty doing real police work!'

'Fuck's sake, Sarge, has he even seen what they did to Andy and Kendra? Is he that twisted in the head that he can't see that we're the best team to deal with it?' added the normally cool Rothwell.

Watts had to step in.

'Alright, calm down, that's enough!'

Watts paused to allow them – and himself – to gather their thoughts.

'I want nothing more than to get the bastards who did this, but the higher-ups have made it very clear, in their typical politically-correct manner, that we have to back off and let someone else take them down. I don't like it any more than you do, but if we go in all guns blazing and something goes wrong, can you imagine the fallout?'

'Sarge, with respect, I couldn't care less what those wankers think,' said Baker. 'There's got to be something we can do, surely?'

'I've given it some thought and the only thing I can think of is to help from the sidelines, covertly,' Watts explained. 'Shake the tree and something will always fall out. Go out there and speak to your informants, gather whatever scraps of intel you can. We can then feed it into the system in a way that doesn't attract attention to us. If the bosses upstairs get wind of it, they will transfer us all back into uniform without a second thought, so be extra careful and speak to me before doing anything, okay?'

There were a few dissenting murmurs, but the team seemed to accept that it was all they could hope to achieve. At least that way, they could contribute to the gang's downfall.

'We could look at new daily crime reports and pick those that may help us with leads,' said Jillian Petrou. 'You know, so we can cherry-pick those where there may be some connection to the ports and lorry parks. Me and Pablo can look at them as they come in every day, including the weekend.'

'Good shout, Jill, you do that,' said Watts. 'Baker and McGuinness, go back to the area near the warehouse and see if you can pick up anything from the locals regarding the shoot-out, maybe they saw some of the gang leaving—but keep it low-profile, some of those may still be in touch with Qupi and his mob. The rest of you just carry on for now, we'll check in every day for feedback and play each day as it comes, okay?'

The team dispersed and went back to the squad room, leaving Watts to ponder on their plans.

Let's hope we don't find anything for a while, he thought. *There'll be hell to pay if the team get hold of Qupi too soon.*

KENDRA HAD NOT ENJOYED the few weeks that had passed since being released from hospital. Although it was something she had pushed for, it meant she had to spend most of her time alone and wheelchair-bound as her leg injuries healed. She tried to rest as much as possible whilst attempting some light upper-body training to keep her busy. It would be dangerous to try to walk too soon, especially with this type of injury. The pain had eased but occasionally returned in waves to remind her, as if to teach her that playing with fire has substantial consequences. She no longer doubted that.

She had tried calling Pike a number of times but had not received any replies, despite leaving messages. She was worried for him, and desperate to help—and her guilt was growing with every passing day.

The team had been great, popping over frequently to check in on her, bringing small gifts to try and cheer her up.

On each visit, the first question she would ask was, 'Have you heard from Pike?' The responses so far had all been the same, that they hadn't spoken to him or heard from him. He had shut himself off from the world, angry and bitter, with nobody to vent to, and had refused all offers of help. According to Watts, the only people who had made any contact with Pike had been the police counsellors at the hospital. He was still receiving treatment but was allowed home most days, according to Watts' sources there. His treatment was not going well, which meant it was going to take some time.

The Met Police were still paying Pike a full salary for the first six months, which would then drop to half-salary for the second. After a year, it was likely that he would be placed on a police injury pension for the rest of his life. As his injuries were so severe and he was now disabled, they were likely to bring forward the decision to place him on the injury pension, which would be better for him than the reduced salary rate.. It was unlikely that Pike cared too much about this whilst he was going through this stage of severe anger.

Kendra vowed to continue her attempts to contact him, it was all she could do while her own mobility was so fragile.

Being at home was difficult at first, navigating the two-bedroomed flat in her wheelchair. Her friends had helped clear enough space for her to move around, storing any unnecessary furnishings or belongings in the spare bedroom. Other than the few exercises she could do, she spent a lot of her time watching television, not really taking it in. In her mind, she kept going over their time in the warehouse and their lucky escape, and her confused feelings about Pike. Their dalliance had been very brief before discovery, more lust-induced rather than anything too emotional. Those feelings seemed more confused than anything else, and all it made her do was think about it more and more, finding no answers and no conclusion.

As the days dragged on, she became more proficient with the wheelchair, and her arms stopped aching. She took to searching the news sites for any information about the gang, especially Guran Qupi. There was very little to be found online and Kendra knew that only the police database, Border Force, or the security services would be likely to have anything of use on him and his cronies. The feeling of help-lessness kept gnawing away at her. It was either guilt about Pike or guilt about not being able to help the team—each as frustrating and painful as the other.

'There's only one thing to do,' she concluded. 'I have to go back to work.'

'ARE YOU MAD? You've suffered a life-changing injury and God knows what else mentally, and you want to come back to work? What the hell is wrong with you, March?'

'Please, Sarge.'

'No, March,' was the distinct reply.

'Please, Sarge, I'm going stir-crazy at home.'

'No!'

'I can sit in the intel office and help them; I'll be comfort-able there and won't have contact with any members of the public. I can get a note from my doctor declaring me fit for clerical work, if you like?' She was trying everything she could to change his mind.

Watts paused, and Kendra knew she had a chance. She

had no idea of the team's plan to covertly gather intel on the gang.

'If you can get a doctor's note saying you are fit to carry out light office duties, then I will think about it.' Watts hung up.

Kendra pumped her fist in delight. 'Now we're getting somewhere,' she murmured to herself. She immediately picked up the phone and rang her doctor's surgery, hoping that her cousin Tracey was still the receptionist there.

———

JILLIAN PETROU PICKED Kendra up the following Monday. She had a doctor's note in her pocket, a pair of crutches and a wheelchair in the boot, and a determined smile that belied the pain she was still in.

'It's great to see you, chuck,' Jillian said as she helped Kendra into the front passenger seat. The deal was that someone would pick her up and drop her off each day. Initially she was only allowed to work four-hour shifts, until she could prove that working longer days would not adversely affect her. It would then be increased by an hour at a time, until she was fit enough to complete a full shift.

'I'm good, thanks, Jill. I missed you guys a lot; it's been a rough couple of months.'

'You'll be back to normal in no time, I'm sure.' Jillian kept her fingers crossed as she helped with the seat belt.

The drive to the station was slow and deliberate. Jillian was being careful not to make the journey uncomfortable for Kendra, and she wanted to probe a little deeper.

'Have you spoken to Andy?' she asked, going straight for the tough question.

'No, he won't answer my calls or messages.' Kendra had half-expected the third degree on the way in. She didn't mind; she knew that Jillian only had her best interests at heart. 'How about you? Heard anything?'

'No, he seems to be ghosting us all.'

Kendra slowly shook her head and looked down in disappointment.

'Don't stress about it, Kendra, I'm sure he'll come around soon.'

'I just want to talk to him, Jill, that's all. Make sure he's alright and see if there's anything I can do to help.'

'We all do, love, but if he's shutting us out, what can we do? We can't force ourselves into his life, can we?'

'He must be hurting really badly. And he must be brutally angry with everything and everyone,' Kendra said, 'including me.'

'Don't be daft, girl. Why would he be angry with you?'

'Because I'll still be able to walk, and I'll still have my job. He won't have either. I just feel so guilty and keep thinking that it should have been me in that position, not him,'

'Kendra, can you imagine how Andy would feel if it was the other way round? Come on, be realistic here, it was just bad luck, that's all. Nobody is to blame.'

Kendra felt differently.

'I guess you're right,' she replied, 'but I hope he reaches out soon.'

They arrived at the station shortly afterwards. Pablo was there to meet them and helped with the wheelchair and getting Kendra out of the car with minimum fuss. They fit snugly in the lift going up to the squad room on the third floor. The team wanted to say hello before she went off to the intelligence unit.

As soon as they wheeled her into the office, the room erupted with cheers and applause.

Nick McGuinness was the first to approach, picking her up gently. 'It's great to see you again, K.' He put her down, and before she could say anything she was picked up again, this time by Wilf Baker. 'Welcome back, Auntie Kim,' he said, grinning.

Rula and Norm followed, but with regular hugs—and a kiss to the cheek from Norm. It was back to the hug with Pablo, though, who said, 'I've been wanting to do this for ages, K.'

'Welcome back, March,' said Watts, the last to greet her. There was no hug or kiss, just a respectful arm on the shoulder and a nod of acknowledgment.

'It's good to be back, Sarge,' she replied. 'Thanks for putting a word in for me.' Which Watts had done to the Chief Superintendent, who had then authorised her return to work having read the doctor's glowing report. A report that her cousin Tracey had helped with.

'Not much I could say, was there? That doctor of yours was very convincing!' Watts gave her a knowing look that said he guessed some serious manoeuvring had taken place.

Kendra smiled, knowing that her sergeant would support her now that she had official permission to return to work, albeit with reduced hours and restricted duties.

'Sarge, before you pack me off to the intel unit, can I have a quick word in private?'

'Sure,' he said, 'come into my office.' Kendra wheeled away and followed him towards his office.

'Out with it then, March, what is it?' He was back to being serious.

'Well, first off, I haven't been able to reach Andy and I'm worried about him. Have you spoken to him?'

'You're not alone there, March, he's ghosting us all at the moment. Word is that he's still very angry and bitter and doesn't want to speak to anyone, apparently he wants to be left alone to suffer in peace!' Watts seemed just as frustrated as Kendra. 'He's bang out of order, you know. I appreciate he's been through hell, but damn it, we're his friends as well as his colleagues and he knows damn well we're all worrying about him.'

'I hate feeling this helpless, Sarge. When I get a chance, you know, when I can move around a bit easier, I'm just going to turn up at his house and see him.'

'Well, good luck with that. I tried it half a dozen times and he doesn't even answer the door to me.'

Kendra didn't know what else to say about the matter, so she decided to change tack.

'Is there any news on Qupi?'

Watts paused, knowing full well that this conversation could turn very quickly.

'No,' he said. Nothing more. Kendra saw a flicker in his eye.

'Sarge, I'm going to be stuck in that intel office for months, looking at nothing but criminal records and crime reports. Please give me something to work on while I'm in there, otherwise I'll go stir crazy. I can help.'

'You planned this all along, didn't you, March? You want to get stuck in as soon as possible, like some kind of avenging angel, don't you?' He leaned in. 'Vengeance can lead to very bad things, Kendra. You make one mistake, and it could have ramifications like you've never seen or experienced. Are you sure you want to go down that path? It could change you and everyone around you in the blink of an eye, I assure you.'

Kendra didn't flinch; she was past that stage now and understood that this was the moment when things would change forever, possibly for the worst. She was determined to take that chance, in the hope that she could right some wrongs and make the world a better place while she was at it. She was aware of the irony, that it would take bad things to make the world better – and she was looking forward to it.

'I'm ready. Just tell me what you need.'

———

WATTS EXPLAINED the plan that he and the rest of the team had spoken about. 'More than anything else, we have to remain covert; we cannot be seen to do anything involving Qupi, do you understand?'

'So, what can I do from the intel unit, how can I help?'

'Well, the first problem is that if you start looking through the records whilst you're signed into the system, it'll flag it up, and it records all the logs and users. There's a definitive audit trail that's regularly monitored. We need to find a way of doing it without attracting attention, so let me think on it.'

He shot her an intense look. 'You need to be really sure about this, March.'

'I'm committed, Sarge, I just want to help.'

'Just do what they ask you for now, while I think on how we can use you in there. It will be boring as hell, but hopefully it won't take you long to get used to the system and its capabilities. Make yourself useful in there and make some friends, they will come in handy later, I'm sure.'

Kendra was confident and her spirits were starting to rise,

knowing she'd be able to do some good again. She was known for her computer skills, legendary in hunting down the smallest of clues and finding pretty much anyone that she wanted. Sometimes she did so even if they weren't in the system, by targeting those close to them and finding devious ways to trick them into showing themselves. She would find a way to track the Qupis down, she was sure of it.

She already had a plan forming in her mind as to how she would log into the police databases without being tagged.

———

PABLO WALKED alongside the wheelchair as they made their way to the second floor and the intel unit. He wanted to introduce Kendra to his close friend Gerrardo, whom he had known for years and who he knew would look after Kendra.

As they walked in, Kendra recognised a few faces from having made many visits for intelligence reports in the past. Gerrardo Salla strode to them purposefully and held out his hand, first to his friend Pablo and then to Kendra. 'Welcome to the exciting world of intelligence,' he smiled ironically. Occasionally exciting, maybe, but most of the time, boring.

'Look after her, Gerrardo, or Rick Watts will have your guts for garters, and you know he's good for it,' Pablo said to his friend, raising his eyebrows theatrically as he turned to leave.

Gerrardo nodded and said nothing, waiting long enough to see Pablo out of the office, and then said, 'Come on, Kendra, let me introduce you to the rest of the team. I know you have met some of them, but it won't do any harm to reacquaint yourselves.

He introduced her to the remaining four people that

manned the intel unit. Two of them, Sam Razey and Paul Salmon, were both ex-police officers who had retired and then been re-hired as civilian staff. Their expertise was invaluable and very much welcome in the small unit. Imran Shahid and Geraldine Marley were serving police officers - Imran with three years' service and Geraldine with eight. Imran was working towards his detective status and Geraldine was on light duties due to being six months' pregnant.

In general, it was a well-respected small team, and now they had the benefit of Kendra's prowess to assist with their work, their stock would only rise.

'And here is your desk,' Gerrardo said, indicating to a typical desk that most dated police stations still used: solid wood with a black top, well-used, and a pod underneath with two large drawers. A standard desktop computer and monitor sat on the desk, and the top drawer of the pod was slightly ajar and had a key in its lock, indicating that it was vacant and waiting for its new user.

Kendra moved to the desk and breathed a sigh of relief when the wheelchair slid underneath the desk without any problems. She would be comfortable there. 'Great, do I use the same login as before, or is it separate for this computer?'

'It's the same login, we're all on the same network, although only a handful of us have full access to the database. They're very strict on it at the moment.'

'Great,' she said, 'what do you need from me?'

'Firstly, I want you to log in to the system and familiarise yourself with it. For now, you'll only be able to access the local database and not the counter-terrorism command one or any of the other agency ones, that will come later. Tomorrow, during our meeting, we can allocate some crime reports for you to go through. You then decide whether they can be allocated to CID or marked as complete or archived – for whatever reasons. Have fun!'

Kendra turned the computer on and waited for it to boot up. She was familiar with the system; every police officer used the same equipment at the station. Only their access was different, some more restricted than others. She was also very familiar with the intel unit and its running, but she didn't want to give too much away and attract unwanted attention. She would take her time, bed herself in, allow the rest of the team to get comfortable with her, and go from there. It could take days or weeks, but there was only one way to find out, and that was to get cracking.

————————

4

REALISATION

KENDRA SPENT THE NEXT THREE HOURS GOING THROUGH criminal records and crime reports. Normally it would have been boring as hell, but she was on a mission and the boring stuff was not a problem. She deliberately steered clear of anything directly related to Qupi and his gang, and instead focused on smaller, lesser-known gangs she had come across in her time here on the division. She would have to be patient for access to the other agency databases, but for now would have to concentrate on local issues. As she went through the crime reports, she noticed a pattern forming.

Many of the crimes that had been committed that were not ordinarily considered major crimes had been written off due to lack of evidence. The majority of these shelved reports were based in clusters in the division and overlapped into the next, where three of the less prominent gangs, considered weaker, were building their empires, in particular around three housing estates. They included crimes such as burglary, robbery, criminal damage, and car thefts. Crimes that were now so prevalent in London that they wouldn't attract much attention, however stat-driven the Met Police were.

Kendra saw this as a positive sign and one to investigate further, and openly, without attracting attention for the wrong reasons. By investigating these clusters and the gangs responsible for them, she would be sure to come across other evidence relating to Qupi's gang, which she could then disseminate through the correct channels. That way, the intelligence on his gang would grow without any direct involvement from her team. In particular, she was keen to investigate car thefts and large-scale commercial burglaries, which were likely to be linked to illicit exports via the Qupi-controlled ports that included Tilbury, Thurrock, and London Gateway. Cars and machinery were regularly stolen to order. On one occasion, a construction gang that had been building a new exit on the M11 had returned to work one Monday morning to find that their entire fleet of excavators, flatbed trailers, bulldozers, dump trucks, cranes, and even a huge compactor, had completely vanished from the site. Stolen in broad daylight, they had been transported on their own flatbed trailers to a site near Tilbury, stripped apart, forklifted into containers, and transported and loaded onto a freighter bound for Dar Es Salaam.

Generally, the gangs would do the honours and pass all stolen equipment and goods on to their regular fences, who were then able to facilitate their sale and ultimate export via the many containers used for that purpose. Small fortunes were made, in particular by the logistics experts, the Qupis, whose global connections meant there were always customers eager for goods.

Another thing Kendra did was to make sure to wheel herself over to each of the intel team members in turn, to ask questions that she already knew the answers to, but primarily to get to know them better and gain their confidence quickly. Her plan required that they be completely trusting in her. She offered to make teas and coffees, bought snacks from the canteen (which fortunately was also on the second floor), and used her time well as she prepared her plan.

Although she was still in a great deal of pain, Kendra went to great lengths to act as if she was perfectly fine. Her recovery was taking longer than she had hoped, and despite understanding the nature of the brutal injuries, she was desperate to get her mobility back.

As she continued to familiarise herself with the system and the unit, one thing struck Kendra more than anything else. She noticed that the success rate on the division was very low, and when the written-off reports were also taken into account, even lower. Robbers, burglars, sex-offenders, wife-beaters, drug-dealers, pretty much the majority of the scumbags that she researched – most of them were never concerned about the police interfering with their crimes - because they all knew very well that the likelihood of getting caught and being convicted was low. They took more chances than ever, because they had modern technology on their side, and the country's weak laws always favoured the criminals. They simply recruited friends and families to use their camera phones to film everything to do with the police, and made sure never to leave any evidence that would convict them. They were savvy and smart, and it worked for them. Simply put, the justice system was failing badly, and the criminals were taking advantage of it.

The more that Kendra researched and investigated, the more she realised this was the case. There was very little justice for the victims, and the police had their hands tied so tightly that they had been hamstrung by a system that was failing them very badly.

She saw more and more reports of crimes being written off, and more and more mug shots of criminals laughing at the camera – and at the police that had temporarily interrupted their day by arresting them. They knew they would be back on the street again within hours. It was a minor inconvenience that they had now turned into a badge of honour. As horrifying as it sounded, it was great PR for them.

Kendra momentarily forgot her task, her mission, and her pain. She could not believe what she was seeing. She had heard rumours that things weren't great but had put it down to the favourite slogan of 'the job's fucked,' which had been around since the 1960s. She'd had no idea how bad it was, and it was clearly getting worse, much worse. It took years for new laws to be introduced, which meant that even if the problems were acknowledged, it was unlikely that anything would be done to fix it for years. Kendra realised that cumbersome institutions, such as government and the police, stood no chance in keeping up with modern crime trends, especially those that were technology-led. By the time action was taken to fix the problem it had morphed into something new, and as such, the criminals were always one step ahead, if not more.

———

At the end of her first day's work, she made sure to say her goodbyes to her new colleagues. Pablo helped her back downstairs, where Jillian was waiting with the car to take her back home.

'How was it, then?' Jillian had expected a little more

exuberance from Kendra, but had instead recognised the signs of a tortured soul.

After a pause, Kendra said, 'Sorry, it's been a very strange day. I was only there for a few hours but what I saw has demoralised the hell out of me. Did you know how low our conviction rates are?'

'Kendra, you've been back one day. Getting upset by that is not a great start, chuck.'

'It's less than five percent in some crimes. Five percent! It bloody well pays to be a criminal nowadays, there's more chance of them getting run over than getting convicted, so they don't give a shit about the police anymore, we don't scare them at all!'

'We can only do our best, love,' said Jillian, knowing that any argument would fail, based on Kendra's clear anger and frustration.

'It's not our fault, Jill, we're doing our jobs, but the law is now weighed so much in the criminal's favour and until that changes, we are well and truly screwed as a society.'

The rest of the journey was quiet and uneventful. Jillian didn't want to provoke any more outbursts and Kendra was deep in thought about the injustices she had read about that day. And this was simply the tip of a very large iceberg.

OVER THE NEXT WEEK, Kendra put all her efforts into learning more about what was going on in her district. She made notes on specific crimes, the conviction rates, the zones most likely to be affected, and so on. She wanted a clear idea as to where things were happening, and made a covert list of criminals she believed were responsible for more than 50 percent of those crimes in her district alone. Occasionally, she would find a tenuous link to Qupi, which she noted separately for later, but in the main, she wanted to isolate the die-hard criminal element that was relatively local. She felt obliged to do something about it and planned to put a folder together with her findings so that she could pass it on to Detective Inspector Damian Dunne, who was in charge of Rick Watts and the team, along with a couple of other specialist units.

Kendra wanted to keep the team out of as much as possible to show that she was doing her job as instructed and keeping away from any Qupi issues. Bypassing the team and going to DI Dunne was an effective way of passing on intelligence that would be disseminated correctly and hopefully acted upon.

Needing a break after another bout of heavy research, she was in the canteen nibbling on a sandwich when Gerrardo sat down opposite her. 'How's it going, Kendra? We haven't spoken for a few days, and I see how busy you are keeping, so I thought I'd pop over now and see how you are, I hope I'm not interrupting your lunch.'

'Not at all, and thank you for asking,' she replied. 'I've been doing what you suggested and familiarising myself with as much as I can. I tell you, it's been an eye-opener, I didn't realise just how much is going on here on our patch.'

'Yep, it's been getting busier each year, too. We keep seeing the increases and we keep passing the intel on, but not a lot is being done about it, unfortunately. The funny thing is that around half the crimes are committed by a small number of known local arseholes, but the job has never got round to doing much about them.'

Kendra was stunned by this revelation. So, it was common knowledge that so many of the serious crimes were committed by known people, but nothing was being done about it? That meant one of two things: a corrupt police division, or incompetence. Some would argue budget constraints, but Kendra thought that was unlikely. It was like being punched in the stomach: how could it be like this in the 21st century? It was not only demoralising but made her angrier than she had been for a very long time.

'So nobody has actioned any operations or jobs against them?'

'We've submitted lots of reports and suggestions, and nothing ever happens. I have a sneaky feeling some of them are informants and nobody can go near them. Even when they get arrested in the street for something trivial, they are out almost immediately for lack of evidence, or bailed to return so that their high-powered solicitors can find reasons to drop the charges. It's been tough.'

Kendra shook her head in dismay, and then the anger returned. *I'm not having that,* she thought. A plan was formulating in her mind; there were interesting times ahead.

SEVERAL WEEKS PASSED and Kendra gradually put her plan into operation. She gathered intelligence and carefully split it into different piles for different reasons and different people. Some of the intelligence would be general work that she was carrying out for the intel unit, some was additional intel on local criminals who had links to Qupi, and the rest was a growing dossier on the local criminals that were committing most of the serious crimes and being allowed to get away with it. Her plan was complicated and slightly deceitful. She would continue her efforts and make herself useful for the intel unit, making herself indispensable to them and gaining more confidence. She would pass on related intel to other units that would help with the investigation into Qupi, as well as pass it on to Watts and the team. And finally, she would gather as much intelligence on the criminals that she would look into in her own time, whilst she decided how to deal with that information and what to do about it. It certainly kept her busy.

It also allowed her to receive unofficial feedback and updates from the team, who were able to let her know what they had gathered from informants and the like, without adding it to the system for all to see. This was very helpful to her as she conducted her own personal operation behind everyone's back. She felt a twinge of guilt, but then determination drove her forward.

Each day that went by, and each dreadful injustice that she came across, simply made her angrier and more determined. Her heart became darker as her plan gained momentum.

———

5

FITNESS

For the first month or so, Kendra had worked the stipulated four hours a day, and she built up a thirst for knowledge and information. Upon returning home each day, she carried on working wherever she could, making notes, updating her plans, and so on. Her dossier on each subject grew thicker each day and was more comprehensive and detailed than even the intel unit had on them. Her meticulous research and computer skills allowed her to glean every scrap of information possible, including associates, partners, favourite haunts, habits, and much more. She wanted to be as prepared as possible for the subsequent operations that she had in mind.

She also made extra efforts to improve her fitness. Her legs had been in a dreadful state, and it was always going to take months for her to make a full recovery. Kendra wanted desperately to bring that forward by weeks, anxious to get out and be fully mobile again. Her upper-body strength was almost as good as it had been before the assault. Her legs were a different matter. She was careful not to overdo her exercises, but always did a little more than what she had been asked. Little by little, the legs healed, and her strength started to return, albeit a fraction of what it had been. The pain was ever-present; even on the good days, it was there to remind her of that fateful day. She didn't mind, it drove her on to do more.

After the first month was up, her hours were increased to five-a-day, giving her more time in the intel unit and more intelligence to sift through. Her colleagues had no idea how skilled she was on computers, and she made sure they never found out. She had found a devious way to get into the system without logging on with her own name, by using one of her colleague's details. Little by little she managed to spy and save the login passwords of three intel unit staff. This would allow her to log in and investigate Qupi and his minions undetected. She had to be careful, though, to do so only a few minutes at a time, on days that her colleagues were working and during their lunch breaks, so as not to attract suspicion.

Every scrap of information went into her dossier on Qupi. She gathered information on all his mob and in some cases, where they had family in the UK, on those people also. Favourite haunts, hobbies, everything she had was saved for later. Some of it was passed on to her team, but most of it was not. She needed an edge and she needed to be one step ahead of everyone for her plan to work.

———

It was time to put another step into place, one Kendra had been dreading since she had hatched her plan, but one that was necessary for her to succeed. She took a deep breath through her nose and exhaled slowly as the doorbell rang. She was expecting a tough hour or so but was keen to get on with it.

'Hello, Dad,' she said, as she opened the front door. 'Thanks for coming over.'

'I'm over the moon, love,' Trevor replied, looking around. He hadn't been there for a long time, he was never really wanted there, truth be told. So this was progress for him, and he would take whatever came. 'Thanks for inviting me.'

'Shall I make some tea or coffee?' she asked.

'I'll take a black coffee, please, no sugar.'

Kendra left him alone and wheeled herself to the small kitchen. She knew he would be taking in all the small details from the flat - he hadn't been there for over a year, and it had changed a great deal since then.

Trevor walked around the lounge slowly, noting a couple of framed pictures of his parents, both with Kendra as a youngster in them, happy and innocent and taken during better times. He nodded in appreciation at two large Miro prints on the wall, along with a fabulous Jean-Michel Basquiat print with vibrant colours and unusual shapes, words and letters placed in random places. The lounge was a spacious one for a flat, with modern décor and tastefully furnished. It had large windows that had a pleasant view overlooking the River Roding. He was proud of his daughter, regardless of their strained relationship, and her flat showed she was more than just a young up-and-coming detective, but a thoughtful, intelligent woman with a love of the arts, and someone who took immense pride in their home.

'Mind if I look around, love? It's been a while since I popped over, it's changed a lot.'

'Feel free.'

As he walked along the short hallway from the lounge he saw more attractive prints on the walls, both sides, including a Jackson Pollock and a wonderful print from artist Aaron Moran, who had been setting the art scene alight recently. Giddings was an art buff, unbeknownst to most people; it wasn't something he spoke about as he didn't want his tough-guy image to be sullied. He glanced into the bathroom and saw that it was also spacious and light, again tastefully deco-rated, in a simple but practical layout that made it comfort-able in its functionality. The main bedroom was dark, with the curtains drawn and the bed partially made. The smaller, second bedroom was also dark, again with curtains drawn. He noticed a large pile of documents on a computer desk in the corner. The computer itself was switched on but locked, with a strange helix-shaped screensaver bouncing gently from one edge of the screen to another, randomly moving around in a mesmeric fashion. Trevor guessed that Kendra did what all hard workers did, and brought her work home.

He wandered slowly back to the lounge and was shortly joined by Kendra, who was delicately balancing a tray on her knees as she carefully wheeled herself over to him. The tray had a bean-bag underside, which allowed it to mould itself to her legs while she moved around. There was minimal spillage.

'Here you go,' she said, handing him an aromatic mug of steaming coffee. It was a strong blend of Arabica from Colombia, he would recognise that wonderful aroma anywhere. 'Thanks, love. How have you been?'

Kendra paused, more for effect than anything. 'It's been tough, to be honest, I'm struggling with a few things, and I was hoping you could help me.' She looked straight at him, noticing the surprise on his face.

'Anything, love, what do you need?' She didn't want to waste time, so she went for it.

'Well, first off, I'm getting frustrated by the lack of progress with my fitness, so I was hoping you could let me use your gym and help out with some workouts. I'll need a lift there and back until I can drive again.'

The gym was in Ilford and not too far out of the way, so she was hoping he would agree to her request; in fact, she was banking on it.

Trevor was delighted that his daughter was finally engaging with him. He understood that it came at a time where she felt some helplessness, but he'd take that, it was a start.

'Of course, darling, I'm more than happy to help. I can set a corner aside for you to do whatever you need. And I'll help with your workouts, too, I've dealt with bad injuries before so I have a good idea of how I can help you regain your strength first and then your fitness levels.'

Kendra smiled, showing some relief. 'And you can pick me up every afternoon after work?'

'No problem, it's not far out of the way.'

'Thanks, Dad, I'm very grateful.'

Trevor shook his head. 'Don't thank me, love, I'm just glad you're okay and that I can help a little.' In truth, he was over-joyed. The feelings of guilt over the years had on occasion overwhelmed him, despite his strength of character. This was a chance at redemption, and better still, a chance at a healthy relationship with a daughter he loved very much.

THE VERY NEXT DAY, after Kendra had returned from the station, Trevor came over as promised and picked her up. They spoke about her grandparents and how they were hoping to go on holiday this year, how they both wished to have seen more of them recently, how they hoped to have a get-together with them soon, and so on. Small talk was the order of the day, with both a little wary of saying the wrong thing or showing too much emotion on this, an immense first day of re-building their fractured relationship. Both had very different plans and ideas about moving forward.

Kendra felt a little guilty taking advantage of her father, knowing there was lots more to come soon that could take things to a very uncomfortable place. She felt less guilty when she remembered just how little effort he had made when she was young.

Trevor parked his matt-black Range Rover in the one parking spot available in front of the gym. Everyone knew not to take his spot. The gym itself was under a large, converted railway arch opposite a 1970s council estate, with a mix of industrial units under other arches, along with a small commercial block nearby. Most of the youngsters who attended the gym were local but there were many who had travelled from across London, based on the reputation Trevor Giddings had. His gym had produced several British champions recently, and his input was the main reason – he was a well-respected and successful boxing trainer.

The gym had been moderately successful financially in the last couple of years, and Trevor had used some of those funds to rent the neighbouring arch from Network Rail, which he had used to start a car repair business that he co-owned with Alvin, a mechanic friend. It was a robust business that supplemented his earnings. It was helped by the fact that many of his underworld connections brought him a lot of business. He left Alvin to deal with it; the less he knew, the better. He liked being on the fringe of things instead of in the middle, it was less risky, especially since he wasn't at all enamoured with the criminal fraternity or any of the 'business' they conducted. It was better, though, to be on their side instead of against them, and that was the game that he played.

'I had Charlie clean out the end of the arch for you, to give you plenty of room. He's also screened it off so the youngsters don't have a heart attack,' he joked.

The arch was surprisingly large and spacious inside, and deep. Trevor had done a good job keeping it neat and tidy, regularly whitewashing the walls and adding enough lighting so that it wasn't the dingy and damp space he had originally rented. It smelled like a typical gym, a cross between old sweat and oils, and there was plenty of activity going on as they walked in. Kendra noticed that most of those training were youngsters, early-to-late-teens, and those training them were not much older, as if the experienced trainees were helping with the youngsters. There were a pair of older men who seemed to supervise the rest, hard-looking types, and both recognisable as ex-boxers by their trademark broken noses. Both looked over as Trevor and Kendra entered, and nodded subtly towards their boss, who returned the acknowledgement.

Trevor wheeled Kendra in and down towards the end of the arch. A few of the teens turned to look at them as they went by, momentarily distracted from their training regimes, but there was no other reaction to them at all. Kendra recognised the respect that her father had here; they were either told to keep quiet or they knew to keep quiet. Either way, they were well-drilled and respectful.

At the end of the arch, Kendra saw that a heavy black curtain had been put up to screen off one corner, an area of around twenty-feet-by-twenty. As they walked around the curtain, a couple of blue vinyl gym mats had been put down, and there were a couple of benches up against the wall. A range of small weights were arranged along the sides, and there were a couple of resistance bands hanging from the benches. Nothing major, but exactly what Kendra needed to get her strength back.

'Here we are,' Trevor said, 'this should be enough to get you started. Once you get some strength back, we can bring in more weights and some other equipment, but for now everything you see here will help you with a bench-based routine, for your upper body. If you're up for it, you can use the resistance bands for your legs, but we need to introduce those exercises slowly, okay?'

'Great, thank you.'

She had come prepared, in her favourite retro blue-and-white tracksuit bottoms, her faded but much-loved Dream Theater t-shirt, and a pair of trainers.

'Where do you want me to start?'

Trevor smiled and said, 'Well, you can warm up first, by doing some stretch exercises, and then move on to some small weights.'

Exercise whilst in a wheelchair was not ideal, but Kendra had become used to it and had been able to carry out rudimentary stretches without too much difficulty. She spent ten minutes on those, and then, with Trevor's help, moved from the wheelchair to one of the benches he had placed near the middle of her curtained-off area.

'Okay, so I want you to lie on the bench but with your feet flat on the ground, and just repeatedly lift these small weights, slowly but methodically.' He handed her the weights. They weren't particularly heavy but after a few minutes of repetitions she could feel her muscles aching and she started to sweat slightly. She carried on for a couple more minutes until it got too difficult, so she slowly brought the weights up to her chest and stopped, waiting for her father to take them from her.

'One more minute,' he said, not touching the weights, 'you need to feel more pain before you see the benefits.'

Kendra looked up whilst still on her back and, seeing her father's grinning face above her, started to slowly lift the weights again. She had resolved not to show any weakness, and she was confident that he liked determination in the people he trained. It would be no different when it came to his own offspring.

'Good, Kendra,' he said, as she laboured with the weights, her sinews stretching more than they had for months, her muscles burning from the exertion.

'And rest.'

Kendra gently handed the weights back and sat up, her forehead now showing a healthy sheen of sweat. She felt good, despite the pain. It was exactly what she needed, much more of this, with Trevor pushing her hard, beyond her comfort zone, so she could come back stronger than ever.

After a short rest she did the same again, and although it was more painful than the first time, it was to be expected. The third round was even more strenuous, and she struggled badly, her arms trembling from the exertion after only a minute. The more she suffered, the more work she realised she had to do, but the better she felt.

After an hour-and-a-half of intense training, Trevor called it a day, much to Kendra's delight. She had imagined she would be in better shape, but this one session alone had proved her wrong and showed her that she had a long way to go. Her breathing was laboured, the sweat was pouring off her, and she found it difficult to move, such was the deep fatigue that had washed over her. Despite this, and the intensely sore muscles, she felt a wave of elation, as if a weight had been released from her shoulders.

'Not a bad first day, K,' said Trevor, as he wheeled her back towards the car. Kendra noticed the same youngsters still training; their sessions were longer and tougher than hers and she was starting to gain a new level of respect for her father. They were here because of him, because he gave them discipline and hope, and he kept them off the streets for a few hours a day.

'The gym is busy, Dad, lots of youngsters. It's a good thing you're doing.'

'Better in the gym than on the street, love, temptation is all around them nowadays, and the police are only ever seen when they carry out raids. You never see a beat bobby walking around anymore, and hardly ever see a patrol car, it's not a safe area anymore.'

Kendra said nothing.

'It wasn't a dig at the police, love,' he continued, 'it's just the way modern life is now. Like you, everyone is trying to do the best they can to survive.'

'I appreciate it, Dad, but it doesn't mean I have to like it,' she replied. And she did not like it at all. She felt a twinge of guilt, having seen things a little differently and up close. She could not deny the police were fighting a losing battle, and their energy was being focused on the wrong people. She felt more determined than ever to do something about that.

KENDRA WORKED HARD on her fitness, continuing with the intense training her father was helping with, along with regular weight-training and a number of stretching exercises designed to get her back to full fitness sooner rather than later. After a few short weeks, her strength and fitness had hugely improved. She was out of the wheelchair for short bursts of training and walking – albeit carefully – around the gym and around her flat. She kept the progress to herself, though, and continued to use the wheelchair for work. She found that it helped with the deception; it was necessary to continue with her plan.

Working in the intel unit was different than what she had been used to. The relationships with her colleagues there were new and - as yet - untested. Fortunately, it didn't take long for them all to get to know each other better. Gerrardo, in particular, helped Kendra with her new tasks, and had warmed to her.

'So, Kendra, who's the lucky fella that you go home to every night?' he asked one day, whilst avoiding her gaze. It was a clumsy attempt at flirting, which Kendra found sweet.

'Well, that would be telling, wouldn't it?' she replied, not giving too much away.

As Gerrardo got to know her better, he became bolder in his questioning, showing a determination that Kendra wasn't sure how to deal with, which she found somewhat amusing. It had been a while since anyone had paid her this sort of attention, and the last time had not ended well.

'We're all going for a drink later tonight,' he said one morning, 'if you fancy coming along?' Kendra had overheard Geraldine and Imran talking about it and the fact that they wouldn't be going.

'Thank you for asking, but I have other plans tonight, sorry.'

'Maybe another time,' he said, quickly turning back to the computer. She could see that he was disappointed but wanted to keep him onside, so she encouraged him in other ways.

'You're very good at this, Gerrardo, and I'm grateful that you have been helping me,' she said, changing the subject quickly. 'It's very useful to have access to other systems, such as the Special Branch records, which give us intel that we wouldn't normally see,' she added.

Gerrardo smiled, back in his element. 'There is so much more intel that we have access to that is restricted, it may look like a dull posting but there is never a dull moment when we get our teeth into a case,' he said proudly.

'I see that now, so thanks again.'

They both heard a snigger from one side and turned to see Sam and Paul, who had noticed the exchange, standing there like a couple of naughty schoolboys.

'She's way out of your league, Gerrardo,' Sam said, nudging Paul.

'Yeah, you need to get back on that Tinder thing, mate, there's bound to be someone on there that fancies a bit of northern stuff,' added Paul. Although they were just teasing and it wasn't anything too hurtful, Kendra could sense that Gerrardo was somewhat embarrassed.

'Don't worry about them,' she said, reaching out and

bringing Gerrardo in close. She kissed him gently on the lips, winking as she pulled back.

Sam and Paul's open-mouthed surprise was all the reward that they both wanted, and they both laughed at the two elder statesmen, who quietly went back to their desks. 'But don't get the wrong idea, Mr Salla,' she said quietly.

'I get it—and thank you for that, it was fun. I'm going to enjoy working with you very much. I have a feeling we're going to be very good friends,' he said.

As a result of her efforts, Kendra was able to pass on selected and relevant information relating to Qupi's generals, their families, and the frequent trips to Albania – typically via Italy or Greece. There were patterns developing that nobody had picked up on, and she was able to use that for the files.

There was a much larger pattern developing involving more than just Qupi's mob, it was a worrying trend. Major crimes were being ignored more and more, and minor criminals and hoodlums were being sacrificed as diversions and distraction tactics to keep the police away from the increasingly successful crime lords – as they were now being called. Kendra kept her thoughts to herself for the moment, deciding to look further before figuring out how to deal with them. There was much to do, and she realised that she needed help, away from her colleagues, to act on what she had found.

She thought long and hard about what to do next and how to achieve it. One part was bringing her father onside more and utilising his skills and connections to further her ambitions to remedy the injustices she was seeing. It would not be easy, and he would be bound to resist, but she was quietly confident that she could bring him around – he had a lot to make up for.

The only other person she could trust was currently unreachable and in a bad place, with no hope of anything changing any time soon. Kendra had to find a way of getting in touch and hopefully bringing him onside – she hoped Andy Pike still had a lot to offer.

———

THE FOLLOWING DAY, when Trevor came to pick her up, he found Kendra waiting for him but not yet ready for the gym.

'It's not like you, love, go and get yourself ready so we can push off.'

'Dad, I won't be going to the gym today, but I do need to talk to you, so please sit down while I get you a coffee.'

'Uh-oh, this sounds serious,' he replied, recognising the sombre tone in her voice.

He sat down at the table and waited for her to return. When she did, walking and using just the one crutch, she put the steaming hot cup of coffee on the table and then turned and went straight back to the hallway. She returned less than a minute later with a large pile of folders and files, of varying colours and thicknesses.

'This is just one pile I have been working on, there are more,' she said, getting straight to business. 'Dad, crime is getting out of control here and it is getting much worse, at a frightening rate. While I've been recovering and working at the station, I have researched months', no, *years*' worth of intelligence, and what I have come to understand is that it is out of control, and nothing the police are doing now is going to change that.'

Trevor's face was a picture of confusion and concern, a look Kendra had never seen before. He recognised that she was serious about it all but had no idea where this discussion was heading, or what Kendra wanted. He indicated to the pile and said, 'Darling, why are you telling me this? I don't know what this is about.'

'I need your help. I can't just sit around doing nothing when I can see what is going on. I want to do something about it, I want to make a difference and make these bastards pay for what they have done to our community. We've been going after the wrong people, and I want to change that. Now.'

'Again, what the hell can I do, love? Honestly, I'm confused.'

'You are already helping me with the training, but I need you to teach me more, much more. I need you to show me how the gangs work, how they're run, who makes the decisions, where they hide their money and their goods, everything. I want you to teach me how to be one of them so that I can be better than them. So that I can take them down.'

It wasn't often that he was left stunned, but Kendra's request made the hairs on the back of his neck raise and he felt a cold chill down his spine.

'Are you serious?' He knew she was, but had to ask.

'I have never been more serious about anything in my entire life.' He hadn't seen much of his daughter, but could confidently say that this was the most determined he had ever seen her.

'Do you know what you are getting yourself into? This is some serious shit you want to get involved in.'

'I'm not crazy. What has happened these past few months has opened my eyes. It's made me sick to my core and I would rather risk everything to make things better than sit on my arse pretending everything is ok. It is not. Please help me, Dad, I know you can.'

'Kendra, listen to me carefully. These gangs nowadays, they don't give a shit about anyone, not even their own families. They will slit your throat at the first opportunity, even if you look at them funny. Please don't do this,' he said.

He could see that she was determined and that she was set on doing something, and he needed to put a stop to it.

'I can't help you, love, not when it will put you at so much risk, sorry.'

'You can't? Or you won't? So, you're happy to sit on your arse while the community around you is destroyed from within? Good one, Dad, that explains a whole lot.'

She turned away in disgust, hoping he would rethink his decision.

'Kendra, I don't want that, and you know it. Why do you think I run the gym? I am trying, in my own way, to help. I don't want you to put yourself at risk, and any parent would do the same.'

'But you're not just any parent, are you, Dad? You are connected to it all in some weird, twisted way, so you more than anyone else can have a huge impact – but you choose not to.'

'Maybe you're right, but how the hell do you think you can turn things around? What makes you think you're the one who can do this when your own police force can't?'

'Because I'm prepared to do whatever it takes to bring these scumbags down, Dad, whatever it takes, including breaking the law. Because it's the only way we can ever succeed.'

Trevor couldn't argue with that. He knew when to stop

pushing. He knew that she would not be swayed. Kendra was set on a course that would change their lives dramatically.

HE LOWERED HIS VOICE. 'I'm not happy about you going ahead with this, Kendra, but I'd rather be with you in your quest for justice than leave you to do it by yourself. And despite what you might think, I do know you. I know you'll go ahead with or without me.'

Kendra smiled a little; she could see he was struggling with it but saw it as an opportunity to make things better, including their relationship.

'Thanks, Dad. I know it's a tough ask but I think we can do something positive, you know? Now, how about we order a takeaway and you can start telling me things?' As ever, she wanted to get stuck in straight away.

'Chinese or Pizza?'

6

ANDY PIKE

Kendra took a cab to Andy Pike's address, deciding to turn up unannounced and stay until he let her in. She could be stubborn with the best of them. This was the next important step in her plan, in addition to securing her father's assistance. It was as important, if not more so, because Andy had skills that few others had. Those skills and his determination would prove invaluable.

As they arrived outside Andy's end-of-terrace house, Kendra could see a faint light coming from the downstairs lounge, through a small gap in the closed curtains. She thanked the cab driver and carefully got out of the cab. Her upper-body strength was now better than ever, and she used that strength to keep as much weight as possible off her feet as she moved towards the house.

She had brought a bottle of water and some snacks in case it took some time, knowing that was very likely. There had to be a way to see him, and she could not think of a better way than this. She was careful moving around, using and relying on her crutches a great deal, along with the sturdy support boots to carefully stand on for the minimum time possible. It wasn't ideal but she felt it was worth taking a chance if she was able to fulfil her plan.

'This is it,' she said out loud. She took a deep breath and rang the doorbell.

As she had expected, there was no response. She rang again, this time leaving her finger on the doorbell for a few seconds longer.

Again, no reply.

She knocked several times on the door, hard enough for anyone in the house to hear.

Nothing.

She knocked again and rang the bell, and then shouted through the letterbox.

'Andy, I'm not leaving here until you let me in.'

Nothing.

Kendra had half-expected this and knew she had to persevere. She knocked, rang the doorbell, and shouted some more through the letterbox.

'Damn it, Andy, it's freezing out here and I'm in a lot of pain. Open the damn door!'

Nothing.

She sat on the low wall and took a breather. She noticed the curtain flicker slightly.

She returned to the letterbox and said, quietly, 'Andy, please let me in. I need help and you're the only one I trust. Please.'

She went back to the wall and sat down. Almost immediately she heard the *snick* of the door being unlocked. She stood up and saw that Andy had opened the door a few inches and stood inside, looking out at her. He looked dreadful, with a scraggly beard that hadn't been trimmed in months, his hair long and unkempt, and had a black patch over his left eye, his long greasy fringe hiding much of it. He wore a stained grey dressing gown that was loosely tied, showing a pair of mismatched pyjamas underneath. Kendra couldn't see his entire body and guessed he was carrying a cane in the other hand behind the door, and his damaged left foot was hidden from view. Worst of all was the grim, dangerous look in his eye as he stared at her.

'Go home, Kendra, I'm not interested.' His voice sounded distant, very different to how she remembered.

Kendra held his gaze. 'Then why did you open the door, Andy? Now stop pissing around and let me in, I need to talk to you.'

She moved forwards and put her free arm out as if to force her way in. As she did so, he instinctively opened the door fully to allow her in, accepting defeat. Kendra walked past him and into the hallway, before entering the lounge. The room was a mess. She didn't expect anything else from a man who had been through hell and was fighting every aspect of life. The TV was on with no sound, a documentary about elephants playing on the 55-inch screen. There were takeaway cartons strewn all over the room, on the coffee table, the settee, and the floor. She saw at least a dozen empty beer bottles and crunched-up empty crisp packets making a colourful splash on the hardwood floor. The smell was rank, and she scrunched her nose as if it would help.

'Well, it's good that you're keeping the place nice and homely,' she said sarcastically, as he came into the room behind her. She turned to him and saw the cane and the left foot, which was in a bulky medical boot of some kind, similar to those that she wore, which kept the foot pointing in the right direction. She moved to the settee and cleared a space on one side with her crutch before gently sitting down. 'How are you doing?'

'Just brilliant, Kendra, as you can see.' The grim look was unmoved.

'I heard that they're likely to medically discharge you, any news on that?'

He paused before replying, the worst part of this experience was not being able to do the job that he loved so much, and which he did so well. 'Still ongoing,' was all he could stomach saying without going into a rant.

'So, what are you going to do?' She could see the grimness fading as he struggled.

'What the hell can I do, Kendra? I'm a fucking cripple!'

The release of emotion, saying those words out loud to someone for the first time, was significant, and Kendra quickly recognised that she could help Andy—and her quest.

'You're only a cripple if you think you are, Andy. There's a shit load you can still do, you just need to want it again. Now, please sit down. I need your help and it may be something that will help you get through this more easily.' Her assertiveness was not lost on Andy, who sat down in his chair and said nothing.

'I don't know if you are aware, but I've been working restricted hours back at the station, in the intel unit. I've been doing it for a couple of months now and I've learned a hell of a lot, Andy. It's pissed me off no end, and the whole thing stinks of corruption and negligence. It's all been hiding there in the open and we've never noticed it.'

'Go on.'

'I wanted to do some intel gathering on the Qupis, so that we could help with the investigation and get them banged up. It turns out that sod-all has been done, there are no leads, no useful evidence, and none of us are allowed to get involved. Basically, they have got away with what they did to us.'

He shook his head slowly. At the very least, he thought they'd be brought in for interviewing and that their statements would help put them away. 'That's pretty fucking shitty. So, it was all for nothing?' Only Kendra's forthcoming request was preventing him from blowing up; he was sure she had something in mind, and he wanted to hear it.

'As I investigated them and all their connections, I found some patterns had developed, where specific types of crimes were taking place, and by who. As well as finding out a ton of intel about the Qupis I also unearthed years' worth of intel on some other major criminals and gangs that have been left, free to do whatever they want. It is staggering how much is being carried out by so few.'

'Have you been to the suits upstairs?' he asked.

'No. I've passed some intel on to our team to help them covertly pass it on to other units, but other than that I don't want to attract any attention to what I have found out and especially what I want to do. That's why I came to you, because I know you can help me, and I know you feel the same way about scumbags getting away with it.'

'So, what do you want to do?' he asked, 'and how do you think that I can help?'

'I want justice,' Kendra replied. 'Summary justice.'

Andy paused, his cold look making it very difficult to guess what he was thinking or feeling.

'I'll ask again, what makes you think I can help you? Look at me, Kendra, I'm a frickin' mess. I've only got one eye and I can't walk properly.'

'You're the best person I know, Andy, and even with one

eye and one leg I know you can do more than most people I know.'

'Kendra, please stop messing me about here, okay? If you've come over to take the piss then just do it and get lost. I haven't got time to arse around.'

'Really?' she said, looking around the room. 'So what *have* you got time for?'

'Well ... I was going to vacuum today, and maybe wash the cat, I'll find something, okay?'

'You don't have a cat,' she said, crossing her arms.

'I was going to buy one. And wash it. I don't bloody know! Look, just leave, okay?'

Kendra walked up close to him. 'Now who's messing around, Mr Pike? I've come over here to ask for your help. If I didn't think you were up for it I wouldn't have wasted your time or mine, okay?'

Andy stared back and changed tack, 'if you don't answer my question properly then I ain't interested. You can say I'm great as many times as you like, but you haven't told me a thing about what I can actually help with. The ball is in your court, Detective March.'

'You can be such an arse, Pike. There's a ton of stuff you can help with, okay? For a start, I know that you're a whiz with the computers. Don't think I never noticed that you were able to find things that most others couldn't. Do you know how I know? Because I'm a whiz too, and it takes one to know one. And I also know that you are very well-connected, all over London, so if we ever needed anything, I know you can find it. Like you did that one time when you found a boat for us to scope from on the Boggis case. You have the knack of getting things done, Andy. And I trust you. That's why I need your help.'

'Yeah, well, that wasn't so hard, was it?' he replied quietly. He knew to expect passion from Kendra, but it was still a surprise to hear so much more.

'I've missed you, Andy, you big one-eyed idiot. Now will you help me or not?'

'I'm going to say no, but thank you for asking.'

'Why not? How many episodes of *Star Trek* are there left for you to watch, for God's sake?'

'More than you think, actually.'

'Stop being a prick, Andy. This is an opportunity to do something good, to make a difference, why would you not want to?'

'Kendra, that is why I joined the police, those two very things. I failed then and that was with the backing of one of the biggest police forces in the world. What the hell makes you think the two of us can do any better?'

She smiled and said, 'Well, for one, there will be three of us, at least.'

'Wow.'

'And also, it will work because we won't be constrained by the law, we will do it our way.'

'So, we'll be breaking the law?'

'If we have to, yes.'

'So, we'll be a couple of law-breaking police officers, committing crimes against criminals?'

'Yep.'

Andy paused and then pointed to the bag of snacks that Kendra had brought along. 'Are you going to eat that Kit Kat?'

'What?'

He shook his head theatrically, paused again, and then said, 'Yes, I'll help you. I may regret it, seeing how feisty and angry you can get, but count me in.'

'Like I said,' Kendra replied, 'you're an arse.'

―――――――――

KENDRA SPENT hours at Andy's house going over options with him, brainstorming and putting snippets of ideas together. They were bold and creative with their plans, some more ludicrous than others and dismissed quickly, but their discussions were enlightening to them both. It reinvigorated their hope and Kendra saw that Andy's demeanour had changed within an hour of her turning up on his doorstep unannounced.

'It goes without saying that there is a lot to do,' she said, 'but we should start with Qupi and his mob, don't you think?'

'Absolutely. But knowing that all the scum are potentially protected means we must be very careful with our approach. Whatever we do must be done quickly, quietly, and without anyone ever noticing. We need to be off the grid, to avoid any subsequent investigations, otherwise it won't be long before we're caught. It wouldn't surprise me if they used our team to investigate.'

'Agreed,' she said, 'and that's why I think I should stick around the intel unit for as long as possible. That way I can keep tabs on everything and subtly nudge them in other directions, which may actually help us in some ways.'

'Well, there's a lot for us to think on. We should meet again tomorrow, if that works for you?'

'Andy, you're stuck with me now. Just do me a favour and have a shower and a shave, okay? This is not a good look on you!' He blushed. She could see that it was a significant turning point. He was back.

A cab arrived shortly afterwards, and as she left the house, she gave him a peck on the cheek.

'It's good to have you back, Andy,' she whispered, as she hobbled away on her crutches.

She couldn't see him smiling on the doorstep as the cab drove away. His remaining eye was no longer dark and foreboding, there was now a glint of hope. He was not as sure of success as Kendra, but she had quickly brought him out of his funk. He wanted to change, and he wanted to be better than he was. Kendra had made him see a different path. It was a path that was full of adventure, but he could see dangers along the way that perhaps Kendra couldn't.

'I guess I can help her with that,' he said out loud, 'so I guess she needs me, which is cool.'

It was Kendra that was the key to the future and Andy had not taken long to realise it.

'Now, do I buy that cat, or not?'

WHEN KENDRA ARRIVED at Andy's the next day, she was amazed by the transformation. The house was spotlessly clean, there was no rubbish, and even the dank smell had disappeared, replaced by flowery air fresheners discreetly placed around the ground floor. But the biggest change was in Andy. The beard was completely shaved off. His hair was still long, but it had been washed and combed, and the eye patch made him look quite dapper and striking. He was dressed in a pair of khaki combat trousers, which hid most of the boot on his left foot, and a light-blue, short-sleeved polo shirt. He carried his cane, which along with the eye patch gave him a mysterious, brooding, but exciting persona.

Kendra smiled when she saw him and said, 'Hello, is Andy in?'

He smiled and gave her a hug as she entered the house. 'I have something to show you,' he said.

He led her to the end of the hall and stopped just before entering the kitchen. They stood next to a door, which Kendra knew led to a downstairs bathroom. 'What are you showing me, Andy? Because the toilet isn't doing it for me.'

He laughed. 'You don't remember, but before I had this turned into a toilet, it was the door to the cellar.'

'You had a cellar?'

'It's still there, just hidden away.' He smiled and opened the door. All she could see was the toilet, facing them, and a small basin that was fixed to the wall on the right-hand side, with a small mirror hanging above it. The wall on the left had a framed print of a pride of lions lounging under a baobab tree, the frame made from driftwood. The room was tastefully decorated in pale-blue-and-white striped wallpaper, with the wider blue stripes edged by a dark blue border.

'I'm confused,' she said, 'what am I supposed to see?'

'Watch,' he said as he walked into the room. He used his right foot to press along the skirting board at the bottom of the left-hand wall and then pushed hard. Kendra heard a click and was then amazed to see the entire wall move inwards, revealing a wooden staircase down into the dark cellar. The moving wall settled against the underside of the staircase leading upstairs, nestling neatly against it. There was a light switch just inside the hidden area, which Andy then turned on.

'This is where I keep my valuables,' he said, smiling, 'but I think we can use it as our base of operations. What do you think?'

'I think it's bloody marvellous, I would never have imagined anything like this, it's really well hidden!'

'Let's go down,' he said. 'Are you ok going down the steps?'

'I'll be fine, just lead the way and I'll be right behind you.'

Andy went down the stairs slowly, conscious of his own limitations and being deliberately cautious for his own safety. Kendra followed, making sure the single crutch was placed in the middle of each step. As she walked down the dozen steps, the cellar opened out and she could see it in its entirety. It was much larger than she had anticipated, a good forty- or fifty-feet long and almost as wide, and seven feet high. At some point, whether it had been Andy or the previous owners, the room had been cleaned out and whitewashed. It was spacious and comfortable, with a couple of bookshelves, a small table and chair, and a safe in the corner. There were a handful of boxes strewn around the room, but in general it was in great shape—and perfect for their needs.

'We have power down here, so we can plug a computer in, and I can bring a Wi-Fi extender.'

'A secret den, it's bloody perfect!' Kendra laughed out loud. Andy smiled, and he looked more like the man she used to know. The man she had respected so much, and cared for. She blushed as the memory of those feelings came back to her, and she turned away, pretending to look around some more.

'Tomorrow I'll start bringing my files over. I'll make a list of some things we may need, like some magnetic boards and stationery. This is a real bonus, Andy, thank you.'

'No, thank you, Kendra, for waking me up from the nightmare I've been having. It went on for too long and I needed this.'

'You just needed some time, that's all.'

'We still need to be careful though, okay? I need to carry on playing the bitter and twisted angry man that doesn't want to speak to anybody and you need to carry on playing the detective who can't quite return to full duties yet. We need to move along like this for as long as possible.'

'Agreed, and it goes without saying that nobody else must know about this room, okay?'

Andy smiled. 'I'm a bitter and twisted angry man who doesn't speak to anyone, remember?' They both laughed.

OVER THE NEXT FEW DAYS, the secret room came together as a functioning operations room with everything they needed for their plans. Kendra had moved the files over from her flat, along with a desktop computer and a spare laptop. Both were scrubbed clean of all data, including licensed software, and then re-booted as stand-alone units that would not trace back to them, should anything go badly wrong. Hopefully it would never come to that.

Three large white magnetic boards were now firmly attached to the walls, waiting for intel, and a box of brand-new stationery sat on the desk waiting to be used. Andy had brought down another chair so that they could both sit at the desk, which was large enough to accommodate them both comfortably. He had also brought down a small fridge, 'From our old beer club on the robbery task force, before they ordered us to remove it.' It was now filled with bottles of water and other soft drinks.

Kendra spent several days going through the files with him, purposely leaving the largest, that of the Qupi gang, for last. She wanted him to have a good overall understanding of the people and organisations they would be looking at and then targeting. She also wanted him to know how some of them were loosely connected to each other, to Qupi, and to legitimate businesses she had researched and confirmed.

After a couple of days, they took stock. 'Great job, Kendra, this is some of the most meticulous intelligence gathering and reporting I've ever seen. I taught you well,' he added with a smirk.

'You can't take all the credit,' Kendra laughed, 'I did learn a few things at the training school too, you know.'

'So, what are we going to do with all of this?' he asked, 'and when are you going to show me the file you've been keeping back?' he smirked knowingly.

'Don't fret, I was leaving it until you had a good idea of what everyone else is doing.' She then lifted the hefty file containing years' worth of intelligence on every aspect of the Qupi gang and their operations in East London. 'Here's your homework for tonight,' she smiled, and dropped it with a loud thud on the table. 'I have to go and train with my dad for a bit, so we'll catch up tomorrow after work, okay?'

She had tried to cram everything into her days: work and training, and now Andy, and it had been tough. She had dropped the odd training session, much to her father's disappointment, and she had asked for earlier starts at work so that she could get some extra time in with Andy. After a while, it was smooth, and she was able to fit everything in.

The cab was on time, and she went straight to the gym, as arranged with her father . She saw him talking to a couple of young boxers by one of the rings as she walked into the gym, and he waved to her before giving an instruction to one of the trainers and walking towards her. He wasn't his usual smiling self, and gently guided her to his office near her sectioned-off area at the bottom of the arch.

'This must be serious,' she said with a smile, hoping it would help take the edge off a little. 'Things have changed, love,' he said, closing the door behind him and speaking in a low voice. 'The Qupi gang have been showing their faces again, much more than recently, where they were keeping a low profile after the run-in with your mob. Rumour has it that most of them went home to Albania and came back with more men. It looks like they're getting serious again, and stronger, so I wanted you to be aware of it.'

'Thanks, that's good to know. Have you heard if they've set up anywhere new? I doubt they'll use that warehouse again.'

'Well, there are more of them down at Tilbury Docks now, and there is a rumour that they've set up a new warehouse in the Sterling Industrial Estate, just off the Rainham Road in Dagenham. I've asked my mates in Tilbury to find out and get back to me about the docks. As for Dagenham, if it's true that they have acquired the warehouse I've heard about, then it confirms that their operation has grown, which is bad news for everyone else. Luckily, I have good connections there too, one of the garage owners on the estate is a great mate of ours, so we'll be able to keep an eye out.'

'Okay, whatever you can find out would be great, thank you. Now, how about a quick workout, I need to fix my legs.'

Trevor smiled. 'No rest for the wicked, eh?'

'You would know, eh, Dad?' Trevor pretended to be offended but took it well. They left the office and moved over to the curtained-off area to begin another gruelling training session.

THE FOLLOWING DAY, Wilf Baker and Nick McGuinness picked Kendra up for work. As they drove to the station there was the usual banter between them. 'You're taking the piss,' said McGuinness, 'having us cart you around like Miss Daisy all the time. I bet that wouldn't have happened if it was one of us.'

'I'm sure your lover boy Baker would have looked after you, wouldn't you, Wilf?'

It was good to be back amongst them, even if it was only for the drives to and from the station.

'All joking aside, how's it all going then, Kendra?' asked Baker. 'Aren't you bored in the intel unit yet? It can't be much fun looking at computers and statistics all day.'

'Yeah, it isn't much fun,' Kendra lied, 'but it keeps my mind busy and I'd rather that than be stuck at home doing nothing. I do miss you lot, though, for some reason.'

'That's not surprising, we're a lovely bunch, aren't we, Wilf?' said McGuinness. 'But don't worry, we'll keep every-thing warm for you, including your special scarf and slippers that you need for your special drives, Miss Daisy.'

Kendra laughed and said, 'You know, I've missed you guys. I've missed the jokes and the banter. It would be great if you had some new material, though, it's getting a little dated,' she replied in a flash.

Baker and McGuinness both laughed loudly. 'See, I told you there was nothing wrong with her,' said Baker.

'Come on, Auntie Kim, tell us some of yours, we've missed them so,' added McGuinness.

Being with them cheered her up and made for a good start to the day.

They soon arrived at the station. Upstairs, she continued her routine of popping in to see her old team before going to the intel unit. It was important to keep the relationships strong and also to update (and be updated on) any developments of note.

'We received a tip from an informant that the Qupis are about to smuggle in a ship-load of Albanians who are coming over from Calais,' said Rick Watts as he and Kendra sat down in his office, coffee in hand. 'Apparently, it's a freighter carrying dozens of containers full of new car spares for Renault dealers in the UK, and they have kitted out a number of the containers to smuggle the people in.'

'I've heard them use smaller ships in the past, but nothing so large. Is there any name or ETA for it arriving at Tilbury?'

'I've got a couple working on that but it's difficult doing it on the quiet. The informant will also keep his ear to the ground, but until then it will be tough to get anything accurate without attracting attention.'

'Nothing has come up in the intel unit, so this could be really fresh info, Sarge. What are you going to do?'

'Well, we have to find a way of getting that intel into the system without it coming from us. I'm going to pay the informant a little bonus to disclose that information to another unit, so that there is no link. I trust him, he's been feeding us info for years, so I think we'll be okay.'

'Great. Hopefully they will take it seriously and put an operation together, surely they can't ignore intel like that?'

'Let's see, eh? Now, get yourself downstairs and to work, young lady, the Dream Machine have crimes to prevent and you're getting in the way!' Kendra laughed and wheeled herself out of the office.

UPSTAIRS IN THE INTEL UNIT, Kendra sat at her desk and pondered on the recent events that had come to light. She made a point to speak to Andy later to see if it was something they could use to their advantage without jeopardising any police operations. In the meantime, her diligent search for information continued, her thirst unwavering. She helped the rest of the unit where she could, making herself useful so that they would want her to stay on, but at the same time being very selective about what she was holding back, for she and Andy to use.

The developments with the freighter intrigued her, and she was determined to find out what the ship was called and when it would be arriving. During lunch, she spent five minutes logged into Gerrardo's account whilst she searched the Border Force, Maritime and Coastguard Agency, and Interpol records. After six minutes, she found something she could use and quickly logged out of his account. She then researched Interpol's procedures on open-source sites before finding an opportunity that she wanted to follow up.

On Interpol's database, she had found a Red Notice for one of Qupi's lieutenants, Roan Dervishi. Dervishi was wanted for the brutal murder of the parents of a ten-year-old girl, who he had then taken and sold to an ISIS warlord in northern Syria. It had made International News and led to a joint operation to rescue the child by the American and British forces in the area at that time. The rescue had been successful, and the child was repatriated and in the care of her grandparents in Tirana, but the cost had been high. Eighteen Islamist terrorist fanatics had been killed, but the cost to the allies had also been high: four killed and six injured. Dervishi had a lot to answer for.

The intel gave background information about him, the

fact that he was from the Tirana region and spoke the Central Gheg dialect, along with Qupi. The last time he had been seen was in the Italian port of Trieste. Further research online showed that this was the port that Renault used to ship its engine components and other parts that were manufactured at their plant in Novo Mesto, Slovenia. Kendra was able to narrow down a number of freighters that were used for the transportation of those parts.

Having made a list of three ships large enough to carry dozens of containers, Kendra then searched vesselfinder.com, which showed every legitimate vessel on the high seas at any given moment.

'Bingo!' she exclaimed, before looking around to see if anyone had heard her.

The *Golden Ray 2* had left the port of Trieste fourteen hours earlier and was currently in the Mediterranean Sea, en route to the Atlantic Ocean and then on to the port of Tilbury. She estimated that it would take approximately seven days to reach Tilbury, giving them more than six days to decide what to do. She wondered whether anyone else had managed to make the same assumption, and decided that almost certainly, someone would have. Without wanting to make things worse, she and Andy had to come up with a plan of action before the opportunity was lost.

7

INTERCEPTION

'DAD, SOMETHING HAS COME UP AND I NEED SOME HELP.'

'What's up?' Trevor asked, sitting in his now favoured armchair. 'Don't you want to get to the gym?'

'Yes, but... I've come across an opportunity to do something about Qupi. We had some intel come in that he is on the move. I managed to trace a freighter that is inbound to Tilbury in around seven days, with dozens of Albanians on board. Some of them are likely to be new soldiers for his mob, and the rest are likely to be women, to work in the sex trade. He is growing and bold as brass, so I want to see if we can do something about it.'

Kendra explained the tricky situation about not being seen to be involved in any way, so whatever plan she came up with must be from a distance, and with no credit or pat on the back at the end of it.

'The thing is,' she continued, 'I can point the police units to all the right places so that they can do something about the ship, but I have to do it in a way that I can then follow up afterwards with the gang itself. I want to separate the two so that I can get to Qupi without interference.'

'If you can get the ship boarded before it reaches port, what do you think would happen with the gang?'

'I imagine they'd get a frantic call from their troops on board who would tell them what was happening,' she said, 'but it must be done in a way that is standard procedure and not off the back of an informant.'

'So, they'd get the warning call and then what? Would they close up their operations in Tilbury and Dagenham?'

'I doubt it, their troops wouldn't say anything to incriminate them, and the girls wouldn't have a clue about their operation. They'd have to write it off and take the hit.'

'There you go, then. You've isolated the two problems and can do something about Qupi away from the attention of the ship. I imagine he'll be pretty pissed off and smacking people around, it's a huge hit to take.'

'We'd have to put some surveillance in place to monitor their response, before anything happens, and then we can deal with them when we see their response.'

'I think it's time to do a recce down at their fancy new warehouse,' said Trevor. 'That way, we can figure out how to keep tabs on them.'

'Great, I'll get my coat,' she said, raring to go. She was walking unaided now, with the exception of a walking stick, and felt freer than she had for months. Trevor stopped her short.

'Oh no you don't, missy, you get yourself down to the gym and work on those legs of yours. They've seen you and they know you, so the last thing that is going to happen now is you poking around their new base – not gonna happen. Leave the recce to me and my boys, we know what to do.' He stood and gave her a hug, before heading out.

'Be careful, Dad, and let me know what you do down there.' Trevor closed the door behind him without a look back.

Kendra knew he was right and she hadn't argued the point, but it still frustrated her. On a positive note, she realised that they were growing closer; it had been a while since they had shared a hug like that. He also seemed to be taking this very well, and continued to surprise her every day.

She caught a cab to the gym. It wouldn't be long before she was comfortable driving again, and the gym was key to that happening sooner. After ninety gruelling minutes of exercise under the firm tutelage of Charlie, Kendra caught another cab and headed off to see Andy, mulling over the day's events in her head on the way. There was so much to tell him and plenty more to plan.

'THAT'S GREAT NEWS, Kendra! And great work finding the ship like that. In future, though, let me in on things sooner. I am a dab-hand on the computer and can help with that sort of research whilst you are earning your pay.'

'Fair enough,' she said, 'it will take a while before we get into a rhythm, but I agree that there is a lot you can do when I'm not around.'

'Good, glad to hear it.'

They sat down at the table and went through the day's intelligence. She explained to him that Trevor was going to visit the Dagenham operation to see if he could do anything from a surveillance perspective.

'We can take a handful of miniature cameras and place them around the exits,' Andy said, after she had explained. 'Those cameras are good for weeks, and I can monitor them from here.'

'What we need to do,' said Kendra, 'is get the information about the ship to the authorities well before it reaches UK waters. If we can get Border Force involved along with the Coastguard, that will be even better, and they can deal with all the initial arrests before the police get involved. That will give us some extra time before any attention reverts to Qupi.'

'Can we pass on the information covertly or via an informant, without going through police channels? If we can get one of Watts' reputable informants involved, they can go directly to Border Force, can't they?'

'Hmm, not sure. My concern is that it somehow comes back to our team, and they get caught interfering in something they've been warned off. We have to be very careful. I'll have a word with Rick tomorrow and see what he says. It goes without saying that I won't mention the warehouse or our plans.'

KENDRA'S LIFT the next morning was from the ever-smiling Norm Clark. Nothing seemed to faze him, and he always had a cheerful air about him.

'Morning, K. Where's your wheels?' he asked, as he helped her into the car. She thought it was time to start using her crutches for work and had decided that the wheelchair needed to be retired.

'I thought it was time I made an effort, Norm. My legs feel

a little better and I think using them more often will make them stronger. So here I am!'

'Great stuff! Well, let's get to work, then!'

As they drove off, Kendra asked, 'Have you heard if there's been any progress?'

'Nothing of note,' he said, 'but it's looking likely that something is brewing and then hopefully someone will act on it.'

Kendra did not say anything else more about it, she wanted to save it for Rick Watts and see what he recommended about getting the intel to Border Force and the Coastguard. He was likely to have good connections, especially in Border Force, so she was confident they could achieve their objective.

'I still haven't heard from Andy,' Norm said, changing the subject. I hear that he's been particularly shitty to anyone that calls to check on him.'

'Yeah, I've heard the same. He's completely ignoring my calls,' she added, 'and I'm just going to stop trying now, his message is loud and clear.'

'I agree, best to stay away and let him get on with it in his own time. Still, he's gone from being one of the happiest, liveliest blokes I've ever met to one of the angriest. Not a good fit for anyone, really.'

'No,' she said, wistfully.

'So, what have you heard?' Watts asked, as soon as she sat down in his office, the door firmly closed behind them.

'The ship is called the *Golden Ray* 2 and left Trieste yesterday, loaded with car parts, sex workers and some reinforcements for Qupi. It's due to arrive in Tilbury within the next week. Sarge, it would be brilliant if it was intercepted before it got to Tilbury, it would be a massive hit to his operation – and nobody would be any the wiser that we had anything to do with it.'

Watts paused to consider the intel, trying to see if there were any pitfalls for his team. 'Whatever we do must be done quickly and without anyone knowing we were involved, it's as simple as that. I don't care about credit or gloating in revenge, I just want these bastards taken down. I'll have one of our informants make the call to Border Force, where my mate Darren runs one of their support teams. He may be able to pinpoint the ship and we can get it boarded. I think we'll tell them it is carrying drugs, so it will come as a pleasant surprise when they find the real cargo.'

'That's a great idea, Sarge, getting them intercepted and escorted to a different port would hurt Qupi badly, and Border Force will then call the locals to make the necessary arrests and so on.' Kendra beamed inside, knowing that it was all coming together exactly as she'd hoped.

'Off you go, then, and call me if you hear anything new, ok?'

'Will do, Sarge.' Kendra waved as she hobbled out of his office.

As she made her way to intel, her mind was a whirlwind of activity, back-up scenarios and checking for any flaws in the plan. She was satisfied that they had done everything required. Now, all she and Andy had to do was to come up with a plan for taking out Qupi and his gang, without anyone knowing.

'SOME GOOD NEWS, K. My mate Stav owns a garage on an estate quite close to the warehouse. There's a good line of sight to the front, so you'll be able to see any movement in and out without any problems. There's a back door, which I noticed had some work done on it recently, which is probably now reinforced and prepped for a quick getaway. It comes out to a short road that leads to Pondfield Park, where they can be lost very quickly. There's a couple of other buildings close by that overlook the front, but nothing that I'd use. There are some small trees on the pavement planted every fifty feet or so, you need to make sure they don't get in the way of where you're looking to set up an observation point.'

'Great, any other concerns that you saw?'

'The only thing that may be a problem is that it is all very close to the Dagenham and Redbridge football clubs, so on match days you will have a lot of activity around there, which may obstruct any views you may have.'

'Yeah, that's useful to know, thanks, Dad.'

'Just be sure that whatever your plan is, that it is solid, K. These bastards won't let you off so lightly if they get hold of you again.'

'I know,' she replied. 'Trust me, I know.'

'OKAY, so everything is going to plan so far,' said Andy. 'But that doesn't mean it won't go to shit very quickly. We need something simple, quick and quiet, and we have to plan for alternative outcomes if things go wrong.'

'No shit, Sherlock,' she said, laughing as he paced around the cellar, looking more like a pirate than a detective.

'So, what's the plan, then, smarty pants?'

'First off, we need to get the surveillance in place. Have you found any cameras we can use?'

'I have, they're affordable and freely available online.' Andy clicked on a link he had saved for this very chat. 'These ones are miniature and only really effective within ten metres, so we can stick them somewhere near their doors and shutters. They're not brilliant, but they'll do the job.' He then clicked on another link. 'These are slightly larger but have a much longer effective range, of around one hundred metres. We can have one mounted at the garage that your dad's mate owns, just down the road. The line of sight is spot-on for something like this.'

'Great, that's the warehouse covered, what about surveillance on the shitbags as they leave?'

'Well, as there are only two of us, and they have seen us up close and personal, we should not get involved at all. We can't trust anyone else to help us with this, so the only solution is to improvise.'

'And how do you intend to improvise, Mister smarty pants?'

Andy smiled, which reminded her of the dashing good looks she had been attracted to. She shook those thoughts clear and listened. 'Well, as with the cameras, you can buy pretty much anything online now, including GPS trackers.'

He clicked on another link he'd prepared earlier and showed Kendra a black octagonal-shaped tracker that could fit in the palm of her hand. 'It's easily installed by a strong magnet and has a battery that can last up to three months. It's a really good bit of kit.'

'Great. So how will we do this?'

'Firstly, we plant these on the cars that we know about, for example, Qupi's lieutenants and those that are high-up in his organisation. We can track a car from far enough away that we won't be seen. Even if we lose them, the tracker will give us the route and destination, so we will very quickly get any addresses they visit. We use the first few days to look for any patterns, confirm home addresses, and then we can plan much more effectively later.'

'Okay, so we get some patterns, and we find out how they operate, where they live. What next?' She had some ideas but wanted to see what Andy had.

'Right, so don't get all upset now, but we need something to help take them out, and as you know, we can't use guns.'

'So, what can we use?'

'Well, the internet is very much our best friend again. I've been looking at all sorts of legal kit we can buy, like discreet tactical armour, some outdoor equipment that can do some damage, like a tomahawk axe or even tent spikes, but I don't think that's where we should go.'

'Glad to hear it!' Kendra exclaimed.

'We're both in a bit of a state at the moment, mobility is not our best feature. And these bastards are as tough as they come. The only way we'll be able to take them out is one-at-a-time, using brain power and a few clever bits of kit.'

'I'm listening.'

'We can make sure we have all the protection we can wear without being encumbered by it, so bullet-proof vests, arm guards, tactical gloves, toughened boots, and the like. We can then source some tasers, pepper spray, and cable ties on the quiet, which is pretty much what we'll need to incapacitate them. Once we have the kit, with the surveillance in place, we can plan a solid schedule for taking them out.'

'Which leaves one obvious problem, and a big one,' said Kendra.

'What do we do with them next?'

8

SURVEILLANCE

Two days later, the cameras and tracking units arrived. They decided to get them up and running as soon as possible. Kendra entrusted the larger camera with the longer range to Trevor, so he could get it installed discreetly at his friend's garage. The smaller cameras were tricky, as it meant getting close to the warehouse. They had pinpointed two of the trees as potential hosts to cover the front and decided on a down pipe from one of the buildings close to the back exit for another.

'I'll send the Ismail twins later tonight,' Trevor said. 'They've done stuff like this many a time, so this should be a piece of cake for them. Nobody will suspect them, and they are very discreet and loyal.'

'The twins?'

'Yeah, Mo and Amir. They're good kids. Their dad worked for me at the garage and was killed last year, so I've been looking after them, making sure they stay out of trouble, that sort of thing.'

'What do you mean by *looking after them*?' she asked.

'Well, they're not as disciplined as most of the other kids, so I give them odd jobs to keep them busy. I also helped their mum out; they don't have much, and their dad was a good guy, you know?'

'So, you trust them.'

'Yes, and they trust me.'

'Okay, fair enough.'

Later that night, the twins made their way to the estate on their mountain bikes. As they reached the industrial estate, Mo, the elder of the two by twenty-seven minutes, stayed back at the junction covering the only road to the Qupi ware-house. His role was to look out for police, security patrols or anyone he suspected may work for Qupi, and then phone his brother to warn him.

Amir, the youngest, who was the more fearless of the two, left his bike with Mo and went into the road on foot, walking confidently in case anyone was watching. He needed to look like he belonged there. They had both browsed the internet to see the layout of the road and warehouse, so he had a good idea what to expect. As it was almost midnight, there was nobody around, although they both anticipated a presence at the warehouse. As Qupi wanted to be discreet at his new venue, there was no obvious security presence there, and his goons were all inside, asleep, playing cards, or doing some-thing that prevented them from paying attention to their jobs. Nonetheless, Amir was cautious as he approached.

At the first tree, he had a good look around, and when he was satisfied the coast was clear, he swiftly hoisted himself up to the lowest of the branches, just under seven feet up. He was instantly invisible from the street, the shadows and his dark clothing helping him to blend in nicely. He activated one of the small cameras and placed it at the juncture of two branches, making sure it was directly facing the front of the warehouse. He then used a strip of high-adhesive tape to secure it in place, without obstructing the camera lens. After another quick look around, quietly and with some agility, he dropped from the first tree and moved to the next one about a hundred feet away, where he repeated the process. He kept looking at the warehouse for any signs of movement but could see nothing, noting the absence of any lights. He went around the back of the warehouse and was able to secure the last camera onto a neighbouring downpipe, taping it to the bracket that attached it to the wall, where it would not be obvious to any passers-by. The cameras were now all in place, activated, and good to go.

As he approached the junction where his brother was watching from the shadows, he sent a message to Trevor to let him know the cameras were in place.

'Good job, bro,' Mo said as they met up. 'Now let's get us out of this manor, it's nasty here.'

FIVE MINUTES LATER, having stayed up specially, Kendra received the message she had been waiting for, from her father.

'The cakes have been delivered,' it said, with a smiley face. She immediately rang Andy, who was also up and waiting for the updates.

'We should be good to go,' she said. 'My dad installed his camera earlier this afternoon and I just heard that the others are all in place in Dagenham, so we need to test all four.'

'Great, just give me a sec while I bring up the app,' Andy said. She could hear him typing away.

'Okay, first up is the camera from the garage with the longest view. The low-light feature is working perfectly, and I can see that there are no obstructions or concerns, good job, Trevor!'

'And the rest? The smaller ones?'

'Yep, all three are up and running. Not as sharp as the other camera, but we will be able to see any movement quite clearly and there are no obstructions. We are good to go, Miss March!'

Kendra smiled. 'Well, if they're set up, we can leave them to do their job and move on to the next part, which is not as easy.'

'The cars.'

'Yes. We need to find a way of attaching the GPS receivers without being spotted, in broad daylight, when the cars are there. Got any thoughts?'

'Maybe, but you need to ask your dad to enrol the twins again, I think it's a job for them.'

'What did you have in mind?' she asked.

'Well, how else can we approach the cars during the day without attracting any unwanted attention or arousing suspicion?'

'You've lost me, I have no idea at all.'

'Okay, so the warehouse has a car park at the front, which is unobstructed and open for all to see. It fits six cars and the rest need to park in the street, right?'

'Keep talking.'

'If we can park a handful of friendly cars out the front, we can send the twins in to wash them. I'm pretty sure your Dad's garage mate has a car wash, so we can make out that they've come from the garage, wearing their overalls, and that these are client cars in need of a clean. Once they start, Qupi's mob will either come out to see what's going on and then go back inside when they see nothing of concern, or they'll have a look out of the window and just ignore them again. Either way, one of the twins can go and knock to see if they want theirs cleaning, and on the way, they can attach two of the GPS magnets in seconds. If they say yes, then it's easy to attach the rest, or if they say no, and we need more tracking, then he can attach a couple more on the way back. We can give them some cards from the garage to leave with them, too. You never know, they may go for it, especially if they want to stay in the area.'

'I suppose it's worth a try. Even if we only attach to four of them, that may be enough for what we need. We have to make sure that the twins are selective as to which ones they target.'

'And don't forget,' Andy said, 'now that the cameras are up, we should know when Qupi turns up and which of the cars is his. I reckon it could work. We can have the twins out there for a few days working on different cars, they will blend in nicely.'

'Okay, I'll speak to my dad and see what he thinks. I'll call you later, get some sleep.'

'You too, Miss smarty pants, today has been a good day!'

———

THE NEXT DAY, after speaking with Trevor and handing over the GPS tracking units, they put the second part of the surveillance operation into action, sending the twins out bright and early to park four of Stav's dirtiest cars from the garage in the street outside the warehouse. It wasn't anything out of the ordinary; the road often filled up with cars belonging to workers from the estate. Getting these in early was not a problem, and was a necessity to ensure they had the right spots reserved, much like annoying holidaymakers with sunbeds.

'If they ask why you have started doing this, then you just tell them that Stav is having some work done at the garage and needs the space for a few weeks,' Trevor told the twins.

'Don't you worry, Mr T,' Mo replied. 'We got this.'

Later that morning, shortly after nine, when most people in the estate were at work, the twins rolled up with their wheeled stainless-steel buckets filled with water and sponges. They played the part well, making sure each car was drenched with cold water first, before returning with warm soapy water to start sponging them clean. They took their time with each car, making sure to do the job well and in the correct order, rinsing and then drying, whilst checking covertly to see whether they were being watched. After they had cleaned the first two cars and dried them, they decided to put their plan into action, which was somewhat different to Andy's.

Firstly, they stopped work and turned on a radio while they sat in one of the cars, the doors open and their feet on the pavement while they ate their sandwiches, the music nice and loud. Hiding in plain sight, as the experts regularly say. After a leisurely lunch, they brought out a football and started kicking it at each other, using the full width of the road to give them some distance. They were surprisingly talented with the ball and kept it up using all parts of their bodies: heads, shoulders, knees, and, indeed, toes. There were lots of exclamations and congratulations as they tried to outdo each other with their trickery. A few minutes in, Amir, who was facing the warehouse, nodded at Mo when he saw that there was no activity at any of the windows. Mo nodded back.

Amir's next effort was sliced and went over Mo's head and into the Qupi car park, much to Mo's feigned amusement. The ball rolled up against a sleek metallic grey Mercedes S 500 Coupe, which was the largest, fanciest car in the car park. As Mo leaned down to pick up the ball, he removed one of the GPS trackers from his sock and gently placed it under the rear bumper near one of the twin exhausts. The strong magnet took hold immediately and stuck fast. Mo grabbed the ball and returned to Amir, laughing and shouting abuse at him for his errant shot. The whole thing had taken just a few seconds, and nobody had seen a thing.

The twins repeated the trick twice more before ending their pretend lunch break. One car was a brand-new electric-blue Audi A8 and the other a menacing BMW M5 in matt black. The three cars they had chosen were the most likely candidates for Qupi and his lieutenants, but the twins were prepared to do the same the following day if required. They also went up and down the street leaving cards for Stav's Garage under each windscreen, as a further show of legitimacy. They had neither seen nor heard a thing from the warehouse, and so the plan was, for now, working perfectly well and according to schedule.

A few minutes after they left, a pair of mobsters came out of the warehouse, looked up and down the street, and then walked to the rear of the cars to check for any damage. They found none and went back inside, content that there was nothing out of the ordinary.

The twins, in the meantime, had sent a message to Trevor,

which he had relayed to Kendra, who was in the intel unit when it arrived. She quickly messaged Andy to let him know that three GPS units were in place, and to ask him to check that all three were active and ready for tracking.

Two thumbs-up emojis followed.

9

HUMAN TRAFFICKING

USING AN ONLINE APP THAT SHOWED WHERE EVERY LEGITIMATE ship on the seas was currently located, Kendra was able to keep track of the *Golden Ray 2* so that she could estimate more accurately their arrival into British waters.

As it was travelling from Trieste, a reputable Italian port, instead of the disreputable Albanian Port of Durrës, some six hundred miles away, it was unlikely to attract any unwanted attention when it arrived, which is why Qupi had utilised this long-winded but seemingly safer method. They had planned it carefully and used their contacts in both countries to facilitate the operation. Qupi was conscious of the recent negative attention he had attracted in London and wanted to keep a low profile. He had ambitions for his UK operations that were unmatched by anyone else, and he was confident he would achieve them – and soon. This was one small part of it, bringing in extra soldiers along with dozens of new sex workers to increase his holdings in East London especially.

What most of his gang were currently unaware of was that several other containers on the freighter were filled with more cargo bound for his warehouse. Three specially-adapted containers had been set aside specifically for the transport of middle-eastern refugees who had paid tens of thousands of pounds for safe passage to the UK. The containers had been refitted to include a false floor, raised eighteen inches from the floor, with several hinged hatches along both sides. The Qupis had done this to create a void underneath with a dozen or so compartments, where waste could be stored, along with other goods they wanted to transport that didn't belong to the passengers. It was a clever system designed to maximise profitability whilst attempting (ever so slightly) to ensure that all passengers stayed alive.

They had crammed thirty people into each container, in typically atrocious conditions. The refugees were to endure seven days of sweltering, stinking conditions with nothing more than buckets and toilet paper, and a few cases of water that they would need to ration. They had also been given stacks of plastic bags and string, to ensure that all waste was bagged up and stored in the floor compartments until their arrival. They had quickly realised that to prevent them from gagging for the entire trip they would need to double- and sometimes triple-bag, and even then, the smell was unbearable.

They had been pre-warned to bring their own food, enough for a week's journey, and to keep their belongings to a minimum so that they would be more comfortable, but they were all very aware of the discomfort ahead of them. All that was provided for comfort were the twenty or so mattresses for them to sit or lie on, and a pile of rough blankets to keep them warm. Included amongst them were many children, but no babies or toddlers were allowed as they were likely to attract unwanted attention with their crying. Only children over five were allowed, as they could be kept quiet when required. The families were under no illusion that it would likely be the worst trip they would ever have to endure.

The crates had been stacked at the farthest section from the bridge amongst the legitimate cargo, the car spares, so the air that made its way to the refugees was fresh enough to keep them going. The passengers spent most of their time lying down and sleeping, praying for the journey to end.

Along with the refugees, there were two further containers that held the sex workers from Albania. The majority of them had been sold by their dirt-poor families when younger, and they had later been held in what could only be described as *human camps*, set up specially to ready them as sex workers for overseas markets. The gangs had much experience in farming these poor women out to maximise profits in what was a lucrative trade. Forty girls in total were kept in more comfortable conditions than the refugees, with screened-off areas for privacy whilst they used the portable toilet, clean mattresses and bedding, and a variety of food and drink to keep them going until they started their new lives in the UK.

The sex workers were also in containers in an isolated area that couldn't be seen by the freighter sailors, but at the opposite side of and farthest away from the refugees. This allowed for Qupi's soldiers to check on them regularly, to open the container doors for fresh air and the occasional dalliance in exchange for cigarettes and chocolates. The soldiers were enjoying their trip, it had turned into a fun cruise for them, a holiday before their new careers were about to start in East London. They too were kept in similar containers, again experiencing much better conditions than the refugees. Their instructions had been very clear, not to attract any unwanted attention whilst travelling. Both the sex workers and the soldiers were being looked after by three of Qupi's trusted men who had flown to Italy specially to supervise the precious cargo on this trip. They were strict with them and ensured that nobody strayed so far as to be seen by the sailors on board. All three were known to the freighter personnel and so their presence was overlooked.

By the time they were one day out from their destination, all parties involved were looking forward to being on land again, and, in the case of the refugees, breathing in fresh air. Qupi's men were confident there would be no hitch when they arrived, as they now had tight control of the docks and almost everyone working there, especially the decision makers. Qupi looked after them and looked after them well, and as such, each delivery so far had gone smoothly.

There was nothing to suggest anything would go wrong in the case of the *Golden Ray 2*.

KENDRA MET with Rick Watts during their morning coffee ritual. They were both excited and nervous in equal measure, in light of what was supposed to go ahead that day.

'Well, everyone is up to speed. Darren and his Border Force buddies will be intercepting the *Golden Ray 2* just as they enter British waters,' Watts said. 'I think they want to see what the score is before making a decision about their next move. They will be looking for drugs that have been hidden in random containers, which is what the informant told them, so they will start looking pretty quickly once they board the freighter, to avoid any potential loss overboard.'

'That's great, Sarge. Hopefully they will find Qupi's men quickly.'

'They have all the kit they need, including drug dogs and special thermal cameras, which will show up any bodies. It'll be spot on,' he said.

'I'm guessing that once they have boarded and make their discovery, it will be hours before the ship is secured in port and prisoners taken into custody.'

'Yes, Border Force and Kent Police will probably take that on, as the ship will likely be escorted into Folkestone to be processed.'

'Great, so now we just wait. Is there an ETA to intercepting them?'

'Darren and his team are geared-up and just leaving now, so I reckon within the next couple of hours we will know.'

Kendra smiled, hoping that the operation was a success. The damage to Qupi would be significant and make it easier for her to deal with him in the aftermath, as the gang tried to hold everything together. Her plan was to continue causing damage to his empire until he could no longer function here, and if there was a way to take him out of action completely, even better. That was a bridge to be crossed when the time came and they had somehow managed to have Qupi in custody.

'Right, I'm off back to work,' she said, limping away on her single crutch.

'You're making decent progress, Kendra,' Rick replied, 'hopefully it won't be long before you're back with us.'

'I hope so, Sarge, but the legs have taken a battering and it will be a few months before I'm fully fit.' And that is how she left him, knowing it gave her some breathing space to carry out her plans with Andy. All being well, that was.

IN THE SECOND-FLOOR INTEL OFFICE, Kendra tried to act as normal as possible and carried out her duties as expected. Inside she was trembling with excitement, counting down the minutes until there was some news about the ship.

'Kendra, could you give me a hand with something, please?' asked Paul Salmon, one of the retired detectives that had come back to serve as a civilian.

'Sure thing, Paul, what do you need?'

'Sam and I have been asked to put together some intel on an Albanian gangster, and I think he is involved with the chap you had a run-in with, Qupi?'

'You know my team has been warned off that lot, don't you?' Kendra said, her expression turning serious.

'Yeah, I know all about that, but nobody needs to find out that we've spoken about it, do they? Also, you're in the intel unit now, so technically they can sit and spin.' The old-timer smiled at Kendra. He knew how the system worked and didn't care if anything went south. Each day he worked was a bonus to him; he didn't need the money, he just wanted to keep himself busy doing the work he had loved for more than thirty years. His colleague-in-arms, Sam Razey, was exactly the same. Kendra knew they would be true to their word.

'Okay then, glad that's out of the way!' she said, with a beaming smile. 'Who is it and what do you need?'

'His name is Roan Dervishi,' Paul said, 'and he is one nasty piece of shit. There's an Interpol Red Notice on his head, so he's up there with the best of them. He killed the parents of a young child back in Albania and then sold the little girl to an ISIS warlord. He's as nasty as they come. The girl was rescued but it cost the lives of four soldiers and eighteen of the warlord's men, so he is wanted by a lot of people.'

'I've come across his name a few times, but nobody seems to know of his whereabouts.'

'Well, the geniuses upstairs are putting some sort of operation together and apparently he is their main target, and not Qupi. It doesn't make any sense, going after someone who is effectively a ghost, when there are others right here on our patch we can go after. Something stinks, and I was hoping you could fill in some of the gaps.'

Sam had started making his way over. Once he had taken a seat, Kendra looked around to check they were out of earshot of anyone else.

'Guys, you know what happened that night, with Andy, and you know my team have been warned off this gang. Apparently, we are a risk to any future prosecution case against them, which is utter crap.'

'Yeah, we're aware of all this, Kendra, but we think something upstairs smells bad about this whole business and we don't trust anyone enough to ask,' said Sam. 'So what do you know?'

'Well, we have our suspicions that someone upstairs is looking after Qupi and his mob, we don't believe any of that bullshit about our being a risk, it's bloody convenient for them, though. Roan is as bad as they come, and it's unusual that they are putting an operation together on him, it sounds like he is being sacrificed to keep the rest of them safe. Or they are doing it to show they are making an effort, knowing full well they will never find him. That's my opinion.'

Kendra had some intel on Dervishi but had no idea of where he was, with no known hangouts or family anywhere in the UK.

'What is it they are actually asking for, from you?' she asked.

'They want to know where he is currently living so that they can get a warrant for a raid, but we have absolutely nothing, and it feels like we're being sent on a wild goose chase to keep us away from the other scumbags. We know where they all live, why not ask about them?'

'Yeah, that doesn't sound good at all, does it? Let me do some digging around and I'll let you know if I find anything.' Kendra wasn't confident, though, her stash of intelligence at Andy's house was comprehensive, and Roan Dervishi's folder was one of the slimmest. Maybe it was time to dig deeper, and have Andy delve into the darker areas of the worldwide web.

'Thanks, Kendra, we appreciate it.'

The ex-detectives walked back to their respective desks, murmuring as they left. It made her proud and restored some of her faith that there were people like Sam and Paul still around, but they clearly sensed the same rotten things she did, which simply reinforced her belief that justice had failed in this country. Still, this was some interesting information that she would put to good use.

At her next break, she hobbled outside and called Andy. She explained the conversation with her colleagues to him and expressed her ongoing concerns that there was a bad fish in the pond upstairs.

'It's interesting that they are putting something together on the one person we know the least about,' said Andy. 'I think you're right, this is a paper exercise designed to keep people off the right track.'

'I think it's time you showed me some of your infamous extracurricular skills, Mr Pike, and get yourself on the dark web. I think that's where we will find Mr Dervishi.'

Andy had mentioned his skills with computers, which were a match for Kendra's, but he had an advantage over her with his knowledge of the dark web, where he was able to find people and equipment whilst remaining anonymous. There was a cost, but that was expected —and well worth it, if it meant you were never traced.

'If he's on the dark web somewhere then we need to find a way of drawing him out into the open, or at least find a way of confirming he is still around. I'll use a special program called *Hades* to search for him there.'

'Hades?'

'He is the unseen god of the underworld, so a pretty apt name, eh?'

'Ah-ha,' said Kendra, feigning amusement.

'I think that finding him will help us with Qupi, especially if the nonsense operation from upstairs then goes ahead because they have a confirmed location for Dervishi,' Andy said.

'So, while they go after Dervishi, we can quietly go after Qupi.'

'And the elephant in the room is...'

'What do we do when we find Qupi?' said Kendra.

'Yep.'

'I think that will depend on whether or not we have any solid evidence that will guarantee a prison sentence, doesn't it? We'll have to think on our feet, Andy. I do have a back-up plan if things don't work out and we don't have any evidence, though.'

'What's that, then?'

'It will mean calling in some big favours from my dad, which may be tricky, as I have asked an awful lot of him recently.'

'Well, there's only one way to find out.'

BACK IN THE OFFICE, Kendra was conscious of the fact that the Border Force operation was about to come to a head. She decided that it would be better if she were upstairs in the Special Crimes Unit with Rick Watts, so that she could get first-hand news of any updates.

'Good timing,' Rick said as she entered his office. 'They're about to board the *Golden Ray 2*.'

10

RESCUE

IN THE ENGLISH CHANNEL, HAVING RECENTLY ENTERED BRITISH waters, the freighter *Golden Ray 2* was entering the final leg of its journey to Tilbury Docks. Captain Philippe Pires, a veteran sailor of thirty years, was just settling down with a cup of piping hot, super-strong black coffee, when he noticed the approaching Border Force vessel, with its blue light flashing.

'What is this?' he boomed, just as channel 16 on the ship's radio squawked harshly into life.

'This is Captain Darren Richards of Her Majesty's Cutter Vigilant. You have entered British waters and we have a warrant to board and search your vessel for controlled substances. Please slow to a stop and prepare to be boarded.'

Captain Pires froze, knowing that he had three passengers on board who could bring an almighty avalanche of unwanted attention to him and his ship. He had insisted on correct paperwork for them, but he had no idea what their cargo containers had in them and what nefarious business they were conducting. His delay in responding elicited the same message from the externally-mounted speakers on the sleek 42-metre cutter, which was now running alongside the *Golden Ray 2*.

'Captain of the Golden Ray 2, this is Captain Darren Richards of Her Majesty's Cutter Vigilant. You have entered British waters and we have a warrant to board and search your ship for controlled substances. Please slow to a stop and prepare to be boarded by UK Border Force agents, who will conduct a search.'

This started a chain of events on the ship that were almost comical, had they not been incredibly serious. The three Qupi goons ran and made sure that the sex slaves and soldiers were all warned to remain silent and that all container doors were shut, before securing them with industrial-sized padlocks to give the impression of security. They quickly scanned the deck to see if there were any tell-tale signs of activity, before casually making their way to the crew's quarters.

One of the men used a satellite phone to send an urgent message. 'We are about to be boarded by the police, I will check in later if all is well.'

Pires decided that there was little choice other than to heed the warning and cooperate with the cutter's request, so he acknowledged Captain Richards on the radio and then proceeded to slow to a stop, which, with a ship the size of the Golden Ray 2, was more difficult than it sounded. The cutter launched its seven-metre rigid inflatable boat from its stern slipway, loaded with eight Border Force agents, a drugs dog, and the pilot. As they pulled up alongside the freighter's pilot ladder, the crew went to assist the embarkation and Pires himself went on deck. The RIB pulled up effortlessly alongside the freighter, which had slowed to a crawl, and nudged the hull as it neared the pilot ladder. When it was in position, the well-drilled agents climbed up the rope ladder that led to the slanted pilot ladder and swiftly boarded the ship, carrying the kit that they would need for their search duty. Last to board was the drug dog and its handler, who needed some assistance as he had the dog strapped in its harness on his back.

'Captain of the ship?' one of the agents asked, as he came forward to meet the crew.

'I am the captain,' Pires said, coming forward, 'Captain Philippe Pires. What is the meaning of this?'

The agent retrieved a document from his pocket, protected by a see-through sleeve, and handed it to Pires, who reluctantly took it, glanced at it without reading it, and then looked up at the agent.

'My name is Captain Darren Richards of Her Majesty's Cutter *Vigilant*, sir. We have a warrant and the authority to board your ship to search for illicit drugs that we believe are on board. Before we start the search, is there anything that you wish to tell us that will speed things up?'

It was always asked and never responded to, but it did sound polite and professional.

'There is nothing here for you, Captain Richards, we are carrying car spares for Renault. Where did you get information that we have drugs on board? It is scandalous!'

'Captain Pires, we are simply responding to the warrant that has been issued as a result of information received. If there are no drugs on board then I'm sure there won't be a problem, will there?' Richards turned to his men. 'Teams of two, split up and start below, you know the drill.' One of the men stayed with Richards as he turned back to Pires. 'Captain, may we please see your manifest?'

'Of course,' was the reply. 'Come with me.' He led

Richards to the bridge, leaving the single agent below to keep an eye on the crew. Pires knew that it was only a matter of time before they found something they did not like the look of.

Back on deck, three men were feeling particularly vulnerable. Qupi's men could not do much other than watch and hope they weren't picked out. They had thrown their weapons—and all other incriminating evidence that they had on their persons—over the side. The man with the satellite phone managed to get another message off unseen, saying, 'They have a dog with them.' That message was loud and clear for Qupi to understand that it was most likely that his precious cargo would be sniffed out by the highly trained dog. The best they could hope for was that the three overseers were not also taken into custody. They had been given papers showing them as ship's crew, but any further investigation into their legitimacy would quickly show they were not employed by the freight company. It was a tense time for them, especially since the agents would not find the cargo until they had finished below and started on deck.

Back on the bridge, Richards was looking through the freighter's manifest, which showed that it was carrying a lot of Renault car spares, hundreds of millions of pounds' worth. As he had spoken with Rick Watts several times, Richards knew the real reason they were on board and was going through the motions to attempt a deflection away from the Serious Crime Unit's suspicions. He could sense that Pires was concerned and thought he'd pile on the pressure.

'Captain, it is just the two of us now, so nobody will know anything of our discussion here. You know as well as I do that something is not right on your ship. We can go through the motions here and find out the hard way, whereby you will be held directly responsible for any illegal activities on your ship, or you can help me find those that are truly responsible. It's your choice.'

Pires looked at Richards and knew that he was a beaten man. 'Captain Richards, I wish to cooperate in every way I can, but I must have assurances,' he whispered.

'What assurances are those, Captain?' Richards asked, knowing he had hit the jackpot.

'I will tell you the men that are responsible, but you must deal with them without any suspicion placed on me or my crew.'

'Captain, you and some of your crew will be placed under arrest and taken into custody, regardless of what you say to me now. What happens after your arrest is dependent on what you tell me and how much you help me. You have my word that I will do my best to see you all released from custody within twenty-four hours and allowed to fulfil your delivery if the information that you give me delivers the right people to us.'

Pires grabbed a notepad from a table and wrote down three names, the three he had been paid a great deal of money to bring on board without any questions.

'If they suspect I am responsible for their detention then I am a dead man, Captain. They know where I live, my family, everything, they are truly very bad people. Please do what you can to protect us.'

Richards looked at the piece of paper, folded it in half, and put it in his top pocket. 'You will all be treated with respect and dealt with correctly, Captain, I have made my promise to you. But know this, if you have withheld anything or have lied to me in any way, I will do my best to see that you serve a life sentence at Her Majesty's pleasure. Now, what is the cargo they are carrying, and what do you know about it?'

'I know nothing about the contents, Captain, you must believe me. What I can tell you is that they have seven containers on this ship, amongst all the spare parts. I can tell you that they have split them into three groups. Two of the groups are close together on deck, but the other group of three containers is at the opposite end and farthest away from the bridge. I have no idea why and I never asked any questions. I did what I did because I fear for my life and for that of my family. I hope you believe me, Captain Richards.'

Richards looked at Pires and could sense the fear in him and saw that he was doing the best he could to save himself and his crew. He believed him. 'Can you tell me where the containers are, the numbers, and anything else about them?'

Pires grabbed the manifest, and from the list, wrote down the seven serial numbers relating to the illicit containers. 'Here you are, Captain. I hope we have an understanding.'

Richards took the second slip of paper and nodded. 'We do, Captain Pires, we do.'

———

BACK ON DECK, where the crew were waiting patiently, Richards decided to address them all, knowing that three of them were ringers.

'Gentlemen, we will try and do this quickly so that you can be on your way again. We have been informed that there is a large shipment of drugs on this ship, which is what we are looking for. The sooner we find these drugs, the quicker you will be on our way. To that end, I am asking you to help me find them.' He looked at them one by one, to gauge their reactions. Almost all had a blank, enquiring, or shocked expression, hardly the look of a guilty person.

'Please raise your hand if you know where the drugs may be. Maybe you heard something or saw something suspicious? Maybe one of your crew has been acting strangely? Anything at all that may help us would be greatly appreciated.'

Almost immediately, at least half a dozen crew turned and looked at the three interlopers towards the back of the group. They quickly looked back, and nobody said anything; it had been a natural reaction that Richards had hoped for. He took note of the three men and said, 'Very well, don't say I didn't warn you. It means you will be held here for some time.'

At that point, the three teams that had been searching below came back on deck. They had an evidence bag that contained a handful of small bags containing herbal cannabis. It wasn't what they were looking for, but it helped with their cause. He made a point of picking them out of the evidence bag and examining them, so that the crew would see everything.

'Okay,' he said, turning to the search teams, 'let's start on the deck, grid plan C as you were briefed.'

He turned to the crew. 'You might as well get comfortable because this will take a while, as I said. If you need to use the lavatory, please step forward, you will be searched and then allowed to go, one at a time.'

Richards then went to join the duo that included the drugs dog. Out of sight and hearing of the crew, he told them what Pires had said. 'Make a show of looking through everything, but these are the serial numbers of the containers of interest.' He showed them the numbers, which they noted, before moving off and finding another team to repeat the same.

The search went on until the silence was broken by one of the search teams shouting loudly, 'FIND!'

Richards smiled, knowing that a container had been detected, so he went off towards the direction of the shout. The drugs dog was sitting looking intently at one of the containers that bore a serial number matching one from the list. His handler said, 'It's a pretty solid find, boss.' He then pulled a tennis ball out of his pocket and lobbed it to the dog, who grabbed it in delight and started chewing away. It was the only reward it wanted, and worked hard for it.

Richards went to the doors and noticed that they were secured by a solid new padlock. 'Get the Beast,' he ordered one of the agents, who retrieved a large battery-powered hydraulic bolt cropper. The agent switched it on, turned to Richards and his colleague and shouted, 'Stand back!' before switching on the cropper. It took mere seconds for it to cut through the heavy steel, and the agent leaned forward and removed the now-useless padlock. 'Ready, sir?'

'Go ahead,' said Richards, stepping back a few paces to give himself more room. The dog became agitated as the agent slowly opened the heavy metal door, releasing an unpleasant smell that could only mean there was something living in the container. The dog went berserk and tried to drag his handler forward, almost succeeding. Suddenly the dog's barking was overwhelmed by the intense screaming and shrieking of many frightened women. Richards shone a torch into the container and saw more than a dozen young women cowering against the far end, still screaming in fear of the dog and their discovery.

'Dear God,' he said, recognising it as a human smuggling

set-up. He brought out his radio and transmitted, 'Gentle-men, we have a smuggling ring here. One container with approximately fifteen-to-twenty young women, with many more to check and many more likely to be found. We'll need some help on deck to manage the crew and also to take these women into protective custody. Contact base and have them send assistance, and also our colleagues at Kent Police HQ, who will need to provide transport for multiple prisoners. Also, please send Nicholls and Price over, we'll need them in the interim.'

Nicholls and Price were a pair of armed police firearms officers Richards had brought along in the event anything was found that could be deemed dangerous. Having spoken to Rick Watts, he had been expecting a container or two full of impressionable young men who wanted to be gangsters, so he thought it best not to take any chances. If this was just one container of the seven, then the situation had turned into something much bigger than they had imagined.

'Gents, it looks like we'll be here for a while. Let's keep an eye on these ladies, don't let them out of the container but leave the door open for now. If they start acting up, then we'll close it again. I don't want to do much more until our back-up arrives, so let's take a short breather and regroup.'

It was going to be a longer day than he had ever imag-ined, as it was a much bigger operation than they had been briefed about.

BACK AT THE warehouse in Dagenham, there was much cursing as the gangsters reacted to the news. After a few minutes, there was a mini-exodus as some of them left, got into their cars, and drove off at a rate of knots. One of those was Qupi, who left in the metallic grey Mercedes as antici- pated. The activity had the knock-on effect of registering on Andy's computer when the cameras picked up the activity, which in turn led to the tracking app being activated by the cars on the move.

'Here we go,' said Andy, rubbing his hands in anticipation before picking up the phone.

'Are you free to speak?' he asked.

'Hang on,' said Kendra. 'Okay, I can speak, go ahead.'

'There's been a lot of activity at the warehouse and three cars have just left, including Qupi. Two of them are heading towards the docks and Qupi is heading north-east on the A12 towards Brentwood.'

'Okay, we think the ship has been boarded but we're just waiting for confirmation. Keep tabs on the cars and let me know if anything changes. Chat later.' She put the phone away and went back into the office where she sat down and continued working. Looking around, she could see that nothing had changed, and nobody was any the wiser. Her heart was pumping hard, knowing that something significant was about to happen, and that she had played a huge part in it. The next day was going to be critical and would determine whether her and Andy's plans were solid, or whether they had done nothing but upset a huge hornet's nest.

BACK ON THE *Golden Ray 2*, help had arrived swiftly in the form of another Border Force cutter, HMCC *Valiant*; Kent Police, with their patrol boat *Alexandra III*; and the Royal Navy's HMS *Trent* and their ninety-metre-long River Class offshore patrol vessel. Between the four vessels, they would be able to handle all prisoners and transport back to Folkestone harbour where they would be processed.

Richards quickly briefed the teams that boarded the *Golden Ray 2* and tasked them. Kent Police were to make the arrests for various offences outlined by Richards, and then take over transport of the prisoners by splitting them up between the various support ships before transport to Felixstowe. He pointed out that there were likely to be many more, so that they were able to plan accordingly. Other Border Force agents would assist with searches that recommenced immediately, and then assist later with transport and the processing of the prisoners.

Almost immediately there was another shout of 'FIND!' as the second container that housed the remaining sex workers was found, very close to the first one. Just a few minutes, and two more shouts of 'FIND!' later, the two containers that held the soldiers were found. There was more urgency in dealing with these and the firearms officers were quickly deployed to cover the agents dealing with them. Fortunately, the soldiers did not put up a fight; there was nowhere for them to go, and they hadn't made this wretched trip in order to die before landing. It wasn't until later when the containers were searched more thoroughly that a large stash of guns was found. There were also a number of bullet-proof vests and night-vision goggles, which suggested that Qupi had been preparing for something huge.

The soldiers were quickly searched and then secured with zip ties whilst waiting for their transport off the ship. Most declined to speak or respond in English when questioned, some replying that they didn't know anything. They had been trained well in advance to deal with the authorities in the UK.

The sex workers were searched by female police officers who had arrived on the Alexandra III and restrained until they could be moved. Many of them were in tears, fearful of what the future might hold for them.

The searches continued as the prisoners were slowly removed. Most of the accessible containers had been searched, apart from those at the far end of the ship. Once they were also searched and dealt with, then they could move on to find the remaining unaccounted-for containers.

'FIND!' was shouted for the fifth time. This time it was by one of the search teams that had gone to the far end of the ship and used a thermal camera to check for any heat coming from the containers.

'Boss, this one is as hot a reading as I have ever seen,' the agent said, pointing to the container in question. Richards checked and confirmed it as one of those on the list of seven.

'Let's get the Beast here and call one of the firearms guys over too, just in case.'

The Beast was quickly brought over and the padlock swiftly dispatched. As soon as the door was open, all the agents present immediately stepped back from the incredible stench that came from within.

'Jesus Christ!' exclaimed the agent with the Beast, 'there's dozens of them inside, boss!'

Richards shone his torch and could not believe what he was witnessing. The container was crammed full of men, women and children, poor wretched things that looked out from under their hands to protect them from the torchlight, too weak to do anything more. They were dirty, dishevelled, and they stank unlike anything he had ever come across.

One man stood up on weak legs, trembling as he did so, and put his arms up in surrender. 'Please,' he said, 'help them,' indicating to a corner where five people were lying motionless on the floor.

'Medics! Get over here, now!' shouted Richards. Border Force, the police, and the Royal Navy each had medical officers on standby at every boarding, so there were enough to check on all of those that had been crammed in containers.

'Sir,' called the agent with the thermal camera, 'I think there's two more with similar readings,' he said, showing Richards the camera. It was indicating a tremendous amount of heat coming from a pair of neighbouring containers.

'Let's get these two open, chaps, quickly as you can!' he shouted. These were the last ones to match the list that Pires had given him.

The beast was deployed, and more medics and agents called for, in anticipation.

Inside the two containers they saw much of the same. Wretched human beings in a dreadful inhuman state, driven to this horrifying existence in search of something better. Richards could only shake his head in disbelief that other human beings could do this to anyone, let alone children.

'Look after them, guys, I need to call this in.'

He went back to the bridge and called the operations room, updating them on their find. More support units were dispatched to assist, and ambulances directed to Felixstowe in advance of their arrival. It was one of the largest human trafficking operations that had ever taken place in British waters, and it was only a matter of time before the press were involved. Richards ended his call and immediately called Rick Watts.

'Jesus Christ, Rick, it's mayhem here. There's almost a

hundred people, including families with kids, crammed into three containers here, it's some sort of human trafficking system they have in place. There's also forty women and forty-odd hoodlums, who we think are the gang reinforcements. It's a massive job, mate, and it looks like there may be some very sick people that need hospitalisation. We're going to be here for a while, so I thought you should know before the press gets wind of it, which they will.'

'Bloody hell, mate, this is much bigger than anything we expected. It's gonna hurt them badly. Thanks for everything, I owe you one.'

'It had better be a bloody good one, Rick!' Richards laughed, hanging up.

Watts immediately called Kendra. 'Can you pop up for a minute?'

FIVE MINUTES LATER, Kendra closed the door behind her and sat down in Watts' office. She had been expecting this update and wasn't surprised to be called in.

'The boarding was a success, Kendra, thanks for your efforts with this. It's turned into something much bigger than we thought, though, a much bigger operation.'

'That's good, right?'

'It is, and Qupi is not going to be a happy man. They found around forty soldiers and forty sex workers in some of the containers, all ready to start work for Qupi upon their arrival. They also found almost a hundred other people: men, women, and children, stashed in three other containers. Some of them are in bad shape and are off to the hospital.

Qupi is involved in a lot more than we thought, human trafficking is the worst of the worst.'

Kendra was stunned. She hated Qupi with all her might
but hearing this took that hatred to a whole new level. She
was stunned but angry beyond belief that he was now
stooping to this to make money for his growing empire.

'Shit, so what are the bosses going to do about this now?'
she asked. Surely they couldn't ignore this.

'I have no idea, Kendra, it's up to them, now. It may be
that it's handed over to other agencies. It's turned into something huge.'

All manner of options and ideas were whirling around
her head as she tried to process this development. She had
anticipated some success but nothing on this scale. Hopefully, it would not impact on anything else she was planning
for Qupi.

'This is massive, Sarge, I mean, we spoke about getting
them in trouble on the quiet, but this? This could seriously
damage their operations here, it's everything we hoped for!'

'You know, I'm a little gutted that this turned out so well
and nobody will ever have a clue that it was our little team
that was responsible,' Watts said, proudly.

'We'll know, Sarge. We'll know.'

11

ANDY AND TREVOR

'Bloody hell, Kendra, that's brilliant news!' Pike said. 'That's really going to sting!'

'I'll stick around at the office to see if there are any further updates. Apparently, there's quite a few people needing serious hospital treatment, so I want to find out exactly where everything is.'

'Received and understood,' he said, 'and I have a bit of an update myself.'

'Go on,' she replied, eagerly.

'So, as we thought, two of the motors went to the docks to see if there was anything going on there. The cars are stationary near the café there, so I imagine they're in there having a catch-up with their stooges at the dock.'

'They're in for a long wait, the Golden Ray 2 is being taken to Felixstowe with everyone on board.'

'Ha! That should piss them off a treat!'

'So, what about Qupi? Where is he?'

'Well, that's where it gets interesting. He stopped at a Holiday Inn at Brentwood, on the A12 close to the junction with the M25. He's parked up there, likely meeting with someone. He's been there for a while now.'

'That's interesting,' Kendra said, 'can you dig around and see who that could be?'

'Already on it,' Andy said. 'I managed to get myself into the CCTV system at the hotel, so if anything happens outside, I should be able to get a closer look. Also, I'm having a sniff around on Hades as we speak. It's amazing what goes on—we need to get on here more often when this job is done.'

'Agreed, but let's get these bastards first, they need to go away for a long time for what they're doing.'

'Let's catch up later, unless anything urgent comes up,' he said, before putting the phone down.

———————

At the gym the next day, Kendra decided to finish a tough self-defence workout before speaking with her dad about her plans. She wanted to think on it more and her workouts had turned into something she thoroughly enjoyed, despite the pain he put her through. Her fitness had improved tremendously, as had her strength. She had mastered new self-defence techniques that would stand her in good stead. Her legs were still weak, but they were greatly improved; she could now stand unaided without too much pain, and she was able to kick the bag without discomfort. She would continue to use a crutch and then a walking stick for another couple of months, in order to give the impression that her recovery was slow but steady, but in reality, she was a couple of months ahead of schedule, thanks to her dad.

In the office after, once she had warmed down, she

decided not to waste any time.

'Dad, I have a plan that I will need your help with.'

'And what's that, love?'

'Qupi's operations are now under threat because of the ship getting impounded and his passengers arrested. But he's still out there doing whatever he wants, and that isn't sitting well with us. We want to go after him and his crew in the coming weeks, which is where you come in.'

'Go on,' Trevor said. He had learned not to second-guess his daughter anymore, and not to disagree or show displeasure at her plans – she was far too headstrong for that now and it would be a waste of time.

'So, we think the best way forward is to take the gang out one at a time, leaving him for last so that he can squirm a little as his operation is destroyed. We need somewhere to hold them until we decide where to drop them off, and I know you have some good connections down at the docks.'

Trevor thought for a few seconds before replying.

'Yes, I do know some people down there, some very good friends, in fact. But so does Qupi, he is paying off a lot of senior people there. There's a good chance he'll find out if we're doing something there.'

'Okay, so what do you suggest?'

'Well, for starters, you just want somewhere relatively remote to keep prisoners, right? Somewhere they won't be heard.'

'That's right. I thought the docks were ideal, with all the containers and empty warehouses there.'

'That's not the only place you can find those, Kendra. Just past the docks and away from prying eyes is the old Tilbury Marine Works, where there are plenty of places where older ships are moored and awaiting repairs or scrapping. There are dozens of old warehouses or buildings left from the boom days of the docks that are just sitting there empty, waiting for someone to make a decision on what to do with them. I know of at least three great buildings where nobody would think of looking. It won't take much to kit them out. Let me ask around and I'll let you know.'

'Great! Thanks, Dad.'

Their relationship had blossomed in the past few months. It wasn't perfect, far from it, but it was significantly better than it had ever been. There was a solid, trusting bond between them now, and an understanding. They had both quickly realised that this was a serious business they were now involved in, and they had to be strong but cautious in how they dealt with it. Planning for all eventualities was important, especially when it came to contingency plans - things were bound to go wrong at some point.

They needed to be meticulous with their plans.

'I think it's time you met Andy,' she said.

'I'm good with that,' he replied, 'Just let me know and I'll be there.'

'How about now? At his house? I'll message him to say we're on the way. He can order pizza.'

'It's good to meet you, sir,' Andy said, shaking Trevor's hand with a firm grip. 'Kendra has been telling me about your help with her training, amongst other things.'

'Yeah, well, it's nice to know she says nice things,' he replied, smiling at his daughter, 'and it's about time we met, with everything happening so quickly.' Trevor looked down at Andy's leg. 'It looks like you could do with some training, too. You should stop by the gym, and we'll sort something out.'

'Sadly, my foot is past the point of no return, sir. They did a good number on it and it's just a useless appendage now. I'm learning to live with it.'

'That's no excuse not to stay on top of your health and fitness, young man. If you're going to be working with my daughter, then I expect you to be fit and strong enough to be able to deal with anything that is a threat to her. Got it?' The smile had gone. Andy looked sheepishly at Kendra, feeling a little smaller than he had an hour ago.

'That's not fair, Dad. Andy's been through a lot and he's actually making great progress.'

'No, he's spot on, Kendra,' Andy piped up. 'I should be able to help you if you need it. I'm a big boy now and I have to find a way of making the best of things, right? I'll tell you what, though, Trevor, you shouldn't mince your words, you know, just come straight out and say what you mean next time.'

Trevor looked at Andy, wondering whether he was being offensive or not. Andy, in his own unique way, was just being funny. It was going to take some time for the two to understand each other's ways.

Kendra was happy to see Andy's mischievous behaviour resurfacing, pleasing her greatly. She was surprised by how much he had come along since she had seen him lurking behind his front door, dishevelled and angry. Surprised by how positive an impact her dad had made so quickly. There was more to him than met the eye, and she was enjoying the unravelling.

'Glad that's sorted, I expect to see you there tomorrow, young man,' Trevor said, placing a hand on Andy's shoulder.

It was a gesture of acceptance and it made Kendra smile. And proud. 'Now, where's this pizza?'

AFTER A QUICK PEPPERONI pizza and chicken wings dinner, washed down with bottles of light beer, Andy showed Trevor the secret operations room.

'This is great,' he laughed. 'I want one!'

They grabbed a spare stool from upstairs and sat down to look through the files and review their plans. It was important that Trevor was aware of everything the duo were planning, so that he could assist at any stage. They were a team now, and communication was key to success.

'Well, you've already put the cat amongst the pigeons and caused Qupi no end of grief, so he's going to be pissed and running around like a blue-arsed fly, trying to find out what happened and who was responsible,' Trevor said, inspecting the intel. 'So, moving forward, if you want to finish their operations off and put them all inside, you're going to have to up your game. Dealing with them from a distance, as you've done, is one thing. Now you're talking about dealing with them face-to-face, which is something very different. You need to be absolutely certain that you're both up for it.'

'Sir—' Andy started.

'And you can start by calling me Trevor,' Kendra's dad said, sternly.

'Sorry, sir, I mean *Trevor*. We have spent many long hours going over our plans, with back-up plans on top of that. Whatever we do, and however much luck we have, good or bad, there will always be an element of risk.'

'We can do this, Dad, but we need your help to be better.'

'You have that, Kendra. I'm not going anywhere, and I know I can help you with this. But it isn't just about this, is it? Once this job is done, you're not going to stop, are you?'

Andy and Kendra remained silent.

'Just as I thought. So, what you must understand is this. If you are going to carry on conducting vigilante operations in the name of justice, then you need to commit to it fully, but you also need to draw the line somewhere. If you cross that line, then you become part of the problem you are trying to solve. You know this, right?'

'Yes, we are very aware of that, Dad. We know first-hand, remember? We're in this for the long run, I assure you.'

'The reason I need to make sure, love, is that I will only help you if you do this properly, which will also mean safely. I will commit to this because I believe your aims to be true and necessary. Just know this, once we all commit and we start on this trail, there is no turning back, and we will always be a target. Not just to the scum out there, but to your colleagues. If you can't deal with that or you don't understand the ramifications, then don't do this, ok?'

The duo looked at each other and smiled knowingly.

'As I told you, we're in this for the long run and we understand the risk.'

'We can't thank you enough for this, Trevor,' Andy added. They shook hands and nodded in understanding.

'Don't thank me, Andy. Just start working harder and be stronger, because the world we are entering is nasty and brutal and unforgiving. If you make one small mistake it will mess you up really badly, really quick. Now, let's get to work.'

The team had just got stronger.

12

DEATH ON BOARD

EARLY THE NEXT MORNING, RICK WATTS RECEIVED A CALL from Darren, who was calling from Felixstowe port.

'Jesus Christ, Rick, this job is getting worse by the day. This is a real can of worms, mate. I've never seen anything like this, and I've seen some shit in my lifetime.'

'Will you stop whining and spit it out?'

'So far we have five refugees dead, including four young kids. And as if that wasn't bad enough, the shit literally just hit the fan this morning.'

'What happened?'

'They started clearing out the containers, which were specially built for these horrible journeys. They have a raised floor with partitions underneath that you can get to via hatches. The hatches were mainly filled with some personal belongings, some food and drink, and some for the rubbish. And then they came across the human waste compartments.'

Darren paused, and it was not for effect but to consider how to pass on the latest news.

'So, under the stinking bags of waste they found a bunch

of firearms, Rick, dozens of them. They were put there on purpose, to keep the refugees away from accidental discovery.'

'What sort of firearms?' asked Rick.

'They found fifty Škorpion machine pistols, fifty SIG Sauer P320 handguns and enough ammunition to start a war. All under the shit.'

'Bloody hell, that's some serious hardware. Are any of them talking?'

'Not a chance, mate. I think we might have to step this up a notch and bring Special Branch in. If we turn it into a potential terrorist threat, then SB can come in and do their thing. These animals will crap themselves if they think they'll go down as terrorists.'

'That's a great move. Keep me in the loop, won't you?'

'Damn right I will, this is all your fault!' he laughed, putting the phone down.

Rick was not laughing when he called Kendra.

AS SHE WAS TALKING to Andy, Kendra saw that Rick Watts was trying to call her.

'So, what have you seen?' she asked, after she had cut Watts off. She would call him straight back.

'I looked through the CCTV footage and it showed someone coming out with Qupi and walking to his car with him. It was dark and the CCTV there isn't great, but I've seen enough that I am confident it is Roan Dervishi. He's a big bastard, Kendra, much bigger than Qupi.'

'So Qupi has left there?'

'Yes, he left in the early hours and went back to

Dagenham where he has been all night. Dervishi is still at the hotel.'

'Damn, I was hoping we'd have a confirmed home address for Qupi by now, but he's been all over the place.'

'It'll come, don't worry. The trackers have at least three months' battery life, we'll be done by then.'

'Okay, keep an eye on him and we'll catch up later.'

Kendra ended the call and dialled Rick Watts. 'What's up?'

'There were five dead people in those containers, Kendra. Those poor bastards didn't stand a chance. Four of them were kids, for God's sake, I'm surprised there weren't more deaths after hearing how dreadful and inhumane the conditions were.'

Kendra was momentarily stunned before her anger got the better of her. 'Qupi has a lot to answer for, much more than we ever thought. So, what the hell are the top brass doing about it, Sarge? Surely they have enough to take them out now?'

'It's not as simple as that. They also found a stack of serious firearms in the same containers. They're debating whether to hand it over to Special Branch as a terrorist incident, to make sure something happens with it. And there is no evidence that ties this to Qupi so we may have nothing, despite this huge operation. Remember, we can't get involved, and the ship was because of a tip-off by an informant, so Qupi is unlikely to come up in any of their investigations unless someone talks, which I doubt is going to happen.'

'Sarge, that can't be right, surely? Nothing at all? None of the soldiers talked, or the sex workers?'

'Honestly, I don't think they even know much themselves,

Qupi runs his organisation very strictly, so it's doubtful. I'll let you know if they find anything else, ok?'

Kendra put the phone in her pocket and walked back to her desk, bitter and angry at the lack of activity against Qupi. She had half-expected it, but it didn't make the anger any easier. Fortunately, they had planned for any non-action, and this had effectively forced their hand.

They were going to have to take them on personally. All of them.

───────

THAT EVENING, Kendra made her way to Andy's house, still taking cabs to keep up the appearance of making a slow recovery. She felt stronger than she had done for a long time.

Despite this, she was still savvy enough to understand that it wasn't her strength and skills that would help her with this operation, but her brains and her guile. The Qupi mob were large, powerful, and armed, so knowing how to kick someone well was not going to be enough.

'Okay, so this has escalated plenty,' said Andy, after their latest briefing. 'The conditions on that ship must have been utterly dreadful for anyone to die—those poor kids.'

'The worst thing, apart from those children dying, is that there is nothing to tie the Qupis to it at this time. No evidence at all. If nobody talks, which they aren't, then he will get away with it. He'll lose a lot, yes, but he will just keep doing what he does.'

'So, we're back to our back-up plan, which is to do something about it ourselves, right?'

'Yep,' said Kendra. 'It seems that is the only way justice of any kind will prevail.'

'Great, we knew something like this was highly likely, and we've made plans. So, what are we doing first? Do we continue to go after their operations until they are out of business or destroyed by rivals? Or just go after the men and sort them out as planned?'

'Things have changed, like you said, Andy. I think we notch things up a little and stir the hornet's nest even more by going after someone that is clearly very important to Qupi.'

'Uh-oh, are you thinking what I'm thinking?' Andy smiled.

'We go after Dervishi.'

13

GANGSTER TAKEOUT

KENDRA HAD SPENT MANY MONTHS IN THE INTEL UNIT enhancing her computer skills, hoping to match Andy's, so that they could delve into those secretive areas on the dark web. When Andy had started using the Hades program it had allowed him entry into the dark web underworld where the likes of Qupi and his cronies did business, away from the prying eyes of the police up above. With his help, Kendra had learned how to access those areas that could only be reached by specific programs like Hades, or other specialist browsers that operated through specific network configurations.

All communication here was encrypted, and allowed for anonymity. Using a virtual private network and the Tor software program, they were able to look around freely, knowing they could not be traced. As Andy had a useful stash of crypto-currency – which Kendra did not ask him about - it enabled him to make anonymous purchases. This allowed him to show as a genuine buyer in some nefarious auctions where you could buy drugs, firearms, bootleg programs, personal data and more.

It was how Andy was able to purchase Cyclops, a program that gave easy access to any type of CCTV software, such as the hotel in Brentwood where Dervishi was staying. Cyclops also allowed for entry into the hotel's server where all bookings and other personal data were 'securely' stored, according to the hotel privacy notice that outlined their data protection obligations. As a result of the 'insecurity' that was quickly exploited by Cyclops, Andy was able to scroll through the current bookings and isolate the possible options for Dervishi. The CCTV coverage within the hotel itself was limited to the main concierge areas, the entrance and exits, and on the floors covering the lifts. Using the coverage that he was able to plug into, Andy quickly worked out that Dervishi was in a first-floor room, 124. The hotel's booking records showed that he had booked in a week previously and had paid in advance for four weeks, which was great news.

'Okay, he's booked in as Mr Cristiano Traore, and used a Spanish passport as ID. He's already paid for the room, using a visa card in the same name. The hotel shows that his car is a two-year old Grey BMW 6 series, which is parked in the hotel car park directly under his room and hasn't moved in days. The car is registered to a shell company based in East London. He has some connections, this bloke, to get these IDs to such a level,' said Andy as they huddled around one of the terminals in their subterranean hideout.

'He must be here for the Golden Ray 2 shipment, don't you think? I mean, why is he just sat in a hotel for weeks if he's not doing something for Qupi? That's why Qupi went to see him, to let him know what's going on.'

'Those guns that they found were probably coming to him, would be my guess,' Andy surmised.

'I think you're right.'

'Well, now that he knows what's happened to the ship it is likely that he will be spooked, so if we're going to do this, we have to do it very skilfully, otherwise it will be bad news for us again.'

'Don't worry, I have a plan. We just need to figure out a way of drawing him out of the hotel without suspicion and without the hotel security seeing anything.'

'I can fix the CCTV, remember?'

'Okay, so I think it's time to get Dad and the twins involved again.' Kendra smiled, the plan coming together neatly.

'Are you sure about this, love?' asked Trevor.

'Yes, he wasn't there when the twins did the whole car-washing routine, so he wouldn't have seen them or know about them.'

'You're convinced he will fall for it?'

'His car is expensive and pretty high-spec,' she said, 'so when he hears them messing around in the car park, he'll definitely want to come out to have a word.'

'Okay, well, you'd better be sure, because this guy sounds like a monster on steroids, and he'll need to be taken out quickly.'

'It's all part of the plan,' she said, smiling confidently.

'Okay, but I'm not taking any chances with this one, so I'll be there to help out as well. Just to make sure.'

'To make sure we don't screw up, or make sure he gets taken out quickly?'

'Both!' Trevor grinned in response.

'I don't know whether I should thank you or be angry with you, Dad,' Kendra said, feigning annoyance.

'Don't flatter yourself, young lady,' he said, 'I want to make sure nothing happens to the twins. Their mother will kill me if they get so much as a scratch.'

They all laughed and sat down to go over the plan. They had to be precise. They had to be very precise indeed.

———

THE NEXT MORNING, just after rush hour, a battered old Ford Fiesta with a dodgy exhaust, and an old Volkswagen Golf with blacked-out windows were driven into the Holiday Inn car park. As most vehicles had been driven away by workers trying to avoid the rush hour, the car park was relatively empty, and, luckily, so were the two spaces either side of Dervishi's fancy two-year-old BMW. The drivers locked the cars and walked away. Nobody had paid any attention.

Just before midday, when the hotel was readying for the lunch break, the twins walked into the car park. Unlike before, they did not wear their overalls or carry buckets of soapy water. This time they were dressed like gangster wannabes, with their designer jeans and trainers, their crisp, clean baseball caps, and their gold chains on display. And they hadn't come alone. The drivers of the two cars were with them, similarly dressed, the four of them talking and laughing as if they owned the place.

Kendra, Andy, and Trevor had timed it well. It was important that not too many staff were around, as they were mostly now tied up with lunch. As planned, and on cue, the CCTV camera covering the car park froze, so that anyone looking – which they were not – would not see anything untoward. Trevor had also arrived with Kendra, in a white van driven by Charlie from the gym, and which nobody would notice as being out of place. They parked at an acute angle so that nobody would see them sitting in the front. Andy had stayed behind to deal with the CCTV camera and also to monitor any activity, in case the operation went south.

The entire cast was there apart from the main attraction, Roan Dervishi himself. The signal was given, and the four wannabe gangsters commenced with their roles. They raised their voices slightly and started smoking the joints they had rolled up when they arrived. Within a few minutes it sounded like a small party was underway, and the smell of cannabis was sickly and very strong. One of the twins sat on the bonnet of the Fiesta, and the two drivers sat on the BMW. The second twin faced them, standing in front of the BMW, making that car the focus of their gathering. It looked very natural and somewhat menacing, the sort of thing most normal people would choose to ignore, a group of young yobs smoking weed and talking crap. Kendra and Trevor had banked on Dervishi not being normal, though, and not accepting the yobs even looking at his car let alone sitting on it. They had banked on his coming out to challenge the hoodlums. The whole plan depended on it.

It wasn't long before the curtains twitched in room 124 as the overpowering smell of cannabis reached the slightly ajar window. Coupled with the noise, it wasn't long before Dervishi looked out and saw what was going on. He opened the window further and shouted down. 'Hey, get your butts off my car!'

The group looked up at him and started laughing, shouting back, 'Don't worry, fool, we'll keep it nice and shiny for you!' More laughter. The plan worked like a dream, and it had given Dervishi no choice but to go down and get rid of the yobs messing with his car. Within two minutes, he was out of the front entrance and storming towards them, an angry giant with some excess energy that he clearly needed to get rid of. This was the perfect opportunity for him to take out his fierce anger about losing his guns - they would pay a heavy price.

'I told you to get your butts off my car, shit-heads!' he shouted, as he approached the four.

'That's our cue,' said Trevor. 'Remember, this needs to be quick.'

He and Kendra both left the van. Charlie stayed behind, waiting for his signal to move.

'Chill out, old man,' Mo said to Dervishi, who was now towering above them, just inches away. 'We're just having some fun here, okay?'

'If I tell you one more time then I will break you in half, little man,' Dervishi said as he shuffled towards Mo, chest out and arms in the typical body-builder position, as if holding barbells in each hand. He then turned to the others. 'And then I will break all of you in half, and then I will piss on you. All of you.'

There was no fear in Dervishi's voice, only a vast amount of confidence that he could take them all on and beat them to a pulp.

'Dude, that's some tough words coming from one man against four of us,' said Amir.

Without saying a word, Dervishi walked up to him and

grabbed him by the collar, bringing him in close. 'You think because there are four of you that I am scared, little boy?'

Dervishi looked at the other three who had converged on him and pushed Amir violently away. Amir fell onto the bonnet of the Fiesta but was unhurt and quickly stood up to face Dervishi again.

'You want to fight me? Come, all of you.' He urged them to come at him. His smile was unnerving, and the four young men knew that a fight would end up with several of them badly injured. They stuck to the plan.

'I thought so,' Dervishi said, looking at them with disdain, 'little boys, all of you.'

As the confrontation was going on, Kendra and Trevor used the distraction to close in on the group. They each carried an American-made Axon Taser 7, powerful enough to take down the strongest of men. They had brought two just in case, as their quarry was a colossal man. They had hoped he wouldn't be high on drugs, as that would make things a lot more difficult.

The group had reacted to the threat from Dervishi by looking at each other and mouthing words of surprise, whilst simultaneously and strategically manoeuvring away, arms and palms out as if conceding, so that Dervishi had plenty of space around him. That had been the plan. That included moving off the bonnet of his beloved BMW. As anticipated, Dervishi walked to his car to check for damage on the bonnet.

He turned to the group of four. 'Now fuck off and don't come back. You know what will happen if you—' That was all that he managed to say as Kendra's Taser released 30,000 volts into his abdomen for five seconds. Dervishi was completely immobilised but did not fall to the ground as he struggled to cope with the electric surge.

Trevor stepped forward and used his to add another 30,000 volts. Dervishi crashed to the ground like a tree, his head making a loud cracking sound as it hit the paving slabs that ringed the car park.

Seconds later, Amir and Mo approached him and used two professional-grade heavy-duty zip ties to secure his wrists tightly, not taking any chances. Simultaneously, Trevor hailed for Charlie to drive the van to their position, which he did. A few seconds more and Dervishi was in the back of the van with the twins in tow. He was further secured with more zip ties for his ankles, and duct tape was used to cover his mouth.

The two shadowing cars were driven away, followed by the van. They left in convoy and headed for the empty building they had prepared for their guests. Trevor and Kendra stayed behind at the hotel, having relieved Dervishi of his room key.

'Let's go,' Trevor said, as they entered the hotel.

As expected, they did not see many staff or guests, who were by now all enjoying their lunchtime treats. Before long, they had entered room 124, which was surprisingly large and luxuriously equipped. Kendra scanned the room and noticed that Dervishi had travelled light, with just a small suitcase and a laptop bag. They quickly gathered his belongings and packed them in the case. The laptop was on the bed, the screen locked. They decided to switch it off in case it could be tracked, taking a chance that no valuable data would be lost. Once the toiletries were removed and the keys to the BMW retrieved, they were ready to go. She took one last look around, confirming that nobody would think that there was anything out of place, and so there would be no suspicion of foul play.

Minutes later they were in the BMW, driving along the A12 and en route to meet with the rest of the team.

'Nice car,' Kendra said, looking like the cat who'd got the cream.

'Yes, it's a shame he won't ever see it again,' Trevor replied, 'there have to be some perks to this job, right?'

14

BESPOKE PRISON

Twenty minutes later they entered the grounds of an abandoned factory less than a mile from Tilbury Docks, but secure, and isolated from passing traffic and prying eyes. They drove down an old pothole-ridden road that hadn't been repaired for many years, and which hadn't seen much traffic, before reaching their secluded and gated destination. The gates had been repaired, oiled, and utilised as an extra layer of defence or shelter should anyone get too close. The factory itself had been abandoned almost twenty years earlier and was not quite close enough to the docks to benefit from the improvements the area had received since, although it was only a matter of time when that ongoing development reached it. It was surrounded by trees and overgrown bushes that made it difficult to spot from anywhere, making it a great place to conduct this part of the operation.

Despite it having been abandoned for so long it was in surprisingly good condition, with no broken windows or leaking roofs. It was a solid building, built just before the start of World War Two, to produce bricks and tiles. It had somehow escaped the ravages of the war and had remained intact.

Trevor had known of this place for some time now and had considered buying it for the land, recognising the potential. Having seen it again now he nodded in appreciation and turned to Kendra. 'This is as good a location as anywhere,' he said. He was also now reconsidering its purchase.

'It looks very secure, perfect for what we need.'

He had sent his trusted team ahead many days earlier. They had cleared out dozens of rooms, most of them on the first floor where the old offices had been. There were also many on the ground floor and some in the basement. Trevor had given instructions for the doors to be checked and secured with new padlocks. The rooms would also be equipped with buckets, toilet paper, and extra-strong garden refuse sacks for the disposal of waste. Much like the refugees had been given on the Golden Ray 2. Each room was checked to ensure there was no possibility of escape, and the ones that were selected to hold future 'guests' would include something to secure them to as additional insurance.

The room set aside for Dervishi was extra special, with his size and strength in mind. It was one of several old storerooms that had been used to store the factory's tools. They would typically be locked overnight and had old prison-type wooden doors with a small, barred window just high enough to look in and make sure everything was secure. There was no window. It was almost perfect for the task. Inside the room, they had placed a large blue gym mat and provided a blanket, along with the bucket that was close enough to reach. The back wall was lined with floor-to-ceiling metal shelving, which was bolted in place, top and bottom.

Dervishi was carried into the room, awake but groggy,

and dumped unceremoniously onto the mat. His left wrist was handcuffed to one of the stanchions that secured the shelving in place, which was almost as thick as scaffolding poles. The handcuff chains were twelve inches long, to allow some movement for using the bucket or sleeping without too much difficulty. His ankles were similarly cuffed, like prisoners are secured when being moved. The zip ties were then cut with pliers and removed, along with the duct tape covering his mouth. He took a deep breath and looked around, confused.

'Welcome to your new home,' said Trevor, as he looked at the dishevelled figure now lying prone on the mat. 'We hope you enjoy your stay with us, which will be for some time. Don't bother to shout or do anything stupid, as nobody can hear you. If you cause us any problems, we shall reward you with broken bones and more duct tape. Do you understand?'

Dervishi glared at him. 'Do you know what you have done? They will tear you all limb from limb when they get you. You cannot get away from them.'

Trevor leaned in close. 'I'm banking on it, you murdering piece of filth.' He then stood back and left the room, instructing his men to lock him in. Kendra had watched from the side, unseen, and was happy they had taken Dervishi off the streets, knowing what was to come next.

'Let's go,' Trevor said.

He gave instructions to his team before leaving. Kendra was impressed by his stature and presence and was glad she had brought him onboard. She had no doubt that her dad was connected to some bad people, but the team were completely in awe of him and appeared fiercely loyal. He had made sure that some of the rooms had been made up for the team and been well-equipped with food, drink, and everything else they needed to be comfortable for the duration of the operation, for both themselves and their forthcoming guests. They would also be very well looked after financially.

After giving the instructions, he and Kendra left the factory and returned to the BMW.

'Okay,' said Trevor, 'we need to get back to town and get this lovely motor to Stav, who will strip it and sell it for parts, which will pay for some of the costs we are incurring.'

Kendra looked at him, unsure how to respond. The police officer in her would instinctively rebuff such a suggestion, but she said nothing. Trevor saw the look his daughter gave and said, 'I know you don't approve of this, but this operation is going to cost a lot of money, which we don't really have, so we may as well let Qupi pay for it, right?'

'What makes you think I don't approve, Dad? I think it's great that Qupi is funding this, the irony is not lost on me, and it *is* summary justice, right?' They both grinned.

They left the factory for one last ride in a very nice car.

'GREAT JOB, GUYS,' said Andy, when Kendra had updated him on the phone. 'There is no movement of any concern at the hotel, no alarm, no police called, which suggests that nobody is any the wiser.'

'Excellent,' Kendra said, 'just as we planned. I like it when a plan comes together.'

'I've switched to watching the warehouse in Dagenham again,' Andy added, 'and so far there's not been anything of note other than a couple of the tracked cars leaving a few minutes ago. I'm hoping that they go to private addresses so that we can house them. Qupi hasn't budged from here yet, but I'll keep you informed.'

'Great. Is there any news on the Golden Ray operation either in the news or on the web?'

'There's been mention of a successful operation in the English Channel where some refugees had been taken into custody, but I think they're keeping the rest of it quiet for now, as they are likely to plan some operations in the very near future.'

'What about the soldiers and the sex workers, anything about them?'

'Nope, nothing. You may have to check in with Rick for that.'

'Okay, will do. Let us know if there is anything else of interest that comes up, and we'll catch up with you later. Dad said he's buying the pizzas tonight.' Kendra turned to Trevor, who was shaking his head.

'I should have walked away,' he said, theatrically, 'but no, I chose to stay, and now I'm the dinner lady!' He rolled his eyes for effect.

'Great, get him to buy the beers, too!' said Andy.

'Absolutely,' Kendra replied. 'But seriously, we need to go over the next step tonight, so have a think about who we should target next, okay?'

'Will do, see you later.' Andy ended the call.

'What do you reckon, Dad? Who should we go for next?'

'We need to take out his lieutenants, one by one, which will weaken him. But we must do it quickly before he realises what we're doing and takes measures to protect his men. I'm going to call in some more muscle for this, I'm running out of gym volunteers!'

'Okay, but be careful not to give them too much info,

okay? We need to keep this as covert as possible for it to work.'

'Don't worry, love, I have a lot of friends who owe me favours. This is the ideal time to call them in, and they will benefit from it too. Also, I have an idea as to what we should do with the scumbags after we have them all. I'll let you know when I've worked out the kinks.'

'Fine by me,' said Kendra. 'Now let's get this car delivered so we can get that pizza, I'm starving.'

15

NCA BRIEFING

KENDRA WAS BACK AT THE POLICE STATION THE NEXT DAY, trying her best to focus on work, but struggling with all the momentous events that were taking place as a result of her plans. She was wary not to get ahead of herself, and careful not to be overconfident, because even the best-laid plans could quickly unravel and turn into something dire and far-reaching. There was too much at stake and too much at risk were they to fail, so she had to keep a level head.

She had spoken briefly with Rick Watts and found that there was no new intelligence or updates of note relating to the Golden Ray 2 case. It was likely the investigators had tightened control of all intelligence leaving their office in order to minimise the chances of disrupting any planned operations, which was standard practice.

'Everyone, listen up. I need you all to be in the briefing room in ten minutes,' said Detective Inspector Damian Dunne, walking into their office briskly. 'Please make sure you're on time, and don't bring your phones or any other recording equipment.' The DI walked back out of the room as quickly as he'd entered.

'Well, that was odd,' Sam Razey said.

'Must be a top-secret operation,' replied Gerrardo, 'otherwise why mention the phones?'

'Yeah, I agree,' said Kendra, intrigued.

'I guess we should make a move now, then,' said Paul Salmon, 'so we get the decent seats!'

They laughed and started to make their way to the briefing room on the next floor.

'Fiver says it's a blue-on-blue operation,' said Paul.

'Deal,' replied Gerrardo, quickly shaking Paul's outstretched hand.

'My money's on the robbery initiative,' said Geraldine Marley. 'We've had one of the largest increases in the Met, so they were bound to do something about it.'

'I have no clue,' said Kendra, 'but we won't have long to wait to find out.'

———

THE BRIEFING ROOM had been prepped in advance, with numbered seats and identifiable sealed briefing packs waiting for someone to claim them. There were two dozen people in attendance and each person had to sign an attendance sheet and confirm the seat and briefing pack they'd been allocated.

'Don't open the packs just yet,' said DI Dunne, standing at the front with a pair of suited men who each carried a folder. A wooden lectern had been provided for their folders and notes.

'Listen up, everyone,' said DI Dunne, as the murmurs came to a halt. 'This is Detective Sergeant Eddie Duckmore and Detective Sergeant Dave Critchley from National Crime Agency working out of the South East office. They're here to give a briefing on a recent human trafficking operation that also involved a substantial firearms cache that was confiscated. According to their investigations there is a lead to our manor, hence the briefing. Gents, over to you.'

Gerrardo leaned over to Sam. 'You owe me lunch.'

'Thank you, Detective Inspector Dunne. My name is Detective Sergeant Eddie Duckmore, NCA, and I am the lead investigator in what we are now calling *Operation Flounder*. You may have heard of a successful interception of some trafficked refugees in the English Channel recently. Please open your packs and you'll see some imagery and intel on what went down on the ship.'

There was a rustle and a tearing of paper as everyone in the room did as they were instructed and took out the briefing packs. Inside were photos of the containers, showing the degrading conditions the refugees had endured, compared to the much better conditions the soldiers and sex slaves had had to tolerate. There were photos of them in their groups as they were being led off the ship, mug shots of the unnamed soldiers, and pictures of the firearms found the next day. Including some intelligence, it was all that anyone in the room needed to see to understand the seriousness of the operation.

'The reason the NCA are now involved is that in addition to ninety-odd refugees, of whom five were found dead, Border Force also secured forty sex workers and forty combatant types, who we believe were making their way to the UK to reinforce one of the gangs here as they prepare for a large conflict with other gangs. As you can see in the photos, we also found a large stash of firearms, including machine pistols. We have been tasked to find out where they were heading, which gang, and what their intentions are. Our job is to stop them, arrest them, and put them away for a very long time, because it's what we do.'

'What a douchebag,' whispered Kendra. Gerrardo smirked and nodded.

'The reason we are here is because we have one very tenuous lead from the ship, as none of the passengers gave any information of any use,' continued Duckmore. 'One of the yobs had a small piece of paper tucked in his sock, containing details of an address on your patch. We checked it out and it is a rental property that is occupied by Albanians, not far from Chadwell Heath station. We have secured a warrant and will be heading over there in just over an hour, where we'll be met by the TSG who will force entry on our behalf. Once the door is in, Dave and I will be first in and will take control of the house as quickly as possible. It won't take us long.'

'Again, what a douchebag,' said Kendra. She had come across his type many a time, and it had never been a pleasant experience.

Duckmore continued. 'Behind us will be your support team of detectives and a search team. We will turn the house upside down, I don't care how much damage we cause, these bastards need taking out.'

'Blimey, what a douchebag,' said Gerrardo, as Kendra smirked.

'Detective Inspector Dunne, I believe you mentioned that

your intel unit was present? Can you put your arms up so we can see who you are?'

The intel team did what they were told, without grinning too much. Kendra felt as if she were at school again, being ordered by an overbearing teacher.

'You've probably been asking yourself why you are here, right? Well, the reason we've asked for your presence to this briefing is so that you can support us with intel before, during and after the operation. We need as much intel as you can find on the house, its occupants, and anything we find there. We'll call it in and expect a swift response, okay?'

Only Imran nodded, the rest remained stoic and unmoved. They weren't probationers and knew what was expected.

'Okay, you can leave the briefing now and start on that before we leave,' Duckmore said, dismissively. 'There's a couple of loose ends that I need to tell the rest, but you don't need to be there for that.'

The intel unit rose as one and left the briefing room, muttering as they left.

'Bloody hell, it was like listening to someone from the 1970s again, what a complete douchebag!' said Sam Razey, as they made their way back to their office.

'Yes, wasn't he?' agreed Kendra, whose mind was working overtime trying to figure out how she would help the investigation without hindering what she, Andy and Trevor were doing. She decided that the address must be a safe house for Qupi's people who came to the UK, somewhere to crash whilst waiting for permanent accommodation. It was unlikely that anyone important would be staying there and almost as unlikely that they would know anything about his operation. Not enough to cause him any problems, anyway.

Kendra went outside and made the calls to Andy and Trevor to keep them in the loop. They both agreed with her summation and agreed that the best thing to do was to help the NCA with their investigation. She made her way back to the office and got to work. She was champing at the bit, for tonight, they were going after both the lieutenants.

16

LIEUTENANTS DOWN

LATER THAT AFTERNOON, AFTER THEY HAD WORKED FOR SEVERAL hours on the NCA research, it became evident there was very little intelligence that would help the NCA in their investigation. The raid had led to the arrest of seven people: three men and four women, five of whom were of Albanian descent, and it had quickly become apparent that the raided property was a brothel. The four young women had been the most recent arrivals to the UK and were finishing their last shifts in this particular house before being moved elsewhere to make room for the new arrivals. Two of the men arrested and quickly released under caution were locals that had been there for a good while. The other man, the Albanian, was identified as the pimp, and would not say a word when arrested or under caution in interview. So, the raid was quickly becoming a dead-end.

The NCA duo kept calling the intel unit with snippets of information that they came across during the search of the house. They investigated the women's passports that were found, some receipts for goods bought locally, but only one mobile phone was found – on the pimp. It was an older iPhone that required a four-digit code and not one of the newer models that required a face-scan or a thumbprint. As such, only ten attempts were allowed before it permanently locked them out. Getting anything from that phone would be a nightmare and take more time than they had. In reality, it was only likely to connect to a burn phone, which would be destroyed if no pre-appointed contact was made, rendering any potential tracking useless.

The intel unit were able to trace two of the women as having been reported missing in Albania, via Interpol searches Kendra had made. The only stroke of luck they had was relating to the pimp's car, which was parked close to the address. Inside it, they found several petrol and grocery receipts from a Texaco petrol station in Beacontree, not too far away. This was an indication he was living close to that area. His car keys also had two door keys on them, one for the house that had been raided, the other assumed to be for where he was living.

Kendra went for a leg stretch and called Andy to update him. He quickly accessed Cyclops and was able to access the feed which showed the pimp's vehicle at the petrol station two nights earlier. The stroke of luck came when the man was seen coming out of the kiosk carrying two bags of groceries. Using the CCTV software, the petrol station had plenty of modern cameras covering all parts of the forecourt, but also, crucially, parts of Beacontree Avenue and parts of Neville Road. Andy was able to follow the car's movements into Neville Road, where its brake lights came on just about a hundred yards into the road, indicating that it was about to park.

'I think he lives in Neville Road, K, one of the first houses on the left as you enter from Beacontree Avenue.'

'That's great, thanks, Andy. See you later.'

Kendra went back to her desk and focused on the Texaco garage. She was able to bring up a Google Maps feed that showed the first part of Neville Road from the petrol station. Sure enough, she could clearly see the pimp's car parked partially on the footway on the left-hand side outside one of the first houses on the left. 'Gerrardo,' she called, 'isn't that the pimp's car?'

'Bloody hell, how did you manage that?' he asked, leaning over to see the screen.

'I always consider the obvious. I figured they'd have a good CCTV system because that area is rough, and when I went to check to see how up-to-date the cameras were, I just had a hunch to look at the surrounding roads, and there it was.'

'Great work. I'll get it over to the douchebag right away. He may even smile and be nice.'

'I doubt it, he doesn't seem the type to smile at anything, unless it is something evil,' she said, recognising the type.

As a result of finding the car, a search warrant was quickly obtained and a team was sent to the address in Neville Road, accompanied by the pimp. The search team made entry and began a comprehensive search of the address, where it was clear that he lived alone. Although they initially found nothing linking his operation to anyone else, they did find half a kilo of cannabis, a loaded Glock handgun, and a holdall full of cash, which, when counted later, amounted to more than fifty thousand pounds. The cash had been rolled into thousand-pound bundles tied with elastic bands and had likely been due to make its way to Qupi very soon. It was another hit on his operation, albeit a much smaller one.

The search team then found a list of women's names on a piece of paper, which was found in a zipped side pocket in the holdall. It was later confirmed that the names matched most of the women found on the Golden Ray 2. It linked the pimp and his operation to the sex workers on the ship and was the first solid lead since the operation had started. It was a small breakthrough, but a breakthrough, nevertheless.

The douchebag never did smile, but it kept the NCA busy for many days.

KENDRA, Andy, and Trevor met later that evening, after she was able to get away from the station.

'Well,' said Kendra, 'that will keep them busy for a while. It's also another kick in the balls for Qupi, so although they haven't found anything linking to him, it means his operations are taking another hit.'

Trevor nodded. 'We need to move fast, guys, before he gets spooked and goes underground. We must take the lieutenants out tonight, both of them.'

'Agreed,' Kendra said. 'So how are we going to do that?'

'We have their addresses now, so we move on both at the same time. It's not ideal but I have some muscle to help and another van for transport, so as long as it's clean, we can get them both.'

'Okay, but again, *how* are we going to get them? We're hardly going to knock on the door and ask them to come with us, are we?'

'What's wrong with that?' Trevor smirked.

Kendra knew better than to ask.

The trio went over all the intelligence they had on the two lieutenants, Amar Hoxha and Altin Kola.

'These are the two main lieutenants other than Dervishi,' said Andy. 'Amar Hoxha drives the black BMW M5, and Altin Kola drives the blue Audi A8. They both live in quiet suburban roads in the Romford area, not too far from the new warehouse. There is one other possible lieutenant who works for Qupi, a chap named Jetmir Marku, but we think he is down the pecking order after these two as I can't find much about him at all.' Andy then proceeded to give the addresses and confirm the vehicle details for both.

'Interestingly,' he said, 'they both live in houses alone, and just like most of these Albanians, they have left their families back home so that they can earn their crust here and support them from afar. It's pretty normal.'

'That's great news, it means that there won't be anyone to interfere or get in the way, right?'

'Not necessarily, Kendra. They typically have mistresses, so expect them to have company, just in case.'

'Okay, we have everything we need, I'll call the teams and we can get cracking. Kendra, you take the BMW goon and I'll take the Audi one,' said Trevor, seamlessly taking control.

'Will do,' she said. 'Andy, please have a look and see if there is any camera coverage in that area or nearby, just in case.'

'No problemo.' Andy got straight to work as the other two left. 'Be careful, both of you,' he hollered behind them.

THE TEAMS MADE their introductions when meeting at the factory to pick up the vans and personnel, where Trevor spelled out the plan to take the gangsters out. Simple was best—and Trevor's plan was just that.

'Okay, at exactly eleven pm, three of us from each team will go to the respective houses, where only one person will go to the door and ring the bell. The other two will stay out of sight and wait for the signal.'

'What will the signal be, Trev?'

'When you hear them sizzling from the taser,' he replied, laughing. 'As soon as he is tasered, the other two come to the door, and between all three, you get him back inside the house and close the door. Don't touch him while the charge is still on!' More laughter.

'One of you then makes a check for anyone else being present, and you secure the target with zip ties. You then call the van in, which parks in a way that obscures the door, and when you're happy that all is clear, you get him in the van and head the hell out of there. One of you will grab the keys and drive their car, and you head back to the factory ASAP, got it?'

'Also, if you see anything of value, like cash or jewellery, or any notebooks that might hold some intel, just grab it,' added Kendra, conscious of the costs involved. 'It will all help.'

'Great stuff,' said one of the team, 'are we taking anything back for Brodie?'

'Don't worry about Brodie for now, mate, we have an agreement, and I will look after him when the time comes, okay?' Trevor nodded towards Kendra, assuring her that it was all under control. It was a conversation to be had at another time.

—————

KENDRA and her three assistants parked the van just around the corner from McIntosh Close in Romford, where Altin Kola lived in a bungalow at the very end of the close. On a positive note, it was very quiet, with no passing traffic, but the downside was that the neighbours would hear any noise. It was one reason why Trevor had been careful with the timing, to coincide with most of them being in bed, but early enough for the gangster to still be up and about.

Kendra and two of the helpers walked into the close and towards the end bungalow, trying to look as though they belonged there, which they most certainly did not. Luckily, most houses were in darkness and being the end house meant fewer neighbours within hearing range.

'Jack,' she said, turning to one of them, 'this guy may remember me, so I need you to ring the doorbell, okay?' She handed him the large bunch of flowers they had brought along especially for the occasion.

'Remember, he is likely to ask who it is before opening the door, so it's important that you apologise and tell him you just want to speak to Grace, okay? He may tell you to piss off, that you have the wrong house, or something like that, so just keep ringing the doorbell until he gets angry and opens the door. As soon as it is fully open, you taser the bastard, and we'll come and help.'

'No problem, Miss.'

Jack approached the door whist the rest of the team held back, just out of sight. He rang the doorbell for a few seconds and stepped back. The front door was made of solid wood and had no peep hole.

A few seconds later came a gruff, harsh response from within. 'Who is it?'

'Sir, I just want to speak to Grace for a few minutes,' pleaded Jack.

'There is no Grace here,' yelled the man, 'now go away!'

'Sir, I will only be a few minutes, I promise.'

No response.

Jack rang the doorbell again, for a little longer this time.

The man was clearly not happy. 'I told you, there is no Grace here, so fuck off!'

'Sir, I'm not leaving here until I speak to her. I brought her some flowers. Please, sir, I promise I won't be long.'

The door opened quickly to reveal a very angry man wearing boxer shorts and a vest. 'I told you, you little shit, there is no—' was as far as he managed to get, when the taser struck him in the chest. As with Dervishi, the 30,000 volts were very effective, but unlike Dervishi, who was much larger, he collapsed backwards like a tree in freefall. He collapsed in his hall with a heavy thud, the back of his head bouncing once before settling back onto the carpeted floor.

As soon as Jack had fired the taser, the rest of the team had made their way to the front door and all three were inside within seconds, dragging the unconscious Kola further into the house. He was immediately zip-tied, and his mouth taped, ensuring he could neither escape nor shout for help. As planned, the others had scanned the bungalow and found nobody within. His car keys were taken, along with a healthy roll of cash. There was also a loaded handgun, his passport, a pair of mobile phones, and a bunch of paperwork that was all quickly placed into a pillowcase from his untidy bedroom. They also found a jewellery box that had no fewer than five

Rolex watches and plenty of heavy gold. A cursory glance under the bed revealed a Tupperware box with much more cash in it, along with a bag full of gold sovereign coins. It was a very tidy haul and well worth the search. They took everything of value and of use and within minutes were ready to go.

Kendra called for the van, and as planned, Kola was bundled through the side door, out of sight of any potential witnesses, with no signs of anyone being bothered enough to take a look. Kola's door was shut behind him and very quickly Jack was in the driving seat of his car, who then calmly drove it off the driveway and away. It was a textbook operation that had gone exactly to plan, as they drove away in convoy and headed back to the factory.

'Let's hope the other team were as successful,' said Kendra. 'You did really great, guys, well done.'

———

LESS THAN HALF A MILE AWAY, in Dunton Road, another cul-de-sac – there were many in Romford, and it seemed criminals liked living in cul-de-sacs where they felt safer – the other lieutenant, Amar Hoxha, was having a rougher time of it. When he was struck by the taser, he had fallen backwards and hit his head hard on the radiator in the hallway. The force of the blow had cut his head open and possibly cracked his skull, so another few minutes was added to their time in the house to wrap his head in a makeshift bandage.

Trevor's team also left with a stash of goods, including cash, firearms, and jewellery, and because of the extra time spent in the house, the team stripped it of everything they could comfortably carry. They took his brand-new Audi, adding to the growing list of fancy vehicles that would be taken apart for spares.

Within twenty minutes, both teams and their substantial hauls were back at the factory near Tilbury Docks. The lieutenants were both secured in rooms far away from each other so that they couldn't communicate; both were warned of the consequences of any such actions. Fortunately, Hoxha's injuries weren't too bad, and once Trevor treated his cut – he had experience from his time as a corner man – other than potential concussion, there was no risk to his life.

'That, my friends, was a good night's work. Well done, all of you,' said Trevor, once they had seen to their duties. They had also checked on Dervishi, who was just as grumpy and angry as they had anticipated.

'So, we have his three most-trusted lieutenants,' said Kendra. 'We have their phones, which I will get to Andy so that he can monitor them, in case they carry any useful information.'

All the phones taken from the two most recent guests were current smartphones and were easy to unlock, using face recognition from the prisoners. Once unlocked, the settings were changed to prevent them being secured again, so they could prove potentially useful later.

'If there isn't anything else, I'll make a move now and go to Andy's, Dad. It would be good to have him check these before Qupi hears or suspects anything in the morning.'

'Okay, love, drive safe. As for you lot, get some rest, guys. We'll be back tomorrow with more to do, so make sure you take turns in getting some sleep, you can sort that out between you. Just make sure to keep an eye on the guests, okay?' Trevor said to them all. Strict instructions were left on the continual monitoring of them all, now that there were three, and more to follow. He also gave instructions for all three cars to be taken to Stav as soon as possible, so that he could disable the trackers and start stripping them. He and Kendra took one of the vans and left the factory, exultant in their success.

'Great job, Dad, and thanks again for helping with this.'

'Don't you worry, love. Clearing this scum out is a good thing. And I know they'll be quickly replaced, but we can have a say in who replaces them and make sure that none of their shit is repeated again.'

'I guess that's where Brodie comes in, right?'

'Yeah, but it's all good. He's helping me out because he knows that when we're done, he can move in and take some of the territory. He'll do very well out of this, don't worry.'

'I know that, Dad, I'm not naïve anymore, remember? I guess in this instance it's better the devil you know, right?'

Trevor nodded. 'You make sure to rest too, young lady, you have work tomorrow.'

'Don't worry, as soon as we drop these phones off, I'll be heading for bed, I'm exhausted.'

17

THE REST OF THEM

THE FOLLOWING MORNING, KENDRA WENT TO SEE RICK WATTS in his office, to find out for herself whether anything had changed overnight.

'It's all going well,' he said. 'That was a good catch yesterday with the pimp. He's in deep trouble but still not talking. Not that anyone at the NCA is telling us much. I think they've stalled on everything else, so the pimp's going to take the fall and go away for a very long time.'

'Qupi must be screaming at the walls about now,' she replied. 'We've cost him a lot of money and caused a lot of hassle for his organisation. It will be interesting to see what he does next.'

'I'm not sure what else we can help with now. We've led everyone to where they should be, and the results have been great. I guess we can breathe a little, now some justice has been served, don't you think?'

Watts was looking carefully at her for her reply. Her response was cautious and measured.

'I'm not sure yet, Sarge. I'm not as angry as I was, because there's a lot of satisfaction considering what we have done to him since. But I still think about poor Andy, and I just don't think justice has been served. If it's okay with you, I want to keep probing into Qupi and his organisation. I want to see if we can do even more damage to him.'

Watts nodded. 'I guessed as much. I just don't want you to be bitter and tunnel-visioned so that nothing else seems to matter, okay?'

'Don't worry, Sarge, I'll be fine. Like I said, I've already had lots of satisfaction from this, I just want some more.'

BACK AT HER DESK, Kendra went through the usual tasks, whilst also checking on any new developments that may be connected to Qupi. So far, nothing had come to light, but it didn't mean nothing was happening. She left the office to make a call to Andy, anticipating some activity at the warehouse after their late-night successes.

'Qupi left the warehouse last night, just before you hit the houses, and he hasn't been back yet. The tracker has pinged his car to a Beauly Way, in Collier Row, next to a golf course. It's been there all night and hasn't moved yet. I'm pretty confident that's where he is living.'

'That's great, that we have an address for him. We have to be careful, though, he must be making phone calls and realising that something is up by now, right?'

'I agree. What would you do if you were him?'

'I'd be very cautious and looking over my shoulder, that's for sure,' she said.

'If you can get away from work early today, it may be worth meeting with your dad and figuring out the end game here, because it's going to start getting more dangerous now if Qupi is wary.'

'I've been thinking that I should take some annual leave, maybe a week, to see this through. Let me see if I can pull it off and I'll catch up with you later.' Kendra ended the call and went back inside. Instead of her office, she went straight upstairs to Rick Watts.

'Sarge, I'm having some problems with my legs, so if it's okay with you, I need to go and sort out a doctor's appointment and get some physio. Also, can I take a week off as annual leave? It's been quite hectic recently and I could really do with a break. I think it's why my legs are playing up.'

Watts looked up from his desk, scrutinising her request.

'Are you alright? It's a bit sudden, so if there's anything you want to talk about, well, I'm here, okay?'

'No, I just need a short break, that's all.'

'Okay, fill out the request form and I'll sign it later. If you need anything in the meantime, just call me.'

'Thanks, Sarge. I'll see you in a week or so.'

Ten minutes later, she was in a cab en route to Andy's, her mind working overtime as she considered all the options. They had caused Qupi a great deal of damage, but the job wasn't even halfway done yet. What Kendra wanted and was determined to complete, was for them to systematically bring down the entire organisation, remove all his henchmen, remove Qupi himself, but most importantly, bring them all to justice – Kendra March style.

It was going to be a long and dangerous couple of days.

TREVOR MET up with them an hour later, having checked in with his teams to make sure everything was okay.

'The factory is in good shape. The guests are behaving very well, thanks to the sleeping pills we have been grinding into their food. It's keeping them nice and placid, and nobody has been bold enough to do anything stupid yet,' he told them.

'Qupi must know something by now,' said Kendra, 'so we need to be careful of our next steps.'

'I agree. I think he will be getting very wary now and will probably take measures to protect himself more,' said Trevor.

'We have some great intel on them now, and we have the advantage of knowing when they are on the move, and where the boss lives. I think we should be flexible and move quickly as and when we need to,' Andy added. 'For example, if we know they are away from the warehouse or any of their other known haunts, like the café or their associate addresses, then we hit whichever one is unguarded. We do the same with the personnel, we just take them out one- or a-couple-at-a-time. It will freak Qupi out no end.'

'I'm with you on that,' Kendra said. 'We take them out as and when it is convenient for us, we play the game and bend the rules to our liking, not theirs.'

'We have some people helping us now, so we can start speeding things up if we need to,' said Trevor, 'but do not forget these are dangerous people, all of them. Don't expect everything to go to plan every time, always expect and plan for the worst.'

'Agreed. So, what's the next step?' asked Andy. 'We know he is at home, and we know there are a couple of cars at the warehouse and around four of his mob there. Do we know what they do in there, or what they even store there?'

'No, but if Qupi is worried then he won't go anywhere without any extra muscle now. And we know he is getting short of people to call upon. Is there anything we can do to piss him off even more?'

'Ideally, what we need to do is draw his men away from the warehouse so they can go and protect him or one of their other venues. Once we know the warehouse is unprotected, then we can go in and plant a few cameras, maybe cause a bit of damage, basically do whatever we want,' said Kendra.

Andy had thought ahead and had ordered another dozen cameras, as the operation gained traction and more venues were identified. He had also ordered some personal tracker discs for them all to have on their person in case anything went awry. At least they'd have a chance of finding them, within reason and dependant on range. They had also installed apps on their phones, which would allow them to be traced. In the eventuality that anyone was captured, it was likely that phones would be taken from them. It was hoped that the captors would hold onto the phones and not dispose of them quickly, which would still allow Andy to trace them.

'I'd go with the option of cameras first. If you start changing the environment, and they know someone has broken in, they'll just abandon it and go underground,' said Trevor.

'That's true. What would be very useful is if we find out where all his other operations were based so that we can clean him out completely. Or even his financial information, I can do a lot of damage to bank accounts if you can get me some account numbers,' said Andy.

'Okay, so let's work on a plan to draw the men away from the warehouse. Got any ideas?' asked Trevor.

'Does Stav have any black cars with blacked-out windows,

or something menacing that we could loan?' asked Kendra, an idea forming.

'I'm sure we can find something,' Trevor said, 'what do you have in mind?'

'Nothing fancy,' she said, 'but Qupi is most definitely spooked now, right? What if we send someone in a car like that down his road, where he or his cronies will most likely be looking out of the window? He will almost definitely have some back-up there with him by now.'

'He'll be worried, for sure, and may call for back-up. It's what I would do,' said Trevor.

'Great! Let's crack on, then,' said Andy. He had his own ideas about damaging Qupi. With the intelligence they had, and hopefully more that they would get from the warehouse, he could get into Qupi's bank accounts and cause all manner of chaos.

'I'll call you from Stav's,' said Trevor, making his way out. 'Let me know if you notice any changes, okay?' And with that, he was gone.

Kendra got up to leave, contemplating the next steps.

'I can't believe how much we've come with this so far, Andy. How is it that we can do so much damage to these bastards, but the police can't? Where has it all gone wrong?'

'Where it's gone wrong, Kendra, is that when the police get caught out doing something wrong or making mistakes, they change the bloody laws to favour the criminals, not thinking that they are only making it harder for the police to do their jobs. It's always been that way, and the laws and the justice system are now heavily weighted in the criminal's favour. That's why it will always be difficult for our colleagues.'

'I guess you're right,' she said wistfully, wishing things

were different. 'Well, it's up to us, then, isn't it? Let's give 'em hell!'

———

LESS THAN AN HOUR LATER, Trevor called to let them know they had a car, and it was on its way to Collier Row to spook Qupi. It would be driven by two more of Brodie Dabbs' men, who had been given instructions on what to do and what to look out for.

'Thanks, Trevor,' said Andy. 'I have eyes on the warehouse and will let you know if there is any movement.'

'Okay, I'm on my way back towards the warehouse with the twins. As soon as you see any movement out of there, call me straight away and we'll go and take a look.'

'Will do,' Andy said. 'Kendra said she'll meet you there to give a hand.'

'Understood,' came the reply. 'We'll see you later.'

Andy turned to Kendra and handed her a small holdall that contained the new cameras he had acquired. They were miniature wireless Wi-Fi cameras that could be hidden anywhere and still pick up motion and audio, so they would work well inside. As they were wireless, the battery life wasn't great, just a few hours when activated, but there was still a chance they could capture some invaluable information.

'Be careful, K. I still don't know how many are inside, so even if the cars move off, assume they will leave someone behind, okay?'

'Don't worry, Andy, I'm sure it will be fine.' She waved and left the basement, to make her way to Dagenham and the warehouse.

A SHORT TIME LATER, Trevor received a message from the Collier Row team in the dark Mercedes with blacked-out windows that had begun its slow run along Beauly Way.

Going in now, all quiet so far

The Mercedes was driven slowly towards the end of the road where Qupi's house was located. The driver kept a lookout on the offside and the passenger on the nearside, as if looking for a house. As they got to the end, they saw Qupi's house and noticed that there were lights on downstairs. The downstairs blinds were closed, but they still allowed for some light to show.

The driver nudged his passenger when he noticed movement at an upstairs window; movement they had been told to look for. He indicated with his chin and smiled. They had been spotted. He slowed the car and came to a halt, before slowly reversing back, giving the impression they were being covert and hoping not to be noticed. He reversed the car to the bend in the road and went out of sight of the house. As instructed, they then parked up in Rise Park Boulevard, where they would be able to see any cars going towards the address or coming from it.

'*Movement at the house, have parked nearby to maintain watch,*' was the next message.

'Now we wait,' said the driver.

JUST A COUPLE OF MINUTES LATER, Trevor received a call from Andy. 'We have movement at the warehouse,' he said, 'five goons just came running out, and one of them locked the door, so it looks like they're leaving it unguarded.'

'Received and understood,' said Trevor. 'Kendra is with us now so we can go and have a look at putting a few cameras in.'

'Remember, the best option is probably that back door, or one of the upstairs windows at the back. Nobody will see you there and hopefully you'll have enough time to do what needs doing.'

'Okay,' said Trevor. 'Keep us informed of any movements, we'll need a couple of minutes' notice.'

'Will do, and good luck,' came the reply. Andy was getting used to being the support now. He had been the lead investigator for so long during his service that he had found this role strange at the beginning. Now, though, he was enjoying it tremendously, and realised he was very good at it indeed. His computer and dark web skills, coupled with his experience and knowledge of criminals and how they operated made him an invaluable resource. He was still disappointed that he wasn't very mobile but was slowly coming to terms with it and was thriving on these challenges that they were going through.

'Give them hell,' he muttered to himself, smiling, and realising that he was finally in a good place after such a long time.

———

BACK IN DAGENHAM, Kendra had given the twins and Trevor a camera each, with instructions on how to activate them.

'Remember, we want them placed where we are likely to benefit from some good intelligence, okay?'

They all nodded in agreement and exited the van they had been using. They had parked close by the rear of the warehouse, and so were not likely to be spotted by anyone leaving it. They walked to the alleyway where Amir had placed one of the earlier cameras to keep watch on the rear exit. They cautiously tried the door and found it be secure, with no likelihood of entry from the outside. Mo looked up and nudged Trevor in the side.

'That's our way in,' he said, pointing to the first-floor window and then turning to Amir.

'Just because I'm the youngest doesn't mean I get all the shit jobs,' he said, smiling knowingly, as he took off his puffer jacket and threw it at his brother, who caught it before it hit him in the head.

Amir intertwined his hands and stretched his arms, whilst looking up at the window above. He took out a small pocket knife and pulled out the three-inch blade, before placing it in his mouth. He then shimmied up a drainpipe as if he were a gymnast, stopping some three feet from the window ledge. He looked at the ledge and timed his jump to perfection, leaping agilely and holding on to the ledge with his fingertips, his feet against the wall supporting his weight.

'He loves it, really,' Mo said proudly to Kendra, as he looked up at his brother. 'That parkour training has paid off many times.'

'Don't get too confident, Mo,' Trevor said, 'he isn't inside yet. Hopefully the window isn't too secure.'

They didn't have to wait too long. As Amir went to try and pry his way in, he noticed that the window didn't have a lock, just a simple latch. He slid the tip of the knife into the frame where the latch was, jiggling back and forth a couple of times, before he was able to get it through and then flip the latch up, allowing him to pull the window open. He looked down, smiled, and then leapt inside with ease, closing the window behind him.

Less than a minute later, the rear door opened, revealing Amir standing there with a big grin on his face.

'Table for three?' he joked.

'Good job, Amir, now let's get going,' said Trevor.

They closed the door behind them and went into the warehouse. The door had opened onto a corridor that had the external wall on one side and internal doors to two toilets on the other. Just beyond the toilets was another room that was being used as a storeroom for cleaning products, toilet paper, and other janitorial equipment. At the end of the corridor was a fire door, leading out into the warehouse itself. Before entering, Trevor made sure to pause and listen for anything unusual, just in case Andy was wrong about nobody being there. He turned to the twins and Kendra and nodded, indicating that it was clear.

They entered the main warehouse, which measured more than a hundred feet square, and was a decent space for storing goods. It was evident, though, that not a lot had been stored here just yet; they hadn't been here long enough to fulfil its storage potential. They noticed that one wall was entirely covered with metal lockers, at least forty of them, waiting for someone to use them. There were three pallet-loads of electrical goods stacked against another wall, along with a pallet containing different types of spirits. There were also two tables with chairs spaced some ten feet apart from

, close to the mostly empty lockers. One of the
was topped with drinks and plates of unfinished food,
dicating that it had been abandoned quickly by the
recently departed gang of five.

A forklift was parked up against the main shutters, in
readiness for the next delivery.

'There's not a lot down here,' Kendra said. 'We should
look upstairs.' She indicated to the metal staircase leading to
the first-floor mezzanine.

'Mo, go and see if you can find a nice spot for one of the
cameras to cover those tables,' Trevor said, figuring that the
soldiers would let something slip at some point when things
went wrong for them, which was always the plan.

'Sure thing,' replied the elder twin, setting off towards the
table set-up.

The rest of them went upstairs where two large offices
were located, along with a small kitchen area. One office was
being used as a meeting area, with a large table and ten
chairs, along with a pair of sofas and a large wall-mounted
TV. The TV was squeezed between two shelving units that
were filed with random things such as DVDs, a few small
spoof trophies, a PlayStation console and games, and a
number of small ornaments that were reminders of their
home back in Albania. Next to the table was a wheeled
trolley with refreshments to one side. There was also a ceil-
ing-mounted projector, indicating that this was used as their
briefing room.

The other room was clearly Qupi's. It was plushily deco-
rated, with a dark-green leather chesterfield sofa to one side,
an ornate brass trolley bar next to it, well-stocked with spirits,
nuts, and chocolate biscuits. The room was dominated by a

heavy oak desk with leather inlay, along with a black leather office chair. There was a 27-inch Apple iMac computer on one side of the desk and a laptop on the other. Along one wall was an oak sideboard that hosted a large printer. Next to that was a pile of recently printed receipts and invoices.

'Okay,' Kendra whispered, 'make sure not to move things around too much. We're looking for something that will help us fight these bastards, so look for bank info, forms of ID, anything like that, okay? Split up and let me know if you find anything of interest.'

Kendra went to check the receipts and invoices and quickly ascertained that there was financial information on them, probably the bank account that the crooked organisation used to launder their funds. She took several photos on her phone, making sure to get everything that Andy could use. 'That's a good start,' she said out loud.

Trevor looked in the bin under Qupi's desk and found some screwed-up bits of paper that he took out and inspected. There were a few petrol and food receipts, nothing of much use. He took them anyway, to determine whether the accounts used to pay for fuel were the same as those on the shipping receipts and invoices. It all helped, even partial numbers.

'Bingo,' said Amir, pointing into an open drawer in Qupi's desk. Nestled at the top of some random stationery were two visa debit cards. One was in the name of Tirana Imports and Exports Ltd, which was the name that had been used to lease the warehouse. The other card was in the name of Jetmir Marku, one of the names Andy had mentioned earlier as a possible lieutenant.

'This is great, it's exactly what Andy was hoping we'd

find,' said Kendra, carefully taking photos of them in situ and then individually, along with the reverse of each. 'I have no clue who that is, I'll send these to Andy now and he can check them out.'

They quickly checked the rest of the office and found nothing more of any use. They couldn't get into either computer as they were both password-protected, so they thought better than to try.

'That'll do for now. Let's put these cameras in and scarper,' Trevor said, not wanting to stay any longer than they absolutely had to.

Kendra placed her camera on the printer, wedging it under the paper feed at the top, towards the back, where it would be out of sight to any casual observer. It was unlikely to get much in the way of images, but any audio picked up could prove invaluable. They'd probably have to run it through a translator program but at least they'd have something.

Trevor placed his camera in the meeting room next door, hiding it amongst the random trinkets on the shelving units. As he left the meeting room, he saw Amir coming out of the kitchen, where he had placed his camera on top of one the units there. 'You never know, they might talk in here,' he said, shrugging.

They met Mo downstairs, where he told them that his camera was in one of the empty lockers near the tables, taped securely inside the door, and hopefully able to view through the slats.

'Okay, everyone, let's get the hell out of here,' said Trevor.

They retraced their steps to the rear exit, where, after confirming there was nobody around, they left the warehouse and made their way back to the van.

As they drove away from Dagenham, Kendra received a thumbs-up message from Andy, indicating that the cameras were active and would start streaming when they next picked up motion or audio.

'Good job, everyone, that wasn't nerve-wracking at all!' said Kendra, smiling, as the rest laughed in relief.

———

18

QUIP

'Come on, then, tell us what you know!' asked Kendra.

'So, first off,' said Andy, 'the gang is using a legitimately registered company, Tirana Import and Export Ltd, to conduct its business over here. It's clearly a front for their operations but they get through a lot of financial transactions, which has been illuminating. At the moment they have almost half a million pounds in their account, which, considering their turnover of eighteen million in just the past three months, is a pittance.'

'So where does their money go, then?' asked Trevor, 'back to Albania?'

'Some of it does, yes, around a million in the past three months. But most of the remaining money has gone into one personal account, almost six million in that period. I checked the account, and it has almost fifteen million in it.'

Trevor whistled. 'Wow, business has been very good for this lot.'

'Is that the account of Mr Jetmir Marku, by any chance?' asked Kendra.

'Yep. And guess what?' Andy said, with a smile, 'I have a passport photo of Mr Jetmir Marku!' He twirled in his chair and pressed a key, bringing up the Albanian passport page.

'Well, if it isn't our old friend, Guran Qupi.' Kendra smiled.

'So, what can we do?' Trevor asked.

'Well, how about ... we take it all?' Andy laughed.

'Seriously?' Trevor asked. 'How the hell do you do that?'

'Well, firstly, you need some special skills, which you know I have,' said Andy, mock polishing his hand on his chest, 'and then you have to have a few untraceable crypto accounts along with a couple of overseas accounts, as I have set up in the Cayman Islands, where they look after your accounts with vicious zeal!'

'Well, what are you waiting for?' said Kendra. 'Crack on and take their bloody money!'

'Already on it, don't worry. I want to do it in stages to attract as little attention as possible. Keeping this lot busy will help with that, so we need to keep them on their toes and worried about the next steps.'

'Don't worry about our friends,' said Trevor, 'we're about to move on to the next phase and thin their ranks just a little bit more.'

'Andy,' said Kendra, 'while we're doing our thing, keep an eye out for their other haunts and associates, they may be calling in favours, and I don't want us to be outmanoeuvred or outmuscled. Luckily, nobody likes them too much, so they haven't got that many people to ask for help.'

'I've called our friends in the scary car and pulled them out before they get caught out down there, so they're near Qupi's address but out of sight and out of the way. They should be able to give us an update if there is any movement there. Once Qupi realises the coast is clear they'll probably all move down to the warehouse for safety in numbers. We can then start picking off the stragglers and screwing with them a little more.' Trevor rubbed his hands together in anticipation.

'Can you work your magic on their broadband connection at the warehouse?' asked Kendra, 'because if we can do something to screw with their signals it'll buy us more time.'

'I can do that, sure. I've got a highly illegal mobile phone jammer that we can use to play with them a little bit, you know—turn it on and off every few seconds. They'll crap themselves.' He went to one of the cupboards and retrieved a small laptop case, passing it over to Kendra. 'You know how it works, show one of Trevor's mates how to use it and that should do the trick.'

Kendra looked inside and saw what looked like a black box, around ten inches long, with four small antennas sprouting out of it. She had seen them before when she and Andy had taken down a vicious drugs gang that had been using them to block their rivals' signals. Andy had been impressed with the gadgets and had purchased one on the dark web.

'It may need a charge, so check it before you hand it over,' he added.

'Great, we'll catch up with you later, let me know if you find anything new.' Kendra waved as they left.

'This is a lot of fun!' she said, as she and her father walked to his car.

Trevor shook his head theatrically. He had his reservations, but inside he was also enjoying this. He was also wondering what they could do with fifteen million pounds.

BACK IN COLLIER ROW, Qupi's anger was showing no signs of abating as he furiously challenged his men to tell him what they knew or what they thought was going on.

'First, we lose the shipment, then Roan disappears without a trace, we then lose Amar and Altin, and now they are stalking me at my fucking house? What the fuck is going on? Who is doing this? Who are these people?' He threw an empty mug at one of his men who was able to dodge it before it smashed into the wall.

'Guran, we have asked everywhere, but we have not heard anything, we do not know,' answered the brave henchman.

Qupi, despite being shorter, grabbed the man by his collar and shouted, 'then do something to find out! Call everyone and ask them again!'

There were now seven of them in Guran's house, crammed into the small but tastefully-decorated lounge. One of the men continued to look out of the window for any movement. They had checked the surrounding roads but had not seen anything remotely suspicious.

'We must get our guns from the safe house and then regroup at the warehouse. We can decide what to do there, when we are all together,' Qupi instructed, having calmed down, 'and then when we find out who they are, we will attack those bastards with everything we've got. You two go and get the guns, and then meet the rest of us at the warehouse. You,' he said, pointing to one of the men, 'call the rest and have them meet us at the warehouse.'

They all left the house together, taking the two newly-arrived cars along with Qupi's Mercedes.

As the convoy turned into Pettits Lane North towards the

A12, they were spotted by Trevor's associates in the dark car with the blacked-out windows. As they got to the roundabout, they had a stroke of luck. Qupi and one of the other cars turned right onto the A12, but the third, a grey Jaguar, continued straight over into Pettits Lane and continued towards Romford. The two associates made the decision to follow the single car at a distance, gambling on the driver not having seen them from Qupi's house earlier on. The passenger called Trevor to update him.

'That's good news, boys. Give them some space but don't lose them. If the opportunity arises, I want you to consider taking them out. In the meantime, I'll send another car to back you up. Be careful, okay?'

'You got it, Trev,' said the passenger, grinning at the driver in expectation of some action. 'Let's do this!'

They followed at a distance, using other cars for cover.

The grey Jaguar finally turned onto Junction Road, near Carlton Road, where they turned into a narrow alleyway at the side of an off-license, leading to some garages at the rear. The driver tailing them decided to park out of sight, and Trevor's men both left on foot to go and investigate further, splitting up to cover more ground. There was a small council block next to the alleyway, and the Jaguar had parked alongside one of the garages. The two gangsters got out, and one of them proceeded to open the wooden garage doors. There seemed to be a large heap of junk in the garage, a couple of old motorcycles and lots of boxes stacked up, nothing particularly attractive or worth stealing. The two men looked around before starting to move some of the boxes to one side, making a path towards the far end.

'Brad, they're looking for something, bro,' the watcher,

Kevin, told his colleague over the phone. 'We'll need to move quickly so that we can grab them here,' he added.

'Our back-up will be here in a couple of minutes, Kev. I'll call them and let them know what's going on.'

'Tell 'em to park the car in the alleyway as if they're popping into the off-license, and then get them to come and meet me in the block next door. The scumbags won't be able to move, and when they get out of the car to investigate, we can take them out. We've all got our tasers, so it should be easy-peasy, bro.'

'Will do. Keep an eye on them and call back if anything else happens.'

Kev had a good line of sight into the garage. He could see that the Albanians had cleared a path to the far wall, where a wardrobe and some kitchen units were exposed. The gangsters opened the doors of both and pulled out a heavy box and a number of well-stuffed holdalls.

'Well now,' Kev said, 'I wonder what nice things they have stashed here.'

The gangsters took the bags back towards the car, looking around before placing them in the boot. The box followed, and they shut the boot securely. They then went back into the garage and started putting everything back where it had been, making it look like it was just a pile of junk. It was while they were doing this that a silver Volvo turned up and reversed onto the forecourt in front of the alleyway, facing away from the garages and blocking the alleyway completely. The back end of the Volvo was almost in line with the building, only a couple of feet away, so anything that happened in the alleyway would not be seen by anyone except those who were directly in line with it, which was unlikely. The two

Volvo occupants quietly made their way to the block next door, where they met with Kev. Brad soon joined them.

'Listen up, boys,' Kev said, 'I think these guys are armed, so we need to be really careful, you know? When they see the car parked there, hopefully both of them will come out to see where the driver is and will probably be pissed off. That's when we get them, before they get to the road, okay? Get your tasers ready and get into position by the wall there. One of you call me and wait for my signal on the phone. When I tell you, I want you to jump over the wall quietly and come up behind them. Before they turn around, I want you to taser the bastards, and I'll come and back you up. So will Brad. We'll put them in the boot of the Volvo and fuck off quick time to Tilbury. Got it?' His associates nodded and slunk off to get into position. In the meantime, one of them called Kev and kept the line open.

Alongside the alleyway and separating it from the council block was a low wall, maybe four feet high. Kev's associates followed the instructions and were soon out of sight behind the wall, hiding between two cars, one of them with a phone to his ear. Brad moved towards the front of the Volvo, in readiness to assist when the tasers were fired. They each carried a couple of zip ties with them, and Brad had retrieved some gaffer tape from their car.

Just a minute or so later, the gangsters finished their business and locked the garage doors. As they got in the car and started the engine, they noticed the Volvo blocking their way. The driver moved the Jaguar forward slowly, stopping about ten feet from the back of the Volvo. It was clear there was nobody in the car, so they waited a few minutes in the hope that someone had gone into the off-license for a quick stop. After a couple more minutes, the passenger and then the driver got out, both impatient to get moving. The driver stood by his door, lighting a cigarette, whilst the passenger went to investigate. It was then that Kev gave the signal and his two associates quietly jumped over the wall. It was not quiet enough, and the driver turned to see what had made the noise.

One of the back-up men went for the driver and quickly aimed the taser at his chest and fired. The driver dodged the taser, which attached itself to his jacket without touching any part of his body. He quickly ran towards his assailant, fumbling for a gun that was tucked in his waistband. His attacker pulled the trigger a couple of times with no effect, and before he could adjust, the driver was upon him. The gun now in his hand, he could see that there was no need to shoot, and simply struck the young man on the head with a vicious blow, knocking him instantly unconscious.

The passenger had not fared as well and had been tasered to the ground by the other attacker, who stood over him and ensured that the volts coursing through his body did their job. He looked up to see his colleague being pistol-whipped and dropped the taser, running towards the driver.

'Calvin! You bastard—'

The driver turned quickly and fired his gun at the rushing attacker, hitting him squarely in the chest. The young man was dead before he hit the ground, just as Kev and Brad arrived and attacked the driver with both tasers. He didn't stand a chance against both and slumped to the ground next to his victim, his gun falling with him.

'Shit!' shouted Kev, looking around to see if anyone was watching. They didn't know their back-ups very well, but were devastated by the result.

'Shit! Stevie!' he repeated.

They both attended their colleagues, one dead and one seriously injured by the driver.

'We need to get them out of here, quickly,' said Brad, 'someone was bound to hear the shot.'

'I can't fucking believe this, Brad, he didn't stand a chance.'

'Mate, we need to deal with this now and get the hell out of here quickly, okay? Snap out of it!' His friend nodded, respectfully closing the dead man's eyes as he did so.

They lifted their dead colleague and put him in the back seat of the Volvo. The unconscious colleague was placed in the passenger seat and strapped in. Kev carefully picked up the gun and wrapped it in a discarded hoodie that was in the back seat of the Jag.

The two gangsters were both zip-tied and then unceremoniously dumped into the boot of the Volvo, where they were quickly searched, and mobile phones, wallets, and keys were all taken from them. It took just a few seconds and Qupi was down two more men.

'Let's get the phones unlocked before we leave,' Brad said. 'Open the boot and I'll scan their faces.'

When the boot was open, he removed the gaffer tape to scan their faces, causing a painful yelp from each man, which unlocked the phones. Kev waved the taser in their faces to prevent them from shouting out or doing anything stupid. The phones unlocked, Brad quickly scrolled through each one's history and address book, noticing that both had very little on them, typical for burner phones. As there was nothing of any use to the team on the phones, they were both crushed underfoot and disposed of in some bushes adjacent to the alleyway so that they couldn't be traced.

Brad got in the driver's side of the Volvo and drove off,

followed by Kev in the now-seized Jaguar. They would return later to pick their car up once the mess had been dealt with. As they drove off, they could hear police sirens in the distance – they had left just in time. Half an hour later, they arrived at the factory, where the two gangsters were further searched and secured in their temporary cells. Trevor was there to meet the team and to help with their casualties.

'Damn it!' he said, when he saw the dead youngster. 'How did this happen, guys?'

'It was just bad luck, Trev,' came the reply. 'The plan was solid; it was just bad luck.'

Trevor shook his head, saddened by the loss. 'Take Calvin to the hospital,' he told one of the helpers, 'tell them he was hit on the head by a swing or something, and stay with him until he's awake, okay?'

He looked around at the group of young men who had volunteered to help them with their cause. He could see both sadness and anger in their young faces.

'Guys, this is a setback for sure, but we're going to have these along the way when we take on horrible fuckers like this, okay?'

'What are we going to do now?' asked one of them.

'We carry on, that's all we can do. We try and stop this from happening again, but you need to know that what we are doing is dangerous. Now that you see how dangerous, you need to make a choice about whether you want to carry on. I will understand completely if you don't want to and will help you in whatever you decide. That's a promise.'

Not a single one of them left. Trevor nodded and said, 'I appreciate you more than you know. Let's look after our people and meet back here in a couple of hours, okay?

IT TOOK a while to sort everything out before they regrouped at the seized car. Young Stevie was taken to a vicarage in Romford and left near the front door, covered with a blanket as if he were sleeping peacefully. The gun that had killed him was placed in an envelope and left in his hands, with a note – *To the police. My name is Stevie Perkins from Stanley Road, Hornchurch, and I was killed by this gun. The man who killed me has been taken care of. Please tell my mum that I didn't die for nothing and that I love her. I'm now with Dad, he's not alone anymore.*

It was the only respectful way they could get him taken care of. The police would have fingerprints from the gun but would never find the perpetrator, hence the message. This way, his mother would be informed quickly, rather than not knowing for weeks or even months - giving some comfort.

'Let's see what these bastards were willing to kill for, shall we?' Trevor said, making his way to the back of the Jaguar. He opened the boot and unzipped one of the holdalls. It was full of brand-new handguns, SIG Sauer P320's, like those found on the ship. Two other holdalls were filled with the same, and the fourth was filled with the deadly Škorpion machine pistols. It was a deadly haul. The box contained enough ammunition to cause problems for any army.

Trevor whistled loudly. 'Look what we just took off the streets, boys. Stevie didn't die in vain.'

'Bloody hell,' said Brad, leaning in to take a look, 'are they looking to start a war?'

'I guess they are, especially with what we've been doing to them recently. They must be crapping themselves, not knowing what is going on or who is doing it to them.'

'What are we going to do with these, Trev?' asked Kev, hoping that they'd be dished out to everyone at the factory.

'I haven't decided yet, but we won't have anything to do with these, okay? So don't get any ideas. Just because those bastards are happy to use them doesn't mean that we will, look at the damage that it has already caused.'

'Fair do's,' came the reply, accompanied by a heavy shrug.

'Right, make sure you check our guests again, keep giving them the crushed tablets, and keep a good eye on them, okay? These guys are animals and will try everything to get away.'

'It's all under control, Trev, leave us to it. What's the next step?' asked Brad.

'I need to call this in and warn the rest of the team that they have taken it up a notch, so everyone needs to be careful while we decide what to do next. I'll call in later, after I take the Jag to Stav,' he added, before taking the latest trophy and driving off, the guns still stowed securely in the boot.

'OH NO, that's awful. Poor Stevie, he's one of Brodie's men, isn't he?' Kendra asked, back at the flat. She was shocked by the news; it was not all plain sailing for them, and this was a reminder there were some rough seas ahead. 'Does Brodie know yet?'

'Yeah, I called him straight away. He's properly pissed off, but he knows the dangers and it won't stop him from chipping in. He sent his men to take care of the body, and will be looking after Stevie's mum, helping with the funeral and with some money, that kind of thing.'

'What about Calvin, is he okay?'

'He's already out of the hospital, he just has a nasty bump and a few stiches on his head. He was lucky. He's feeling gutted about Stevie, who was his best friend, so he's keen to come back and help soon. Not sure if that's a good idea, though, with Stevie's killer here at the factory.'

'I agree. Maybe have a word with Brodie to see if he can keep him busy there instead.'

'That's a good shout, I will do.'

'Despite the setback, you've all done a great job, Dad,' said Kendra. 'That's, what—four cars and a bunch of money we've taken from them, along with five of his top men? And Andy might still be able to deprive them of all the money in their bank accounts, too. It's turning out well, isn't it?'

'Don't get too cocky, darling, these guys are desperate now. Apart from killing Stevie, just look at the guns they were about to release, and don't think they haven't got more, either. They're desperate and they're vicious.'

'I know that Dad, but we still have the upper hand and we're outwitting them at every turn. We have to press on, to give Andy the time he needs to clean them out, and for us to take the rest of them out of circulation.'

'Yes, darling, I know that, but after each piece we take, it gets that little bit harder. What I'm trying to tell you is that we haven't won the war yet, just a few skirmishes. We need to keep our wits about us and not get too complacent.'

'Got it, and I agree, so what's next?'

'Qupi and his crew are now back at the warehouse, where they'll probably remain while they decide what to do, safety in numbers and all. We need Andy to check the feeds and see if he can get anything that will help us. Can you check in on him?'

'Sure. He's a busy boy, isn't he?' Kendra smiled proudly.

'Be careful, love, he's doing great, but give him time to get through things, okay?'

Kendra blushed, recognising that she'd inadvertently shown a sliver of emotion. 'Don't worry,' she said, flustered, 'it's all cool.' She got up and walked to the other room to make the call. Trevor smiled, knowing that he'd embarrassed her just a little.

ANDY WAS STUNNED by the casualties when Kendra updated him on events. 'Bloody hell, Kendra, this shit just got serious,' he said. 'They're going to pay a heavy price for that, the bastards.'

'I agree, but let's focus on what we're supposed to be doing now, okay? We expected problems along the way and they just hit us like a train, but it won't stop us.'

'I wish I had a couple of extra arms,' Andy said, nodding as he indicated to his monitors.

'There's been some comings and goings at the warehouse.'

'Go on,' she said.

'Qupi turned up with the other car in tow, so there were five of them in the factory until about five minutes ago, when two more cars turned up with four more goons.'

'So, there's nine of them now?' she asked.

'Yes. They're just making some hot drinks and starting to meet up in the meeting room upstairs. I can't see much but I can hear them quite clearly. I'll have to record them and find a way of translating later, so it won't be instant, I'm afraid.'

'Don't worry, just do what you can.'

'I've ordered a bunch of extra kit, by the way, so our secret operations room is going to get a steroid-inducing makeover tomorrow,' he said. He gave a rueful smile; in light of the bad news, he was still very positive about their venture. It was good to hear him content and confident again. 'Wait 'til you see what I'm doing with the place,' he added.

'Looking forward to it,' she replied.

'Kendra,' he continued, straight-faced, 'despite the setbacks, I'm really enjoying what we're doing here and just wanted to thank you. It's taken me back to a much better place and I'm thinking ahead positively now. I dread to think what I would have turned into if it wasn't for you.'

'You don't have to thank me, Andy, you were always there, you just needed something interesting to do to get your juices flowing.'

'Well, this is interesting for sure. And I'm glad you know about the dark web now, I dabbled in it for years but was worried it would get me into trouble. It is a horrid place, but it has helped us no end, so if we can use it for the power of good, then I'm all-in.'

'I'm with you on that, Andy. We just couldn't do any of this officially without taking years and risking a lot more lives and careers, and then taking a chance that someone would believe us in court and convict the bastards. This lot don't give a shit about anyone, they are brutal and inhumane killers, as far as I'm concerned, so I'm more than happy to do anything it takes to get them out of the way.'

'Yep. Although I'm loving this and it's working really well, I still miss the actual hands-on work, you know? I'm thinking of seeing a specialist about my foot to see if they can do anything.'

'I thought the nerves were too badly damaged to be repaired. Isn't that what the hospital said?'

'Yes, but I want to see a specialist who deals with the proper, nasty war injuries, to get their opinion. If they can't do anything, at least I'll know.'

'Fair enough, there's no harm in asking. Hopefully we'll be done with this lot in the next few days, and we can all have some time off!'

'Fingers crossed,' he said. 'Now let me get back to the cockroaches so I can find out what they're saying.'

'Alright, catch you later.'

As she sat back in her chair, she thought back to the few brief moments of joy she had experienced with Andy in the back of the van, on that fateful day, which seemed such a long time ago now.

'Listen to yourself, Kendra,' she said out loud, 'back of the van indeed. You tart!' She was laughing, but in the back of her mind she was hoping she would one day experience joy like that again.

19

TIME TO STEAL

THE NEXT DAY, ANDY CALLED KENDRA EARLY TO LET HER KNOW what he had been able to translate from the Qupi gathering.

'Honestly, it was really tedious getting anything from Google Translate and not a lot of it made sense. I was able to isolate some words, though, and I caught the gist of what they talked about.'

'Go on, I'm meeting Dad in a while, so I'll update him then.'

'Well, Qupi swore in about a dozen different languages and shouted at everyone in the room, which was quite impressive. He is a vicious bastard to his own people, Kendra, let alone outsiders. Anyway, he mentioned guns and missing men a few times. He also mentioned the ship, which I assume meant *Golden Ray 2*, and men on the ship, which I assume is the group of soldiers that were coming to join him. And then he kept going on about people, and he said the word *thousands* many times. I think he's been smuggling people into the UK but wants to expand the business.'

'We've put a huge dent in his operation, and we can do a lot more to him,' she said.

'Then it got interesting. He mentioned another ship, the *Svanic,* and the port of Durrës, which is in Albania. I think he's sending another shipment over, K. It would be horrible if more people died, like the last lot.'

'Shit, he doesn't mess about, does he? I'll let Dad know and we'll have a chat about how to pass on that info without attracting attention. Talk to you later.' They needed to put an end to this gang quickly.

Trevor picked up after the first ring, 'Alright, love, what's going on?'

'Qupi is sending another shipment over, he isn't wasting any time at all. It sounds like he's expanding his operations over here significantly and is determined to succeed at all costs. We need to find a way of getting that one intercepted also,' she said, the anger in her voice quite evident.

'Damn, he's a feisty bastard, isn't he?' Trevor replied. 'Are you thinking of telling your boss again?'

'I want to, but I need to do it in a way that doesn't shine the light on what we have been doing. So far, it's been great, not a peep from anyone, and nobody is any the wiser, just as we hoped. I checked in with Gerrardo earlier and he told me.'

'Isn't there a hotline set up for anything to do with human trafficking?' Trevor asked.

'Not really, people are advised to call 999 or *Crimestoppers*, but that's a great idea, because all the *Crimestoppers* tips for our area come into the intel unit. As long as the caller mentions our ground, then it will come to us. I'll get on that now and will see you later,' she said, quickly ending the call and calling Andy back.

'Do you by any chance have any burner phones?'

'You know better than to ask that, smarty pants,' he said, laughing. 'Pop over and get one if you need it, you know where I am.'

Kendra smiled and grabbed her coat and keys. She was careful when driving to avoid any old haunts where friends or colleagues might spot her, and had found a circuitous route to Andy's house, parking a little away from it just in case.

A few minutes later she was at the front door, eager to reveal her plans.

'That didn't take long, did you do all the red lights again?' Andy smiled. 'Oh, and don't take this the wrong way, but here's a key so you don't have to wait ages for me to crawl my way to the front door.' He handed Kendra the key, attached to a troll doll keyring, its luminous green hair and pink outfit standing out like a beacon in the hallway.

'Yeah, that's great, thanks, I was going to ask for one,' she said, flustered, walking past him towards the under-stairs entrance to their secret room.

As she went downstairs and the room opened out, she remembered what Andy had told her the previous day, about getting some new kit. She wasn't expecting what she saw.

'Flamin' Nora!' she exclaimed, looking at what was now an entire wall of monitors, four rows of five, tightly-spaced and each with a number neatly written in silver marker in the top left corner. There were seven monitors on at the time, full-colour, showing various parts of the warehouse, both inside and out, where the cameras had been placed. Kendra stared in amazement.

There were now two tables underneath, a couple of feet away from the wall of monitors to allow for better viewing, and on each table were two desktop computers, plus an additional four monitors for those. At the end of one of the tables was a wooden trolley that had been butted-up against the table, making an L-shape of desks. The trolley had two laptops on the top and a number of hard drives on the lower shelf. There were two more hard drives on the desks, neatly placed behind two of the monitors, and linked to all four computers.

'Well, what do you think?' he said, savouring her reaction.

'And look here,' he added, drawing her eyes away from the new set-up to a grey metal cabinet, reminiscent of those found at the police station, which he proceeded to open with a flourish. Inside were four shelves, each now filled with various gadgets Andy had acquired, some legally and some not so. There were GPS trackers, tracking disks, tasers, pepper sprays, zip ties, gaffer tape, extendable batons, and much more.

'Kendra, what we have done in such a short period of time is pretty remarkable, and as a team, we've grown a lot. I figure we should all be well-equipped when it comes to sorting out the trash, don't you think?'

'You don't have to justify your actions, this is fabulous, and as we grow we'll need more of this.'

'And you know the best part? Qupi paid for it all,' he said, beaming.

'Wait, what? You managed to transfer his money? Really?'

'Yes, I did,' he said, bowing with a flourish, 'and not just his, I took the company money, too!'

'How the hell did you manage that?'

'Well, I told you roughly how it could be done, by transferring funds into Crypto accounts and then redirecting to offshore accounts, blah blah blah.' He smiled again, before continuing. 'I mean, don't get me wrong, it was a lot more difficult than that and it is very boring, but we now have control of nearly sixteen million pounds, in two separate accounts in the Cayman Islands.'

'What?' was all that she could say, stunned and open-mouthed.

'I know, I know, I'm pretty cool and all that. And before you say anything, the accounts will be managed by both of us. I created two new companies out there, *Sherwood Management Trust* and *Loxley Investments*, and I am working on due diligence for the time when people start looking at them in the future.'

'Where have I heard those names before?'

'Well, you must know Robin—'

'Robin Hood!' she yelled. 'Robin of Loxley and Sherwood Forest, that's hilarious!'

'Yep, but all joking aside, we'll be using a lot of this money to help with equipment and to fund our operations, but I also want to give something back to the victims and those who have helped us, like your dad. Think what he can do with some of the money, opening other gyms and finding good jobs for the kids. I think that would be awesome, don't you?'

Kendra couldn't help herself and threw her arms around Andy. 'I think *you* are awesome,' she said gently, looking at him affectionately.

'Well, if I knew that this would happen,' he said, 'I would have done it a lot earlier.' He returned the hug and smiled as she let go. He closed the cupboard doors and moved to one of the chairs, sitting down and unlocking the screen.

'Let me show you,' he said, waiting for her to sit next to him. It felt awkward, but also right that they were slightly uncomfortable, almost confirming that there was still a spark between them despite everything that had happened. Neither of them had spoken about the events leading to their capture; they had both assumed it would have been the last time they would connect emotionally and physically, and it now seemed neither of them wanted to have that conversation because they both wanted more of the same.

Andy keyed in a username and password, which Kendra briefly saw contained some letters from her name, along with several numbers and an exclamation mark. She blushed.

'This is one of the accounts, the *Sherwood Management Trust*. As you can see, it has had four lots of funds transferred, each for three million pounds.' He then went to the other computer and did something similar, bringing up another bank account. 'This is the *Loxley Investments* account,' he said, and showed two deposits of two million pounds each, and two more of thirty thousand pounds each. 'The loose change from both Qupi accounts.'

'So, he literally has no money at all?'

'Not in a bank that we know of, no. And as we took a bunch of cash from him as well, I imagine he will have to survive on what little cash he has left or take some money back from his hoodlums.'

Kendra laughed and clapped her hands. 'He is going to hit the roof!'

'Once we had some of their phones and the records from the warehouse, it was easy to pinpoint which was his phone, so I sent him a nice little Trojan virus, which he thought was from one of his men, and now we have control of his funds, his phone, and more! Seriously, though, we can't just leave it like this, we need to go in for the kill, figuratively speaking. We can't give him any time to recover, none at all.'

'I agree. I have some ideas that I want to run by Dad, and

let you know what we come up with. In the meantime, keep an eye out and let me know if you hear or see anything else, okay?'

She went to leave but turned back to Andy.

'Sorry, I've got to keep saying things like that. *Keep an eye out* – honestly.'

'I thought you were taking the piss, it's almost funny.'

She kissed him gently on the cheek and held his gaze. 'No, just me being an arse. Also, thank you, Andy, you're doing some brilliant work.' She turned and left, leaving Andy confused, happy and determined. He looked down at his damaged foot, still encased in the surgical boot, and said, 'We'll sort you out, mate, I promise.'

'Wow, sixteen million quid!' exclaimed Trevor. He seemed elated but then his expression suddenly changed. 'What are you planning to do with that money, Kendra? You're not giving it to the government or anything like that, are you?'

'No, Dad, so don't worry. We will give some to any victims that we come across, but in the main it will help fund our operation here. We've got off to a great start, think of what we can do with the funds in place. And the best part is that all the funds have been and will always be taken from the criminals. They will pay for their own downfall!'

'Now that is summary justice!' he said, repeating what was now their favourite phrase.

'Not quite,' she said, seriously. 'They need to pay more than just in money, Dad. They need to pay for their crimes in a way that no court of law will ever allow nowadays. We will judge them as *we* see fit, not some pompous ass that doesn't like the way the police put handcuffs on, or the way they arrest people. Enough of that shit.'

'Well,' her father replied, equally serious, 'I am close to finalising my plans for Qupi and his lot, and I think you'll be pleased with what I come up with. But before we get to that, we need to round the rest of them up and close down their operations, fast.'

'Agreed. We need to draw them out of the warehouse and find a way of taking them out before Qupi comes up with any ideas about getting more help. We have good eyes on them, as you know, and we have the personnel now to make it more even, but they have guns.'

'Ideally, we need to split them up, but I doubt Qupi will allow that, now that his team have been picked off. Also, I'm sure he'll have a few more men scattered around running other brothels or operations, he may call them in to help, too. I think we should do the thing they least expect.'

'What's that?' Kendra asked.

'We attack the warehouse. They'll never expect it, and we know we can get in really quickly.'

'Are you serious? You want to break into a warehouse full of armed men?'

'Remember, we have access to their broadband, their power, *and* we have eyes and ears on them. It won't be without its risks, but we have the edge. Call Andy and ask him to get some night-vision goggles and tactical gas masks ASAP, and we can go in tomorrow night.' He smiled broadly.

'He's going to love that,' said Kendra, 'more gadgets for his cupboard. You should see what he's got going on in that basement.'

'Good for him, it's exactly what we need at the moment.'

'I'm on it,' she said, picking up her phone.

THE FOLLOWING day started with an anonymous phone call made to *Crimestoppers* suggesting that the police look at a ship sailing out of Durrës and en route to the UK with guns, ammunition, and gangsters, along with more refugees. As the *Golden Ray 2* was still fresh in the authorities' minds, the investigation still ongoing, Kendra was confident they would take the tip-off seriously. The tip-off also gave Qupi and Dervishi's names and Qupi's address in Collier Row, but not the warehouse, which they wanted unmolested until they carried out their plans. This would ensure that the tip would be passed on to the intel unit, who would then try and join the dots as they had done with the *Golden Ray 2*. She expected a call from Gerrardo asking for help with it and was confident that if they used the same tools as before, they would identify the *Svanic*. Once identified, they would simply put another similar operation into place and seize everything before it landed.

'That should get things moving, but I'll keep an eye on it,' Andy said. 'If they're a bit slow putting it all together, then we can give them a nudge.'

'Good call,' Kendra said.

'I fast-tracked the extra kit your dad asked for, it will be here later this afternoon,' he continued, 'and there's something else you should be aware of.'

'Go on.'

'Qupi has been on his phone like a maniac, calling half a dozen numbers more than once. I've made a note of them for later, and I have a feeling they are linked to his other operations, like the brothels and probably a couple of gambling clubs. If he was calling for reinforcements, I think they would have turned up by now.'

'Okay, that's good to know, but to be honest, when it hits the fan later, it wouldn't surprise me if he does call for help, and they probably aren't too far away, so we need to be mindful of that.'

'Don't worry, I'll keep an eye on things like that, but you should warn Trevor to have a plan or two just in case.'

'I will, and thanks. We'll pop over later for the kit, let us know if anything else happens in the meantime.'

'I've been messing with their broadband and lights since yesterday, so they're probably pissed off but used to it now, which will help for tonight,' he added.

'Great, it all helps, see ya.'

Kendra made her way back to her flat, where she was due to meet with her father. Her mind kept going back to the day they were captured, and also what they had achieved since. She was elated that they had made so much progress but also somewhat demoralised by the broken system that had led them to this point. There was no turning back now; they had started something that had grown into a beast, with endless possibilities to do some real good, and she was determined to carry on. There were some niggles in her mind relating to her job as a police officer, and whether returning to full duties would impact on what she was doing. She had some tough decisions ahead, but first she had to clear her head and prepare for what she hoped would be the finale of the operation to get rid of Qupi and his monsters.

TREVOR WAS at the flat waiting for her, sipping from a steaming cup of Columbian coffee. She had given him a key early on; it was the least she could do, being that he had spent so much time away from his own business and club.

'I've been thinking, Dad, you mentioned buying the factory at one point and then kind of forgot about it, was it because it was too pricey?'

'Yes, which was a shame, because I think that land will be very valuable one day, why do you ask?'

'Well, we have that money from Qupi burning a hole in our proverbial pockets. Why don't we use some of it? If we're going to carry this on, which I very much want to, then wouldn't it make sense that we will use it again and again? We could spend some money fixing it up and making it work for us, don't you think?'

'I think it's a great idea, it's brilliantly placed for what we're trying to do!'

'Also, I'm conscious of how much time you are spending away from the gym and your other business, and I think we should use some of that money to expand that operation and get you some help to run it. I honestly can't do this without you, Dad, I've realised that these past few months, and I really enjoy doing this with you.'

Trevor paused for a few seconds, carefully placing his coffee down on the table before replying. 'Darling, I couldn't think of anything I'd rather do than help you put the world to rights.' His eyes welled up. 'When I started this with you, I felt compelled to help you, *guilty* almost, because of our history. But the more time I've spent with you, and seen the passion and drive that you have for justice, the more I want to be a part of it, and most importantly a part of your life. I'm so proud of you, love.'

She walked over to him, and they hugged, both pairs of eyes now filled with tears. They released and wiped their eyes quickly.

'Thanks, Dad. Honestly, at the start, I just wanted to take advantage of that, but not for long. I love spending this time with you and doing something that will help a lot of people. I love making a difference, and the fact you are a big part of it makes it even more special, so again, thank you.'

'I'm very happy to hear that, darling,' he said, 'but before we get too cosy and confident, let's not forget that we still have a job to do, okay?'

'Yes, sir!' she said loudly, mocking a salute. Trevor laughed, and they sat down and started to plan the night ahead.

20

ASSAULT!

Trevor and Kendra were busy on the phone for many hours setting everything up. They collected the new equipment that Andy had ordered for them and then met with the team that would be with them that evening, at the factory.

Amongst them were the twins, Mo and Amir, along with Kev and Brad. Charlie from the gym had also volunteered. None of them were aware of the financial gains Andy had made, or the overseas bank accounts, and it had been decided very early on that they would not tell anyone outside of the three of them. Although they trusted their team, that amount of money would do nothing but bring temptation and bad decisions, so it was best to keep everything that sensitive away from them. The rest of Brodie Dabbs' men remained at the factory, making sure that their 'guests' were secure, and that the factory was prepared in advance to accept a few more – hopefully the remainder of Qupi's gangsters.

'There may only be seven of us and nine of them, but we have the advantage of surprise and a few sneaky tricks that will help us in there,' Trevor started, handing out night-vision goggles and tactical gas masks to everyone in the room.

Andy had ordered a dozen of each, so there were plenty to go around. They were Nightfox Swift Night Vision Goggles that could be worn with a full-face tactical mask. Their ease of use made it a good choice for a bunch of novices. The tactical gas masks were Avon M50 Joint Service masks, usually only available to the military or the police, but again Andy had managed to use his nefarious connections on the dark web to order a dozen. They were sleek and simple to use, but very effective against the worst types of gas or irritants. The goggles would be able to slip over the masks easily with no obstruction at all.

'Use your time to familiarise yourselves with this kit, it will save your life inside when the shit hits the fan, okay?'

'Don't forget, guys, these bastards are armed and extremely dangerous, so don't take any chances in there, please,' added Kendra.

'So, this is what is going to happen and how it's going to happen,' Trevor said, continuing with his briefing. 'At eleven pm, Andy is going to jam their mobile phone signals and fritz all the electric feed going into the warehouse.'

'How's he going to do that?' asked Mo.

'If I tell you I'll have to kill you,' Trevor said, laughing. 'Only kidding, Mo. He will overload the transformer at the end of the street, and it'll blow all the fuses on the block. It won't affect anyone else because they'll all be closed, so don't worry about it. As for the mobile phones, we have a bit of kit that is directional and will only affect the warehouse. Remember that when we're inside, we won't be able to use our phones.'

'That's cool,' said Kev, nodding.

'That will be our cue for Amir to do his magic and climb up to that first-floor window. Hopefully whoever is in the warehouse will congregate when the power goes off, to see how they will deal with it, and they should naturally do that downstairs.'

'I'll be able to tell if anyone is upstairs, and I won't make any noise getting in, anyway,' added Amir, relishing the task.

'With Amir inside, he has a few tricky moments where he'll need to find a way to the back door to let us in. By then, they will have their torches on from their phones, so they'll have some light, which may cause him a problem.'

'How's he going to get past them, then, Trev?' asked Brad.

'That's where my friends from Tilbury Docks come in. I've been thinking of ways to re-locate these bastards when we have them all, and I came up with something that fits the bill perfectly.' He smiled menacingly, pausing for effect.

'Dad, please don't do that now, it's bad enough that we're going into a hornet's nest, seriously,' said Kendra, slightly irritated by the drama.

'Sorry, love, you'll understand why when I tell you. When their lights go out, and before we go inside, I will send a message to my mate, who will drive up to the front of the warehouse in his lorry, which will have a twenty-foot container on the back. He'll reverse up close to the shutters and turn the engine off. He'll then get out of the lorry and walk away.'

'So, is anyone else confused?' asked Mo.

'Think about it, Mo. The lights go out and they hear a diesel engine outside, and then see a lorry reversing onto their lot. What would *you* do?'

'I'm guessing they'll be shitting bricks and getting ready for a gunfight,' said Mo.

'Exactly,' said Trevor.

'Which will leave the coast clear for me to move to the back door,' Amir said.

'Not only that, but they can only see out the front from the ground floor, the upstairs offices overlook the back. They have to come downstairs and get ready for what they think will be a raid of some sort.'

'Which will allow us to sneak in without being seen or heard, while they're all taking cover downstairs covering the shutters,' added Kendra.

'And while they're covering the shutters with their guns, they won't be using their phone torches, will they?' continued Trevor, 'which should leave us with the advantage, because we'll have our night-vision goggles on, and our gas masks, which will save us from their fate.'

'I was going to ask, why the gas masks?' said Charlie.

'We managed to acquire some CS gas, which Amir will release as soon as he has opened the door, and it's pretty nasty stuff,' said Trevor. 'We may not be armed, and we may be outnumbered, but we have the brains and the guile to take these bastards out. As soon as the gas starts taking effect, which will be within seconds, that's when you move in and start tasering. Remember, though, they will probably start firing blindly, so please be careful.'

'And that is also why we've bought some of these along,' said Kendra, throwing each person a sealed bag containing covert body armour. 'These are the ballistic vests worn by covert units such as surveillance officers. They're smaller and designed to fit under jumpers or jackets, so they will give you some measure of protection in case you get hit by a wild round.'

'Blimey, we're gonna look like something out of Star

Wars,' laughed Kev, nodding in appreciation at the kit that they had been given, but especially at the consideration for their welfare.

'Dude, you saw what happened to Stevie; best not take any chances, right?' said Charlie.

Kev nodded, remembering his fallen comrade.

'Alright, listen up,' continued Trevor, 'once they have been tasered, you need to move in fast and secure them with zip ties and gaffer tape. Make sure you use two zip ties on their wrists, tightly, and one set on their ankles. They're heavy-duty ones so don't be afraid to make them really tight,' he added.

'You need to act really quickly, guys,' said Kendra, 'because two of them will be unattended for a few seconds while we sort the rest out, so keep an eye out for each other but especially those two.'

'Make sure you take their weapons, phones, keys, and anything else they have on them, okay? Don't forget that. Once they have all been taken down, we will open the shutters and load them into the container,' Trevor said.

'When they've all been loaded then we can take whatever else we can fit in their cars and our van and get the hell out of there, so don't forget to grab their keys,' added Kendra.

'Do any of you have any questions?' asked Trevor. 'Now is the time to ask.'

They all shook their heads. It was a simple plan that would be difficult to deviate from, so if it all went to plan, it would end quickly and without casualties.

'Okay, people,' said Andy, trying to keep his voice calm as they were about to take their positions. 'Let's get into place before the lights go out and we can't talk anymore.'

The team had moved into position at the rear of the warehouse without any difficulty, using Andy to guide them in based on his feeds within the warehouse. They looked an odd bunch, with the night-vision goggles on as well as the full-face gas masks, almost like a rag-tag team of mercenaries from a video game or sci-fi movie. They were all wearing the ballistic vests under their clothing, so at least they didn't have to look entirely like a team of stormtroopers.

'It looks like there are three of them in Qupi's office and the rest downstairs. They have been taking turns looking out of the windows but appear quite relaxed,' he said, watching the screens carefully for any changes.

'That's good news,' said Kendra, 'it means they'll be shocked and relatively unprepared when the lights go out. They'll panic for a few seconds before they realise they can use their torches.' Despite the masks, they could easily hear each other, which was a relief, as going into a potential hellhole without being able to communicate would not be well received, and far from wise.

'And just as they're sorting themselves out, the lorry will turn up and frighten them witless,' continued Trevor. 'We hope.'

'Okay, all is well so far, there is nothing of concern going on, so I will be frying their electrics in five...four...three...two...one...it's fryin' time!'

It took a couple of seconds before the transformer went and then all the lights in and around the warehouse died.

'I've sent the message for the lorry, let's go!' Trevor said, as they moved to the rear door of the warehouse from their vantage point behind a nearby wall.

Without being asked, Amir scaled the drainpipe as he had done days earlier, looking like a cyborg ninja, and within a few seconds he was gaining entry to the first-floor landing of the warehouse. He could hear multiple voices urgently shouting over each other, trying to figure out what had happened. He hid in the cupboard, the door slightly ajar, waiting for the voices to die down and for the next phase. The night-vision goggles worked brilliantly, and he was able to see clearly if anyone were to approach.

Within a minute or so the voices had calmed, and the gangsters had used their phones, as anticipated, to give some light. There were a few urgent instructions given, mainly by Qupi, but it was more orderly and less panicked. Amir then recognised the change of tone in the voices as they became more urgent, which he rightly assumed was due to their hearing some activity outside.

Downstairs, the men had all moved into defensive positions. Qupi had ordered them to spread out and prepare for action when they had heard the loud diesel engine outside, which was now manoeuvring very close to them.

'It's reversing up to our shutters!' one of the men said, from a window.

'What the fuck is going on?' another asked, clearly rattled.

'Shut up and listen, all of you!' shouted Qupi, as the lorry completed its manoeuvre, and the engine was switched off. 'We are in a strong position here and we are well-armed. They would be stupid to attack us here. It must be a mistake but be prepared for anything, you hear me?'

The men acknowledged their leader.

As Qupi had been shouting at his men, who were intently focused on the shutters, Amir was able to slink downstairs without a sound and move towards the rear exit as planned. He had already switched on the night-vision goggles before moving into position and checked his mask again before opening the door for his colleagues. Not waiting to see what they did, he then quietly went back to the main area, holding a pair of CS gas canisters that Andy had procured for them. He carefully removed the pins and rolled the canisters towards where the gangsters were positioned, making sure to space them well enough apart that everyone in the warehouse would be affected. Just seconds later, the canisters released their toxic compound. As it was dark, it was difficult for Qupi and his men to see anything, and the hiss from the canisters was not too loud that it caused alarm.

The first man coughed uncontrollably and instinctively rubbed his eyes with his free hand, not understanding that he was making things worse. Seconds later, they were all doing it, except one, who had used the few seconds available to him to run upstairs and away from the panic. Qupi's sense of smell saved him, and he recognised the peppery aroma immediately; coupled with the first man's reactions, it was all he needed to know to move quickly. As a result, he was able to escape the effects of the gas. As he ran, he shouted, 'Gas!' but it was in vain. His men were in tatters, confused, in pain, and completely disoriented.

The men were coughing and spluttering, wiping their eyes in an abject attempt to free them from the intense burning. They were shouting, pleading, and as the seconds passed, they deteriorated further. Kendra and the rest of the team entered the main space and fanned out, picking the target they were going to take down. They started tasering immediately, and the gangsters started to fall quickly, their pain intensified by 30,000 volts. Many of them dropped unconscious, some vomited, and several wet themselves. It was more than any human being could handle. One of the larger men instinctively fired towards the shutters, unable to see what was going on. Luckily for Trevor, he had seen it coming, and made sure to avoid the errant gunfire by staying low. It didn't take long for them all to be completely under control. But Kendra had seen one running away, and recognised the shape as Qupi.

'He's going upstairs!' she shouted to Trevor, who looked up towards the mezzanine and nodded. He looked around quickly to make sure everyone was under control. All the gangsters were bound and gagged, as planned. He saw his team taking guns, phones, and other belongings and putting them into the holdalls they had brought along. He indicated for Mo to come to him, and said, 'Get the shutters open and these bastards into the container as soon as possible, okay? We'll sort the other one out.'

Mo nodded and went off to do his bidding, while Trevor moved towards Kendra, who had just finished with her prisoner, one of the unfortunate unconscious ones.

'I saw him, Dad,' she said, 'we need to take him out otherwise he'll just regroup and keep doing what he does.'

'We'll get him but remember that he is armed and a bloody lunatic, so please be careful. I'll go ahead and you come up behind me, okay?'

Kendra nodded and moved towards the staircase. The only advantage they had was that it was dark, and they could see with the night-vision goggles, unlike Qupi. But Qupi was armed and would not give up without a fierce fight, so caution was the word of the day. They went up the stairs slowly, remembering the layout on the mezzanine and knowing that he'd probably hide in the hope that the attackers would leave, and he'd get away with it.

As they reached the top, Trevor made a sign for Kendra to stop while he took a good look ahead. The sounds from the ground floor were muted and it was now relatively quiet, interspersed with instructions from Mo to the rest of the team as they prepared to open the shutters. Trevor heard the shutters squeal loudly as they were being opened slowly and nodded in appreciation that the plan had, in general, worked brilliantly. Only one more, the evil snake in the grass, and they would be home free. If only it were that easy.

Trevor called Kendra forward and whispered in her ear. 'I can't see anything but I have a feeling he's in his office, probably hiding behind that big desk of his. I'm going to get a chair or something from the meeting room and throw it in there, see if I can flush him out.'

He moved stealthily towards the meeting room. Kendra followed for part of it and stopped outside the door while he went inside, waiting for him to come out. The loud squealing from downstairs continued as the shutters made their way slowly to the top.

Suddenly, she heard three rapid gunshots from within the meeting room, and her heart immediately turned to ice as she heard the thud of a body hitting the floor. She quickly leaned forward and looked into the room and saw Qupi standing at the far end of the table, pointing his gun from side to side as his eyes desperately tried to acclimatise to the darkness. At the side of the table, she saw her father lying on the floor, on his side, unmoving. Fearing the worst, she sobbed quietly and then took several deep breaths, remembering the training he had put her through.

Staying low, she crawled silently into the room and under the large table, pausing for a second to listen. She could see Qupi's legs, just ten feet or so away from her. She lifted her goggles away and then removed the mask and placed it quietly on the floor before taking out her taser gun from her jacket pocket. She then re-positioned her goggles, got into a squatting position, and shuffled along, as there was just enough space between the chairs on either side for her to do so. Just a few seconds later, she was close enough to touch Qupi and got ready to taser him. Before she had a chance to do anything, a light suddenly shone down on the floor, moving along before finding Trevor's prone body on the floor.

'There you are, you piece of shit,' Qupi said. 'How does it feel now, eh?'

Qupi started to move towards Trevor, slowly and cautiously. 'I have a friend of mine who would like to meet you,' he continued. From her position under the table Kendra saw that Qupi had – thankfully — put his gun down. But he was removing his now infamous flick-knife from his pocket.

'This is my best friend,' he went on, 'and I always introduce him to new friends, like you.' He laughed, not too loudly, but with a quiet venom. He kicked at Trevor's prone body, the heavy blow striking his back. There was no movement at all. Kendra covered her mouth with a hand to stop any involuntary emotions escaping. She then took a deep breath and gathered her thoughts.

She had little time to think but was glad the gun was out of the picture, albeit temporarily. Just as Qupi was about to kick at Trevor again, she pushed one of the chairs hard to make space for herself and then jumped out from under the table, lashing out with all her renewed strength with her right foot to the back of Qupi's right leg, just below the knee joint, just as her father had taught her so many times. His leg collapsed under him as he turned in surprise to confront his hidden assailant.

'Aaargh!' he screamed, as the joint suffered significant damage. He swore loudly in his native language, cursing in pain; the pain that now coursed through his damaged leg. He was now on one knee and struggling to stand, without luck.

He grabbed the side of the table and pulled himself up, slowly, whilst pointing his phone torch towards Kendra, who he could now see clearly. The light temporarily blinded her, so she moved the goggles up to her forehead.

'You look familiar,' he said with a laugh as he tried to steady himself using one leg, grimacing at the pain.

'Hurts like a bitch, doesn't it?' she said. 'Not nice when someone hits you hard, is it?'

'You think this hurts me, police lady? Don't you remember my little friend?' He laughed, waving his knife towards her. 'Come on, come and get me!' he goaded.

Just as she moved towards him, ready to taser him, he dropped the phone suddenly, disorienting Kendra and limiting what she could see. There was just enough light to show Qupi moving towards her, and had it not been for his damaged leg, he would have caused her a serious injury. He slashed wildly; Kendra tried to dodge the knife by ducking to one side, holding up her arm defensively. The knife caught her and sliced through the cotton jacket easily, cutting deeply into her forearm. She cried out in pain but managed to move out of reach.

'Come on, little girl, it's just a cut. My little friend needs to go much deeper, maybe into one of your eyes. Like your friend, remember?' He laughed loudly as he moved towards her.

Kendra knew she needed to act fast. Although her injury was not life-threatening, it was certainly enough to slow her down, which could prove fatal in this encounter. Holding her arm to stem the bleeding, she kicked out at one of the chairs, which immediately impeded Qupi and caused him to lose balance again. He stumbled backwards, out of control, and then fell to the ground next to Trevor's prone body.

Realising he was in trouble, Qupi thought fast and put the point of his knife to Trevor's back, looking towards Kendra and daring her to act. Kendra slipped the night vision goggles back on and remained calm, recognising Qupi's intentions, and remembering the planning that had gone into the operation.

'Move one more inch and I will stick this pig friend of yours,' he smirked, relishing the challenge. Kendra could see a small pool of blood forming under Trevor's body.

'Go ahead,' she said. 'I dare you.'

Without a moment's thought, Qupi stabbed down into Trevor's back. Of course, he had no idea that Trevor was wearing a ballistic vest. Without blinking, Kendra fired the taser into Qupi's surprised face from just six feet away. The fishhook-like barbs bit deeply into his cheek, shocking him like nothing he had ever experienced. His face contorted uncontrollably as he slumped once again to the ground, this time unconscious.

'And just so you know, you piece of shit,' she said, looking at the now-unconscious body, 'that's not my friend, that's my dad.'

Almost as if on cue, Trevor moaned and then moved slightly as he regained consciousness.

'Dad!' Kendra shouted, momentarily forgetting Qupi and going to his side. She helped turn him onto his back and then hugged him as he moaned again.

'Sod that,' he said, opening his eyes, 'that didn't half hurt, love.'

'Where are you hit?' she asked.

'The lucky sod hit me in the arm, which is burning like hell. He had the whole bloody vest to hit and he missed, the bastard! Aargh!' He was clearly in agony. The bullet had hit him in the upper arm, just below the shoulder joint and gone straight through the muscle without hitting any bone. He had been lucky.

'I think the bullet's gone right through, 'Kendra said, carefully inspecting the exit wound, 'otherwise this wouldn't be here.' She noticed an egg-sized bump on his head and said, 'how did you get that?'

'When he shot me, I ducked down quickly to get out of the way and hit my head really hard on the side of the table. That's what knocked me out, not getting shot, how stupid is that?' He rubbed his temple gently.

Kendra quickly turned when she heard a moan behind her. Incredibly, Qupi stirred and tried to lift himself up from the floor. Kendra noticed that he had dropped his blade. She quickly grabbed it as he went to reach for it. She then stabbed him in his right foot with all her strength, feeling a great deal of satisfaction when he screamed. She then picked up the taser gun and gave him another five-second jolt, which was enough to knock him out again.

'That's for Andy, you piece of shit.'

'Best you get some zip ties on him, love, he is a tough, stubborn bastard, so it's best not to take any chances,' said Trevor as he moved into a more comfortable seated position.

Kendra did as she was told and used two zip ties on Qupi's wrists and one on his ankles. She removed the knife, embedded deeply in Qupi's right foot, which was now bleeding. Quickly rifling through his pockets, she retrieved his car keys, wallet, some loose change, and two mobile phones. While he was still unconscious, she brought each phone to his face so that they could be unlocked. She then put some gaffer tape over his mouth and quickly went through the settings of each phone to remove the security feature.

'We need to get these into a faraday bag to block any signal.'

Trevor nodded in agreement. 'We have some in the van so that we can put them all in there,' he said, thankful for Andy's forward-thinking.

'Before that, we need to patch you up, Dad,' she said, ripping one of Qupi's designer shirt sleeves. She wadded it up and packed it against the entry wound, taping it in place with the gaffer tape. She did the same with the exit wound, stopping the bleeding. She then loosened Trevor's ballistic vest and tucked the injured arm in it to keep it immobile, which would be enough to hold it steady until she could clean and bandage it properly back at the factory.

'What's taking you guys so long?' asked Mo, as he came into the room. 'We need to move out of here. The cars and van are ready, and the lorry has already left, with Kev and Brad in the container to keep watch until they get to the factory.'

They had not heard the gunshots due to the horribly loud squealing of the shutters opening.

He then noticed the blood on the floor and Trevor's pained expression. 'You okay, Trev?'

'All good, Mo, it's just a flesh wound. The bullet went straight through, so I'll just be stiff for a few days, that's all.'

'You got shot and it's *just* gonna be stiff for a couple of days? Man, you're tougher than I thought. Kudos!'

'We're going to give these rooms a once-over and take whatever we can,' said Kendra. 'Can you make sure that all the cameras are removed? You know where they are, don't you?'

'Yes, no problem,' Mo said, and left.

'Let's have a look in his office to see if there's anything useful,' said Trevor, slowly getting to his feet. He winced but was able to steady himself, taking a couple of deep breaths which seemed to help.

They went into Qupi's office and started looking through his drawers, grabbing paperwork and anything of value.

'Bingo!' shouted Trevor, forgetting his pain for a moment as he looked into the large bottom drawer on one side of the desk, leaving it open for Kendra. The drawer was filled by a holdall that contained bundles of cash, in rolls of twenty-pound notes on one side and fifty-pound notes on the other.

'Bloody hell! There must be hundreds of thousands of pounds in there!'

'Isn't that good of him, eh? To fund so much goodness!' Trevor laughed. It was a drop in the ocean compared to what Andy had seized, but this was real cash, untraceable, and could be put to immediate use without anyone knowing.

'Grab the holdall and don't show anyone else just yet, I don't want anyone to lose focus on what we are doing,' said Trevor. 'We can use it to give them all a nice bonus.'

Kendra smiled and retrieved the heavy holdall, zipping it shut. She hefted it onto her back and continued looking for more treasures to take with them.

'You know, if we have time, I may get some of the guys to come back and take all the furniture, too,' Trevor said, looking around at the quality contents in the office. 'We can use some for the factory.'

'I think you'll have to, Dad,' she said, pointing to the inside of a cupboard, which showed the clear outlines of a safe, measuring three-feet-by-two. It was a solid, modern-looking safe that would take some moving. Opening it was a problem that would be addressed once they'd had it removed and taken to the factory.

Kendra smiled.

'We can't leave this here, can we?'

————

21

TIME TO CLAIM

THE TEAM STAYED BEHIND LONG ENOUGH TO STRIP EVERYTHING they could carry in the three gangster cars along with the van they had arrived in. Even then, they realised they would be leaving plenty behind, including a number of the pallets containing electrical equipment and alcohol.

'We won't be leaving them a sodding thing,' Kendra said resolutely, determined as she was to wipe them out completely and not give them a shred of a chance of starting up again. Anything of value had to be removed, however small that value was.

'We'll come back with a couple of vans later and take everything else,' Trevor said. 'It'll be worth it. Brodie will be very happy with the gift of alcohol.' Brodie Dabbs was a criminal, but he was one that Trevor knew well and trusted, within reason. Keeping him close and keeping him relatively happy was the plan. Brodie had helped a lot, but for selfish reasons, in that his gang would be able to take over the Qupi operations and grow rapidly as a result. It may be another gang taking over, but that was always going to happen, so it might as well be a gang that would not exploit helpless refugees or bring firearms and gangsters into the country. It was a case of *better the devil you know*.

Kendra had originally had issues with this, but as she saw the damage Qupi had caused, she had quickly realised the downside to having another vicious gang take his place. Brodie Dabbs was the compromise, and maybe they could persuade him to do some good in the community too, which would likely strengthen his position in the wake of the Albanian mafia's departure.

They crammed everything they could into their vehicles and closed the shutters but did not lock them, making sure that gaining entry upon their return would not be an issue. All the cameras had been removed and given to Kendra, and they made sure not to leave anything behind that would incriminate anyone there or even put them anywhere close to the warehouse – just in case.

'Let's go, guys, great job,' said Trevor to the rest of the team, getting into the passenger side of Qupi's pride and joy, his immaculate Mercedes. 'See you back at the factory.' Kendra joined him, getting into the driver's seat, having discreetly put the holdall full of cash into the boot, along with a couple of other holdalls containing kit and additional intelligence from Qupi's office.

As they drove off in convoy, Trevor looked over at his daughter and smiled. It had been a little shaky at one point, especially with his having been shot, but other than the flesh wound and the painful lump on his head, they had succeeded beyond expectations.

'This is a lovely car,' Kendra said. 'I don't suppose we can keep it?'

He laughed and said, 'Sadly no, Stav will be taking this

beauty apart just like the others and selling the parts off. We discussed this, right? This and all the money we have seized will be used to do good things, K, just as we planned.'

'Yeah, I know. It's just so comfortable,' she said, relaxing into the luxurious leather seat.

UPON ARRIVING AT THE FACTORY, they made sure to search their prisoners thoroughly before giving them the same pep-talk and warning about making noise or attempting to escape. They were all then placed in separate rooms, within which they were secured in a manner that made their stay uncomfortable, with minimal movement that barely allowed for them to relieve themselves. When fed or given drink, they were given the same ground-up sleeping tablets that were making the rest of them continually drowsy.

Qupi had tried to be loud and obstructive when he arrived. 'You think this is over, shit head? When I get out I will hunt you all down and cut you all to pieces. I will feed you to pigs and put the video on YouTube. Everyone will know and everyone will see you turned to pig shit. Remember—'

Trevor gave him a healthy dose of pepper spray to the face, which quickly did the trick and reduced him to a spluttering mess.

'Fuck you! I will kill you!' he spat, his arms lashing out wildly.

He was kept farthest away from the rest of the gang, in case he became alert and bold enough to attack his captors. His foot had been hastily cleaned and bandaged, the wound making him limp severely when on his feet. Kendra thought it fitting, and quietly hoped that it left lasting damage.

The vehicles were emptied and all the belongings taken inside, some stored in one of the rooms, and the smaller items that might prove useful given to Trevor and Kendra.

Kendra yawned and stretched her arms out, exhausted from the day's exertions.

'Dad, if you don't mind, I'm going to call it a night. I'll take all this intel to Andy tomorrow morning and will call you after, if that's okay?'

'Of course, love, we have this all under control, go and get some rest,' Trevor replied, giving her a hug before she left.

Kendra had cleaned his wounds and used sterile dissolvable stitches to close the small bullet holes, before bandaging his arm and putting it in a sling. It hurt like hell, but Trevor was still mobile, and the painkillers helped.

He was conscious that they would only be able to keep the prisoners like this for a short while, so he had put his plans into place for the next phase. He instructed some of the men to clean out the container and then prepare it for its long journey. He gave specific instructions relating to some ventilation that he wanted toward the roof, and also for some storage boxes that would hold both supplies and waste for a journey of thirty days. He made a list of supplies they would need and handed that over for someone to take care of, giving them cash to pay for it. He hoped it would be ready to depart within forty-eight hours, if not sooner.

A short time after their arrival, he gathered a small group to return to the warehouse and pick it clean. He wanted them to start with the lockers, which would prove useful at the factory, and also the table and chairs, along with Qupi's solid oak desk.

He pulled the twins to one side. 'There is something we need to remove from the first floor that is quite heavy and potentially valuable. I don't want too many of the team to know about it yet, okay? So, when you get back, be discreet about it until we decide what to do.'

He told them where to find the safe and sent them off in another van with the tools they would need to free it from within the cupboard, where it had been bolted securely in place.

The operation took several hours, and it was early morning by the time the vans returned with their plunder. Aside from the safe, the vans were quickly emptied, and the contents stored until it was decided what was to be done with them.

'The warehouse is bare, Trev,' said Mo, winking as he entered the factory.

'Great job, guys, but we haven't finished yet. I know you lot must be knackered, but we have a few more houses that need cleaning out. Are you up for it now?'

Everyone present was happy to assist, but Trevor was careful to swap most of them around with those that were guarding the prisoners, who had been rested. He gave them the three addresses that he wanted stripping, which were Qupi's house and the two lieutenants' homes. He gave them the keys to the houses, and told them to act as if the householders had instructed them to remove their goods if anyone asked any questions. He doubted that the neighbours would care too much, they probably feared them and would be happy to hear that they had suddenly moved out.

'Take everything you can fit in the vans, including towels and blankets, okay? And keep an eye out for valuables, they will be well hidden, so look in every nook and cranny. I want these bastards to have nothing left, ever again. What you can't take, just leave outside in the front garden for neighbours and locals to help themselves. Strip their fucking houses clean, boys.'

The three vans left a few minutes later. Trevor had kept Mo and his brother behind so they could address the issue of the safe.

'Leave it a few minutes and then quietly take it around the back to one of the sheds and I'll come and join you shortly. I'll get Qupi's phone and see if he was good enough to leave the code on there for us.'

There were several brick-built sheds behind the factory that had been used to store gardening equipment amongst other things. They were now derelict and so ideal to take the safe away from prying eyes. Trevor was conscious of everyone knowing and getting greedy, as with the cash they had found, and wanted to keep this part of the operation on the down-low, just in case. He quickly located Qupi's phones, both of which had been unlocked and had had all security measures removed.

All phones had had their SIM cards removed, making them untraceable once it was confirmed that all contacts and information had been transferred to the handset. The same had been done with the earlier seized phones that Andy had taken care of. Qupi's phones were no exception.

Trevor scrolled through the notes pages, and, finding nothing, started on the contacts – on both phones. There were more than a hundred to go through, much of it written in Albanian, so it took some time. He had no idea what he was looking for and hoped that something would stand out as he scrolled through, something similar to what he usually did when he saved a PIN number in his contacts. It wasn't very secure but with half a dozen different cards it wasn't possible to remember the secure codes by heart – saving to contacts seemed a decent solution. It wasn't.

It took a while before he finally hit the jackpot, when he got to the contact named '*Thesar*,' on the second phone, which he later found to be an Albanian translation of the word *treasure*. In the contact page, he found a seven-digit code that he hoped would be for the safe, where the phone number would normally be. Before getting overly excited, he googled on his phone what an Albanian phone number would look like, which was nine numbers, so it didn't match what he had here. To be sure, he rang the number and got the message: *this number has not been recognised.* Confidence was high that this could be the safe code.

'Not as secure as you thought, Qupi, is it?' he said, and went to find the twins.

The safe was in one of the sheds, as instructed, with the twins both sitting on it, back-to-back. It was dark in there, so they had both turned their phone torches on.

'We're in business, boys,' he said as he entered the shed.

He quickly moved to the front of the safe, the twins now standing behind him, shining their torches onto the front of the safe. The matt-black *Burton Brixia Tre* safe was an expensive luxury model and Trevor hoped the contents were reflective of its cost. It had been fitted in the cupboard by a couple of bolts, but whoever had fixed them in had done so to the wooden floor of the cupboard, which made it very easy to remove. The digital keypad was in the middle, slightly to the right of the handle.

'Okay, here we go,' he said, rubbing his hands together before continuing, 'seven-seven-six, three-eight-five-one,' he said out loud as he entered the code, willing it to be correct. A second later he heard the sound he was wishing for, a satisfying click, before the handle popped out slightly, inviting him to pull it open. As he did so, the torches illuminated three sections inside, two larger sections at the top, and a smaller one at the bottom. The top section was filled with cash, neat bundles of notes taking up every square centimetre. The middle section also had neatly-stashed bundles of cash, maybe half-full, with a leather-bound folder lying on the top. The smaller lower section had maybe two-dozen prestige jewellery boxes of varying sizes, which were found to contain Rolex watches, gold chains, rings, and all manner of expensive jewellery. Trevor and Amir both whistled loudly, whereby Mo started giggling in excitement.

'Well, boys, it appears that we have literally struck gold. Amir, go and get me some holdalls so that I can empty this beauty. I think we'll keep this safe and use it for ourselves once we have sorted everything out, it's a nice bit of kit. When everyone is back, I want you to gather them all in the main hall and we can start explaining what will happen next.'

'Damn,' Amir said as he prepared to leave, 'we did good!'

'Yes, we did, bro,' replied Trevor, giving Mo a pat on the back. 'Just hang on a sec,' he added abruptly.

'Boys,' he said, looking at them both in the eerie torchlight, 'I need you to think about what I'm about to tell you, okay? What we have been doing these past weeks has been very successful, but I need to know what you want to do moving on from here.'

'What do you mean?' asked Mo.

'I mean, are you happy to walk away with some cash in your pockets and go back to doing what you were doing before? Or do you want to carry on doing some good, taking more scum off the streets, and making those streets a better place for us all, especially your generation. You saw what happened to Stevie and Calvin, and also to me,' he said, highlighting his injured arm.

'Wait,' added Amir, grinning widely, 'you mean we could carry on doing this?'

'Yes, that's exactly what I mean, Amir. But before you decide, I want you to know that we can never let this sort of thing blind us to what we are trying to do,' he said, pointing to the money and jewellery in the safe. 'If we get greedy, it will ruin everything and put us all in danger, you hear me?'

'Come on, Trev,' said Mo, 'when has this ever been about money, man? You know we'd do anything for you, after what you have done to help us and our mum. Seriously, bro, that's out of order.'

Trevor put his hand on Mo's shoulder, squeezing tightly, 'I had to ask, son, forgive me.'

'Nothing to forgive, Trev, you've always done good by us, it's only right we do the same by you. We know you'll look after us, and that's all we ask for.'

'I always will, Mo, you know that,' Trevor said, 'but not everyone will think and feel the same as you two, so let's keep this on the quiet for now, right? We're going to use this money to buy what we need to keep us going and also to help each other out. That's what we want to do, and it will benefit a lot of families. We're going to keep needing help, so I want to keep Brodie sweet, too. He's going to do very well with Qupi out of the way, but we need to keep him onside while we carry on doing our thing.'

'Count us in, Trev,' Mo said. Amir nodded.

'That's great, guys, thank you. Now, go and get me those holdalls so we can get ready for later.'

IT WAS daylight by the time the vans returned, all crammed with goods from the three houses. The teams had stripped everything of value, as instructed, and had also found some extra bonuses along the way.

'Look what we found at Qupi's,' said Kev, proudly presenting a holdall, open for all to see. It was filled with bundles of cash and more jewellery, watches and gold chains in particular. Weirdly, there was even a gold eye patch encrusted with jewels.

'Seriously?' Trevor said, picking up the eye patch and putting it on. 'I must wear this when I pay him a visit!' He laughed loudly.

The team were buoyant from their success, and more holdalls were presented from the other two houses, also stuffed with valuables. The vans also yielded some expensive furniture, paintings, and electrical goods, all upper-end models. It was a great result and would yield a good return for their operation.

'Dude, Qupi had seven TVs in his house, seven!' added Brad, 'including a 55-inch in the bloody bathroom!'

They also claimed dozens of black bin bags containing expensive branded clothing, along with unopened boxes of aftershave and many other luxury items. Their haul was impressive, and the elation was there for all to see. After a short while, when they had taken refreshments and calmed down a little, Trevor called them all together. They were silent as they waited for him to speak.

'Guys, I can't thank you enough for your help these past few weeks, you've all been brilliant. I wanted to let you know that we're almost finished with this operation, and that it has been a bloody great success. I also wanted to let you know that we will probably carry on doing something similar, and I'll be speaking with Brodie about those of you who have helped so brilliantly, to see if you fancy carrying this on with us.'

There were plenty of murmurs amongst those that did work for Brodie. They had thoroughly enjoyed their time with Trevor, and it was likely that many – if not most – would happily carry on.

'Before you decide, remember Stevie and Calvin, you saw what can happen. It's dangerous business, and I don't want you to make your decision without thinking of them and poor Stevie's mum. Nobody here would think less of you if you walked away now, okay?'

'Trevor, please, man,' said Kev, 'if we didn't want to be here then we'd be somewhere else okay? And I know you'll be helping Stevie's mum out, and so will some of us who knew him well. It's cool, man.'

'Again, I appreciate it, guys, I really do. In the meantime, I wanted you each to have something as a gesture of thanks, for all the help recently. This won't make you rich, but it should help you all. I'd urge you to keep it to yourselves and not splash out too much.' He gestured for Amir to bring over a holdall that he had prepared for this chat.

'Okay, who's first?' he asked, smiling broadly as he held out a bundle of fifty-pound notes.

'Each bundle has one hundred fifty-pound notes, which Qupi and his friends were kind enough to bundle together conveniently.' Trevor smiled as he started handing out the rolls of notes. There were whistles of appreciation and plenty of smiling faces as Trevor completed his gesture. Five thousand pounds was nothing to be sniffed at, and it would go a long way; it was more money than most had ever seen.

'We would have done it for nothing, Trev,' said Kev, laughing. 'I haven't had this much fun, ever!'

They laughed and agreed, but it was important to Trevor that he showed his appreciation.

'Guys, there is more money, as most of you will know, but we will be using that to help the clubs and also to help some families who have suffered at Qupi's hand. It's important that you know that, and to understand what we're trying to do, okay?'

More nods, all in appreciation and understanding. He could not see any greed or malice in anyone present, for which he was grateful.

'Okay, so, not long to go now, let's make sure to keep an eye on our guests before they leave us,' he added, 'and all of you, get some rest, you've certainly earned it.'

22

PLANS FOR THE BAD GUYS

THE NEXT DAY STARTED IN EARNEST AT THE FACTORY, WITH plenty of activity around the container and with the prisoners. They had been checked regularly and it had been noticed that they were becoming angrier and bolder, lashing out at times and receiving a jolt from a well-aimed taser in exchange.

'Luckily, they won't be with us very long,' said Trevor, as he spoke with Kendra on the phone, having briefed her about the previous night's findings. 'What have you found at your end?' he asked.

'Nothing much to shout about, to be honest. Andy is still going through it but it's mainly more invoices and financial transactions linked to the bank accounts we've already cleaned out.'

'Well, remember I have that folder that you can pick up later, it looks like it has some addresses and numbers that Andy may be able to figure out. It's all in a foreign language.'

'No problem. By the way, the holdall is safely in the basement now,' she said, referring to the cash they had taken from the warehouse. 'We should bring that safe over to Andy's when we get a chance, we have plenty to put in it and the basement is the best place for it.'

'Yeah, that's a good idea, but I'll wait until you're here so that we can do it together and nobody else sees us. It's best that nobody knows we have taken it.'

'Agreed. How's the prep coming along?'

'Better than I had hoped. The container will be ready tonight, so I'm going to move them in the early hours, I think. It'll be safer.'

'Okay, well, I'll pop over in a bit and help, it doesn't look like there's much I can do here.'

'See you later, love, give my best to Andy.'

The men had made quick work of the container, drilling some ventilation holes up high, and had also fetched two dozen large plastic storage boxes. Most of them had been filled with food and water for the journey, along with bags of less perishable food. They had included a large pile of bedding and blankets from the three houses, and they had set aside a number of storage boxes for the waste, where they put rolls of small refuse bags, cheap toilet paper, and a separate pile of empty plastic tubs.

'We're good to go, Trev,' said Brad as he came over to inspect it.

'Great stuff, well done, boys,' he replied, admiring their handiwork and checking to make sure they had covered everything. He wanted the gangsters to suffer but to survive the journey, so that they would experience their true punishment at the other end. He smiled just thinking about it.

'Summary justice,' he said, softly, to nobody in particular.

KENDRA ARRIVED LATER that afternoon and helped where she could, feeling satisfied with the extent of their achievements. Anyone that was free helped her to re-arrange some of the furniture they had *procured* from the gangsters, smiling with each piece that was put in place in its new home. One of the larger, cleaner rooms upstairs was set aside as the main office, and, as such, Qupi's ornate oak desk was ceremoniously placed there, along with some shelving, a large TV, and other electronic equipment.

The lockers were placed in another large room downstairs for anyone to use as they wished. It was likely that this place would be used for a while now, so Kendra wanted it to be comfortable and well-equipped. Some of the lockers were rightly taken to the gym, along with a couple of TVs and other useful electrical goods.

Trevor had been to the local hardware depot and spent thousands of pounds on new locks, plug extensions, tools, chains, and anything else he thought would be useful for the future. He had plans to make the rooms more secure for any future potential *guests*. Their hope, his and Kendra's, was that parts of the factory would be a sort of holding pen for those that needed removing from society and relocating where they would do no more harm. The rest of it would be utilised to progress their ambitions to make East London a better place, so it would be well-equipped and comfortable for those that would be helping them. As the building would be owned by *Sherwood Management Trust*, Kendra had thought long and hard about appearances, and how it should look to any visitors who came by, whether by invitation or on spec. It was likely to be an important factor in how they would set the place up, so the holding bays would need to be separate from the legitimate business. It was this, without telling Trevor too much, that Kendra had thought hard about. As such, it was likely that they'd need to bring in some construction workers to build new walls to allow for the buffer between the cells and the rest. Well, they had plenty of money, so it was nice to plan ahead.

By the evening, the factory was starting to look like a local club, with a mish-mash style of tables and chairs, TVs, half a dozen different sofas and more. It was easy to see that once the place was formally set up and legally theirs, it would be greatly improved. Andy had confirmed with Kendra that he had made an official bid on behalf of *Sherwood Management Trust* that had been accepted, and so it was just a formality for the sale to go through. She didn't want to tell her dad just yet, wanting it to be a nice surprise. It would cost them four-and-a-half-million pounds of Qupi's money, but it would be worth every penny and would be a great asset to them. Another pleasant surprise, which again had not been mentioned, was to pay off all outstanding mortgages relating to the gym and garage next door, leaving them both free of debt and able to continue flourishing as businesses and – in the case of the gym - a place of safety for the local youth. Kendra smiled at this; it would make Trevor very happy. She and Andy had also spoken about setting funds aside to buy more such clubs and expand that side of things. The world was their oyster, and it was always going to be funded by the scum of the world, which made it even sweeter.

Trevor had sent one of the vans to Brodie Dabbs, fully laden with almost all the alcohol they had seized. He had spoken to him to let him know the operation had been a success and – from tomorrow – there would be very little left of the Qupi gang and their influence in East London. He hadn't told him the whole story, as in how much cash had been seized, that was to remain a strict secret between himself, Andy and Kendra. Brodie was delighted with the news and offered more help for the future when Trevor advised him that they wished to continue fighting certain types of criminals. He wasn't interested in anything controversial; he was just an old-fashioned crime boss who recognised a good thing when he saw it. Brodie Dabbs did not need to get into people-smuggling, or gunrunning, or anything that would attract the wrath of the people. He was happy to handle stolen goods, make some money from protection, and take over the high-end brothels that had become so popular under Qupi. None of the workers would be there against their will, and all those that had been kept under duress would be freed. That was the deal Trevor had made with him, and he was happy to comply. He wanted to be one of those crime bosses that people respected and liked, because he would help with local causes and such.

It was a decent compromise and one that Kendra hoped would last for a long time, certainly long enough for them to make a big impact locally.

And then it was time to say goodbye to their *guests*. They had been fed, watered, and drugged that little bit more than usual, so they'd be drowsy for the transfer to the container and beyond. Trevor remembered the jewel-encrusted gold eye patch and put it on as he went to speak with Qupi. His men had been safely removed from their confinement and moved to the container. They were dishevelled and clearly beaten, with some resistance from the likes of Dervishi and the other lieutenants, who received one last blast of pepper spray for good measure for their efforts. The resistance did not last long.

As Trevor entered Qupi's room, the now-former gang boss looked up and saw someone wearing his prized eye patch. His fury returned quickly as he cursed in his native tongue, reaching out in vain towards the man who was wearing it.

'That was a gift from my wife, you bastard,' he shouted weakly, exhausted from his short burst of anger. He lashed out feebly with his free arm, a futile gesture that didn't even get close. The sleeping tablets had worked their magic, and this was all he could manage.

'Well, it's mine now, and I thank you for it,' Trevor said, bowing in an exaggerating manner. 'I just wanted to see you one last time before you go on a nice trip with your friends, and to tell you that, well, you have absolutely nothing left. Not even a spare pair of pants. We have taken it all from you, everything, and you will never see any of it —or any of us— ever again. You will never hurt anybody again, you horrible piece of shit. All the damage you have caused, all the people you have hurt, it was all for this, so that you can end up shit-ting yourself in the dark while you think about the future. Enjoy it, Qupi, you will love your new home.'

Trevor moved back as a pair of men came forward to move Qupi. Another held back, holding some pepper spray and a taser, just in case.

As they moved him out of the room, Qupi looked back at Trevor. 'You and I will meet again, bastard,' he said, before being dragged away to the container. He tried kicking out but was so weak that the men carrying him didn't even notice.

'No,' said Trevor,' I don't think so.'

The container was locked and then secured with the best padlock Trevor could find. He then stuck the key underneath one corner of the container, as it was accessible whilst on the back of the lorry, using self-amalgamating rubber tape, which would survive the trip and not be found by accident. He would tell those that would meet the container at its end destination where to find the key and give access to the *cargo*.

Trevor smiled as the lorry left for Tilbury Docks with its payload, which would make one last trip.

23

TIME TO EXPORT

Trevor had called ahead to his contact at Tilbury Docks. Bruno was to facilitate the entry of the lorry, the unloading of the container, and then ultimately the loading of it onto the small container freighter that was bound for Freetown, the capital of Sierra Leone on the west coast of Africa. The journey would take up to thirty days, depending on weather conditions, and would be a deeply unpleasant trip for those inside the container. Trevor had explained to his contact what the cargo was, and about the harm that they had done to women and children in particular. There were no questions or concerns at all from his contact, who knew what he was getting into, and who knew exactly where to send the cargo.

'Don't worry, my friend,' said Bruno, 'I know exactly where to send the filth in this container. They will take good care of them, I promise you.'

'Thank you, Bruno, and remember, I will be back again soon with more.' Trevor handed over four bundles of cash to

and he's even worse now, but I thinl
away and see if I can break through th

'Well, good luck with that. And ke
what you decide, okay? Hopefully I'll

'All received and understood, Sarg
call.

'Well, that wasn't very nice, was it?
that, not at all,' said Andy, who had l
the whole time, pretending to be upse

'Did I say anything that wasn't true

Andy thought for a few seconds ar
'No, I suppose not,' he said, and then
infectious smiles.

'And you can be a twat someti
loudly.

'Yeah, yeah, laugh it up, smarty p
you'll get without your genius friend h

It was incredible just how muc
changed into a futuristic ops room. It r
a rocket ship; such was the startling nu
had accumulated over the past few wee

'You really need to stop buying s
said, enjoying the exchange, 'the poor
time he loads his van up, knowing that

'Not at all, Lewis and I have becom
ly,' he said seriously, 'he looks after me
throw things around like the other driv

'Can we get back to work now, p
genius?' she mocked.

'Yes, your highness, let's!'

Kendra laughed, feeling better tha
long time, and feeling happy that her i

help fund the transfer and told Bruno where the key was for
him to pass on.

Trevor watched as the container was hoisted onto the
freighter. It was placed on the deck where it would subsequently have four more containers stacked above it. The ship
was relatively small and handled just sixty containers, but
what it lacked in capacity it made up for in speed and agility.
There would be no difficulty at all the other end, where some
of the funds allocated to Bruno would make their way to the
port officials who would expedite the removal and collection
of the container. Trevor had spoken with Bruno at length for
weeks about this and was finally able to see it in practice. He
was pleased, *very* pleased with the outcome.

'Bon Voyage, arsehole,' he said, waving, as the container
settled on the deck.

He and Bruno walked away, satisfied that the job was done.

Kendra answered the phone to Rick Watts, surprised by the
timing.

'Hi, Rick, I still have a few days left, right?' she said,
mentally counting the days off that she had taken.

Rick laughed. 'Yes, Kendra, I'm just checking in to see that
you're okay and to give you a bit of an update.'

'Thank God for that,' she replied, 'I thought I'd gone
AWOL or something!'

'Not at all. The intel unit did some great work while
you've been off, and Border Force and the task force set up to
deal with the refugees and the people-smuggling seized
another ship. They had the same cargo, same number of

people, both refugees and workers,
think how much of it we have missed

'Well, it sounds like they won't ge
not using those routes, anyway, and
losing out on two huge shipments
smiling to herself. 'How are the rest o

'All is good. We've not made m
mob, the intel just dried up complet
what is going on. Maybe that douch
has taken control and stopped anyth
who knows? Regardless, it means tha
on us anymore and we're back in the
Looking forward to having you back, I

'Yeah, about that, Rick. My legs a
hundred percent,' she lied, taking a de
the physio I will need, as well as psy
haven't spoken about much, I think I
intel unit for a few more months, n
thinking of going part-time so that I c
ery, both physically and mentally.'

'Bloody hell, Kendra, where did al
minute you're set on fearful vengeance
to go part-time? What's really going
better than she thought.

'I just think I need more time t
honestly. And I want to help Andy wit
know? He hasn't got anyone to help
want to be there for him.'

'That was his choice, Kendra, you k
reached out dozens of times and he jus

'I know, and I get it. I just think I
get through his thick skull. He's always

had gone up a notch, almost to the point where they were
flirting with each other again. *And we know how that ended up,*
she thought, smiling mischievously.

'As I was about to say, before we were so rudely interrupted by our dear sergeant,' continued Andy, 'the leather
journal, from what I have briefly looked at, is a list of the
businesses Qupi was running here in East London. I'll
confirm when I've had a closer look, but they had seven
brothels, four gambling clubs, and half a dozen other cash
businesses that they used to launder money. I think they were
getting ready to expand all their operations and their areas,
which is why they were bringing in soldiers and guns, to
remove the other surrounding gang-led operations.'

'It has them all in there? So, is it something we can benefit
from, or do you think we should hand it over to Rick? This
could be a huge boost for the Met, don't you think?'

'I think we're okay for funds, even with what we've just
splashed out for the factory and Trevor's businesses. To be
honest, Kendra, we need to limit the amount of interaction
we have with Qupi's remaining people and businesses; we
need to stay covert and under the radar. I say give it to Rick
and let the team take the glory.'

'Agreed,' she said. 'So how do we present it to them?'

'We'll figure it out, K, the informant route or *Crimestoppers*
is always a good place to start. I'd even go as far as sending
the journal by post to Rick at the station anonymously, he'll
know what to do, won't he?'

Kendra laughed. 'I never thought of doing that, it's
simple, and no questions will ever be asked. Go, Andy! Or
should I say, go, *genius* Andy!'

'I'll take that, smarty pants, now let's get this in a jiffy bag and to the post office, on the hurry-up,' he added, 'I've made a copy in case it comes in handy again later.'

'*Now* who's the smarty pants?' Kendra said.

Fifty minutes later the package containing the journal was handed over the counter at a post office in the Ilford area, to be sent by Special Delivery and addressed to Sergeant Rick Watts of the Serious Crimes Unit.

RICK WATTS RECEIVED the package the next day, and within hours was mobilising teams across the region to raid the addresses and seize any evidence relating to Qupi. It hadn't taken his superiors long at all to accede to his requests to do so, mindful of the fact that the journal had been posted to him personally.

'I don't suppose there's a return address?' the superintendent had asked, knowing full well there wouldn't be, and that they didn't really have any other action to take other than to let Watts and his crew take it on.

'Just remember, Watts, we'll be looking at this very carefully, so don't screw up.'

'I have no intention of screwing up, sir, with respect,' Rick replied, 'and I have no clue who sent this, but it is a gift that we cannot ignore if we want to get rid of the scum, so just let me crack on with it.'

The superintendent waved him out of his office, shaking his head and hoping that Watts would deal with it correctly.

'As ever, I'm too old for this shit,' muttered the superintendent, sitting down in his worn-out chair and wishing he could take a nap.

BY THE FOLLOWING MORNING, all the addresses had been raided, many arrests were made, and evidence was seized. With that, and the likely evidence that would come from records and interviews, Qupi's empire was dead and buried. The Special Crimes Unit would use their skills to delve into his operations with a fine-toothed comb in the hope that it would lead them to him. They would find plenty of useful evidence but nothing that would lead them to the man himself. Eventually, when all was dealt with, the police would consider it a partial victory in that all Qupi's operations were subsequently closed with severe impact, but neither he nor his main cronies were ever located or detained.

Brodie Dabbs would later step in and take over those same operations, with zero resistance or even a raised eyebrow. The plan had worked very well indeed, despite the casualties.

24

MORE ASSAULTS!

LATER THAT EVENING, KENDRA AND TREVOR MET WITH ANDY at his house, to discuss what they would be doing next. They sat in the lounge eating pizza and drinking beer, enjoying each other's company, and all visibly relaxed for the first time in months.

'I think we surely deserve this,' said Trevor, raising a bottle of beer to his daughter and Andy. 'Cheers to you both, and to the rest of the team that made it happen.'

'Cheers!' they replied, in unison.

'Honestly, I never thought we'd achieve as much as we have, so well done to you both for sticking to your guns and being as ambitious as you have been.'

'Dad, we couldn't have done it without you, and to be honest, we probably wouldn't even have tried, so take some credit, please!' Kendra smiled proudly at her father.

Trevor nodded and said nothing more, not wanting to get emotional. He quickly changed the subject.

'So,' he said, rubbing his hands together, 'what are we going to spend all that money on?' He turned his head back and forth to them both, making light of the fact that they had millions of pounds sitting in secret Cayman Island bank accounts.

'Well, actually, we've spent most of it already, Trev,' replied Andy glibly. 'I can call you Trev, right?' he said innocently, taking in Trevor's shocked reaction.

'No, no, you cannot!' Trevor replied angrily, almost hysterically. 'You spent all that money? What the hell did you do, give it to the policeman's ball fund or something ridiculous like that?' He got up and started pacing the room. 'Seriously? You spent it? All of it?'

'Most of it, yes,' replied Kendra, innocently.

'Sorry, Trev ... I mean *Trevor*, but we had some huge bills to pay and everything that I bought cost a lot of money,' Andy said.

'You spent fifteen million quid on equipment?' Trevor was almost apoplectic.

'Yeah, and those factories don't come cheap, you know, and your mortgages had twenty years to go, so they weren't cheap either, and—'

'Wait, what?' Trevor's expression changed once again. He saw that they were toying with him, barely able to keep the smiles from their faces.

'What the hell is going on here? Seriously, what are you talking about? And don't play games with me, boy, don't think I won't take out your other leg,' he hissed. His expressions were priceless.

'You heard him, Dad.' Kendra stepped in, finally smiling. 'We bought the factory and paid off your mortgages on the club and the garage. And we want you to buy a few more clubs and get someone you trust to run them.'

Trevor was speechless. He stood there, unmoving except

for his eyes, which swivelled almost comically from Kendra to Andy and then back again.

'Why have you done that?' he asked, still bemused.

'Because we can't do this without you. Because what you do with the kids is brilliant, and we think you can do it for many more of them. And it's what we always wanted to do, to sort out the scum and help those that need it, because nobody else is doing it. And what you've done these past few months has been nothing short of brilliant and showed us that not only are you good at what you do, but you are also incredibly well-connected. Like I said, we couldn't have done it without you. That's why, Dad.'

Kendra could see the tears welling up as it sunk in.

He wiped them away and looked at Kendra and then Andy, who was now also smiling, and said, 'I'll let you off, you can call me Trev.'

He extended his arms out for his daughter to come in for a hug, and she was happy to oblige. It was a long one, and they were soon joined by Andy who put his arms around them both and said in the most exaggerated and over-the top voice that he could muster, 'Group hug! I love you both so much!'

'Don't push it, boy,' Trevor said, finally letting go, giving Andy a gentle slap across the head.

'Well, that love didn't last long, did it?' Andy laughed, rubbing his scalp.

'And if you tell anyone you saw me crying, I'll poke your other eye out,' Trevor added for good measure. It was his turn to laugh at Andy's expression.

'Seriously, Dad, we need you to help us with this. Are you okay with that?'

Trevor took one of Kendra's hands and looked at her lovingly.

'There's something I never told you, darling,' he said. 'I loved your mum more than any other human being on this earth, until you came along. I got into some trouble with the wrong people and the only way I could protect you and your mum was to stay away. That's why I wasn't around much and that's why you ended up being raised by my parents when your mum died. When you joined the police, I was chuffed to bits, and you never knew, but I was at your passing-out parade and cried like a little baby when I saw you receiving your award.' He looked pointedly at Andy. 'Again, if you tell anyone ...'

He turned back to Kendra, still holding her hand. 'And that's why you didn't see much of me from then on either, it was bad news for you to be associated with someone with known criminal connections. But I was there for you, watching from a distance, seeing you flourish and succeed at everything you did. I just wanted you to know that I stayed away to help you and to protect you, and it broke my heart.' More tears welled up in his eyes, but he kept her gaze. 'So of course I will help you. You will not keep me away now, girl, I am here to stay, and I have a lot of catching up to do.' He leaned in and grabbed Kendra into another hug, this one much tighter than the last.

'Thanks, Dad,' she said, tears forming. It felt like closure. She had already forgiven him, but now that she fully understood he had sacrificed so much to keep her safe, it all made sense.

'Sorry for being a bitch all those times, I feel terrible now,' she said, laughing.

Trevor heard Andy sniff and turned towards him, ready to

slap him around the head again. Andy stood there, leaning on his cane, crying.

'Sorry, it's just that she never knew, and she really did call you some nasty names when she was angry,' Andy said, laughing as he wiped the tears away. 'I mean, *really* nasty names.'

Trevor and Kendra both walked up to him and slapped him around the head simultaneously, both laughing as he shouted, 'Ow! There's just no love here at all, is there?'

THEY SPENT several hours going over their plans for the future. This included planning all the upgrades for the factory, making sure it was to be as secure as possible, not just for holding any future '*guests*' but also for all the equipment they would be looking to store there for their operations. They would spend a lot making sure the perimeter was completely protected with the latest CCTV and sensors, along with some for the track leading to the gates, for advanced warnings. Andy rubbed his hands together glee-fully when discussing potential new kit that he wanted to try out.

'Boys with toys,' Kendra remarked.

'So, here's a thought,' she added, 'we should make one of the clubs a female-only club, where we could protect vulner-able women and train them to look after themselves. I was the only girl working on this operation and it would help us all a lot if there were more girls, don't you think?'

'We have a couple of girls at our club who can look after themselves,' said Trevor. 'They can help with the training.

You're right, it would be great to have more girls on the team, some I know are tougher than most men!'

They planned to set aside some time for sourcing new locations for the clubs and making sure that funds were set aside to allow for their fitting-out.

'This is so amazing, guys, honestly,' Trevor said. The future was looking very rosy. And best of all, it was being paid for by the criminals, which always made them chuckle.

'Summary justice,' Kendra said.

'You can't beat it,' Trevor added.

'You guys are so great, making the world so much better 'n' all,' Andy squealed in his exaggerated voice, mocking them both.

He had clearly deserved those slaps to the back of his head.

EPILOGUE

Twenty-eight days later, the container finally arrived at its end destination. The heat was only just tolerable outside, so it was unthinkable as to what it was like inside the container itself. The slightly rusting container door squealed loudly as it was pulled open, releasing a stench unlike anything they'd ever smelled before. They instinctively pulled back from it a few paces, their eyes almost watering from the horrid smell, strongly ammonia-like with much worse mixed in. Dozens of flies buzzed around the new hosts as they made a desperate attempt to flee the revulsion.

'Dear God,' said one of them in their native language, 'what in hell have they sent us?'

Something stirred from within, and they moved back another pace, their rifles aimed at the door.

'Don't shoot,' said a man in English, his voice weak. A distressed shambles of a man shuffled to the door, shielding his face from the glaring sun above. 'Don't shoot. Please help us.' He stepped outside, looking around at the dozen armed men standing before him.

Several more men, in a similar state, ambled forward and exited the container, all shielding their heads from the unforgiving rays. Eventually they all exited, except for two that lay prone inside the container. They stirred, barely alive, one of them raising his arm weakly to show that he was still with them. Two of the guards covered their mouths and noses with the bandanas around their necks and went inside, dragging the two weak men outside. One of them had a bloodied bandage on his right foot, and many flies still buzzing around it, hoping for more sustenance from it.

'Help us,' said Qupi, his mouth and throat dry and painful, and his voice rasping as a result. 'We need help,' he repeated. His foot had become infected on the dreadful journey and had weakened him greatly. He had lost a great deal of weight and was a shadow of the strong, confident leader he had once been, not so long ago.

'Give them water and then put them in the truck,' said one of the armed guards.

When they had all been watered and placed in the canvas-covered truck, the leader of the guards stood at the back of the lorry, looking inside, and said in English, 'You are now our prisoners. Welcome to the Republic of Mali! You will be taken to a mine, where you will be looked after with food and water. You will work for twelve hours a day and six days a week in the mine. For this, you will be allowed to live. If you try to escape, you will be shot. If you cause us any problems, you will be shot. You have two options, you either want to live, or you want to die. It is your choice.'

The prisoners were in no condition to argue. They had barely survived with the rations they had been given.

'Who has done this?' asked Qupi, still unsure who had vanquished him.

The man smiled, and said, 'I have a message for you all, from your friends in the UK.'

'What is it?' asked Qupi.

'They wanted me to tell you that this is payment for the lives you have destroyed. Oh, and *thank you for the eye patch.*'

Qupi stared at the man, knowing that he was beaten. His head slumped to his chest in defeat as the truck moved off, trundling slowly over the dirt track towards the further hell that awaited them.

THE END

'Fagin's Folly'

Book 2 of the *'Summary Justice'* series
with DC Kendra March.

https://mybook.to/faginsfolly

Or read on...

BOOK 2 PREVIEW

THEY LAY IN WAIT, TWO IN THE BUSHES AND TWO BEHIND THE large oak tree to one side of the path. All four wore black garb, including beanie hats and snoods, which they pulled up to hide their faces, leaving just their eyes visible. They looked like four ninja warriors from a television show, waiting patiently, biding their time, ready to strike at any moment. They had done this many, many times in the past year, it was something that they had become proficient at.

The darkness had arrived less than an hour earlier, partially concealing the poorly lit path that was frequently used by those taking a short cut from the busy eateries in Mare Street, Hackney to the quiet gentrified residential streets beyond London Fields, the park that the path cut through. The four *ninjas* had chosen London Fields as their focus for tonight, one of the dozens of venues throughout East London that they had carefully selected for their ambushes. They were careful to pick locations that were poorly lit, where their victims would not be seen or heard, that had several escape routes, and where it would be difficult for any help to arrive in any good time to help any victims. They had picked their venues well, with significant - and growing - success.

They didn't have to wait long tonight for their victims, a couple in their late thirties out celebrating their eleventh wedding anniversary at a nearby bistro that was a favourite of theirs. Although not drunk, the bottle of wine that they had shared had cheered them nicely and helped them disregard the dangers of cutting through a park so late at night. The husband was a large man, six feet three inches tall and of stout build, almost twenty stone, and at this moment - with three glasses of wine in his system - feeling untouchable. As they approached the bend that was overlooked by a large gnarled two-hundred-year-old oak tree, the four ambushers used their now familiar hand signals to indicate that their quarry was almost upon them.

The couple, cuddled together and enjoying each other's company, stopped suddenly as two of the sinisterly clad strangers stepped out from behind the tree.

'Money, jewellery and phones, now!' shouted one of them, brandishing a machete towards them.

'Steady on, fella,' the man said, sobering quickly as he recognised the threat, 'we don't have anything that you want,' he added, his left arm extended towards them, palm up, as if to fend them off.

'I won't ask again,' the young man behind the mask replied menacingly, 'do it now or we'll cut you both real bad.' The second stranger also held a large knife, which he slowly waved warningly in front of them both.

'Look, mate, we've just been-' The man didn't have time to complete his pleading as the machete man lunged at him and slashed the blade towards his extended arm. The man instinctively withdrew his arm and stepped back, pulling his wife behind him as he did so. They did not see or hear the other two assailants sneak out from behind the bushes on the opposite side of the path to the tree, behind them, both similarly armed with large knives. One of them sliced the back of the man's leg with a large, frequently sharpened serrated hunting knife, slicing through his left hamstring as a knife would slice through a piece of raw chicken. The man screamed and collapsed to the floor, clutching the back of his now furiously bleeding leg, trying desperately to keep his wife safe from the attackers.

'Please, don't! You can have everything!' the woman screamed in fear, handing over her handbag to the nearest attacker. He grabbed it from her but continued to slash her arm with his knife, eliciting a scream of pain from the victim.

'Here!' shouted the man, handing over his wallet with one hand whilst holding the back of his blood drenched leg with the other, as he quickly weakened from blood loss.

The machete wielder took something shiny and metallic from his pocket and put it on his right hand, flexing his fingers as he looked lovingly at his pride and joy. It was a vicious knuckle duster with raised bladed edges marking the letter 'E', measuring two inches by two inches, the back of the 'E' rounded and the middle line slightly longer than the other two, giving the impression of a claw.

'Next time, do what you're told, old man,' he said, before punching the man hard in his midriff, prompting a grunt from the man as the breath left his body, leaving bloody slashes in the shape of the knuckle duster. He looked up just in time to see the attacker strike again, this time flush on the forehead, a blow that knocked him out cold. The attacker turned to the woman and said, 'when you tell your friends this story, remember to tell them that you met the *East London Consortium*, and remember to tell them that we give no mercy.'

She nodded quickly.

'I'll tell you what,' he said ominously, approaching her slowly, 'let me help you with that.'

He stepped forward and placed the knuckle duster gently against her forehead. The woman whimpered, frozen stiff in fear, fearing for her life as the cold steel caressed her skin. She closed her eyes as the attacker pressed hard into her forehead, squeezing first upwards then downwards to ensure that the letter was clear on her skin, drawing blood, painful enough for her to cry in agony. She had been branded.

The four attackers then proceeded to rummage through their victims' pockets and stripped them clean of everything of value, including their wedding rings, credit cards, gold chains, and mobile phones. Within seconds they had taken their stash and vanished into the gloom. The woman opened her eyes and looked around, blood slowly dripping from the wounds on her head and arm, not knowing what to do except scream for help.

It would be thirty minutes before the ambulance finally arrived, along with the police shortly afterwards. Her husband's injuries and blood loss were severe, and he in a coma for three days before finally gaining consciousness and making a start to the slow road of recovery. Their painful injuries, especially the robbers' brands on their bodies, would remind them every day for the rest of their lives, of the fateful walk in the park.

It was not an anniversary that they would ever forget.

Chapter 1

'Okay, listen up everybody, let's make a start,' shouted Detective Sergeant Rick Watts, clapping his hands with authority as he moved to stand in front of the magnetic board that he would be referring to during the briefing. The voices died down to a murmur as the *Serious Crime Unit* sat down to listen to their highly respected leader, the man that had recruited them. He waited patiently, shaking his head as the team took their seats in the briefing room.

'Come on, you lot. Honestly, it's like being back at school again. Let's get a grip here!' he said loudly, eliciting a smile and a few giggles from his team. He grinned back.

'Before I start, I want to clear something up with you all, as I know you're all champing at the bit waiting to find out what the hell is going on. We have been joined today, graciously I might add, by our esteemed colleague Detective Constable Kendra March,' he continued, indicating to the smiling Kendra who had sat near the front. She shook her head, feigning irritation. The rest of the team clapped and whooped enthusiastically, glad to see Kendra back with them in a formal briefing. It had been a long time since that had last happened.

'Don't you shake your head, March, you know I have to do this,' Watts continued, smiling. 'Anyway, as you can clearly see, young Kendra here is recovering well from her injuries of many months ago. It's taken a little longer than she'd hoped but she's getting there, right?'

Kendra nodded theatrically.

'Good to hear, and that's the good news. The downside

is that she has decided to slow things down a little, which is understandable, and has decided to go part time.'

This somewhat surprising announcement was met in silence, the rest of the team unsure of where Rick was going with this and uncertain of how to respond.

'Now as you know we don't have any part-timers on this most elite of teams,' he said, noticing the surprise and silence within the team and stepping in quickly to continue.

'Come on, guys, we are elite, aren't we?' He extended both arms to his troops, prompting more laughter and clapping.

'So, you may quite rightly be asking *then why she is here in this briefing*, right? Well, we have managed to secure permission to include Kendra's honoured presence in our briefings and investigations as a representative of the *Intel Unit* downstairs. So, in a way, she'll still be part of the team, she just won't be able to get involved in anything exciting until she decides to come to her senses and come back to us full time.' Watts looked directly at Kendra and smiled again, nodding slightly to acknowledge that this was what he wanted to happen.

'Anyway, that's enough of that. Kendra will still be around to help with stuff, so before you know it, we'll all be sick of her again.' More laughter.

'What about Andy, boss? Any news?' asked Nick McGuinness, one of the longer serving members of the team. He was keen to hear news of Andy Pike, who had been on sick leave for many months now.

'Well, he hasn't been in touch much, as you know, but we have heard that his papers will be going through any day now for him to be medically retired. I spoke with him a few days ago, he is still quite bitter and unhappy but seems resigned to his fate, which is an improvement on how he was. He is planning to take some trips and will probably then fade away; he doesn't want to engage with anyone at the moment.'

It was the news that they had expected, but it was still a surprise that he didn't want to engage with them anymore, and they were all very saddened by that.

'Shame, that,' Wilf Baker replied, 'he was a good 'un.' There were lots of murmured agreements.

Kendra did not respond in any way, knowing what she knew about Andy and his current status. She didn't like to take credit for anything, but in this instance, she had pulled Andy Pike, her partner on the team, from the depths of depression and inactivity and helped transform him into a Q-like figure from a James Bond film. His progress from agreeing to join her and her father Trevor on the quest for justice had given Andy a new lease of life, made all the more satisfying by them having found out that he had a genius flair for hacking and navigating the dark web, as well as the ability to procure almost everything that they would ever need. Thanks to their joint efforts and with the help of some talented friends, they had managed to secure premises and equipment, more than enough to deal with the types of criminals that had been getting away with their crimes for decades.

It was why she kept the emotion from her face as the team openly and enthusiastically showed theirs.

'Those Albanians have a lot to answer to, the bastards,' Pablo Rothwell had added, still angry that the Qupi gang were never brought to justice for their vicious attacks on Kendra and Andy, which was the cause of Andy's subsequent retirement.

'Right, well if you allow me to continue, I will explain

what this briefing is all about,' Watts said, stepping in to take back control of the conversation.

'You almost spoilt it for me there, Wilf, so thanks for that,' said Watts sarcastically, continuing. 'As you know we were barred from engaging with the investigation into the Qupi gang, because those *higher beings* from the top floor thought it would cause a *conflict of interest*,' he mimicked with both hands as if quoting the bosses. 'Well, it didn't stop us from causing a few problems for the bastards, and the two ships that we sent information about were bringing over a ton of firearms and people that would have caused a lot of problems here in East London when they were seized. We did that, we caused a massive problem for Qupi, so well done us.' They all clapped briefly, accepting what was a covert pat on the back, which would bring no recognition as they had conducted their interference covertly.

'So, why this briefing?' Watts continued. 'Well, it seems that the Qupi gang have vanished from the face of this earth. Now we knew that seizing the ships and the cargo would cause them problems, but they were a solid outfit, so it doesn't make sense that they would just ... disappear.'

'What, you mean they've stopped their criminal activities?' asked Jillian Petrou.

'No, I mean that they have completely vanished. Nobody has a clue where they are. There's no activity recorded at any ports; they have just disappeared. Their warehouse is empty, their houses are empty, their bank accounts empty, their cars gone, no trace of anything anywhere.'

There was silence in the room as the team digested this news. It was very rare for something like this to happen. With modern technology there was always a trace of someone somewhere, so this stumped them completely.

Kendra kept quiet, knowing that the Qupi gang were now in deepest Africa paying a heavy price for their crimes, their wealth taken from them and ready for it to be used to fund operations against other criminals. Her team had done a grand job in taking them off the streets, something that the police were not able to do – such were their hands tied nowadays. It was a pattern that was repeating itself many times all over London, and it was a pattern that Kendra was doing something about, covertly and very much against the laws of the land.

'Well, that's good news, right?' asked Norm Clarke, 'shouldn't we be happy that a bunch of nasty bastards are now off our streets?'

'If only it were that simple, Norm,' replied Rick. 'Personally, I'm delighted that they have vanished, but at the same time I'm pissed off that we can't put them away for twenty years or more. Those upstairs have suddenly become concerned and have ordered us to investigate. How typical is that? One day they order us to stay away on pain of being sacked and the next they want us to investigate!'

'Sarge, if they've disappeared then what is there to investigate? You've already said that they've cleared everything out, including their houses and bank accounts. What do they actually want us to do?' asked Kendra. She was concerned about the direction that this was going, but also relieved that she was here in the middle of it, with knowledge of what was likely to happen.

'Well for one, they want to know where the money has gone, in case we can seize it under the *Proceeds of Crime Act*. And then there are the deaths on the ships of those poor refugees, they're desperate for convictions so that they can show Europe that we are on top of these things. A lot of it is political so we just have to get on with it,' Watts replied.

'Understood,' Kendra replied, thinking ahead as to how she and Andy would deal with this later.

'So, for the next few days, let's put some intel on this board and start searching, people. I'll start the ball rolling with this fella,' Watts added, placing a recently taken picture of Guran Qupi on the magnetic board and then writing *where is Qupi?* underneath.

'Kendra, if you and the intel team focus on all UK ports against Qupi's goons in case we missed any trace of them leaving, that will be a good place to start.'

'No problem, I'll start on that today,' she replied.

'Let's crack on then, team, let's find these people sharpish. Unless there are any other questions, you're dismissed.'

Nobody raised their hand or asked anything, so the team rose from their chairs and left, typically in groups of two or three, discussing the next steps. Kendra held back to speak to Rick privately.

'Sarge is there anything else that we can help with downstairs?' she asked, fishing for more information.

'No, don't worry, K. I have asked for the *Financial Investigations Unit* to help trace the money, but I think it's probably all back in Albania now, paying for large houses and swimming pools.'

'Okay, I'll let you know if anything comes up with the ports. See you later,' she said, turning to leave.

'It's good to have you back here, Kendra, you part-timer,' Watts said as she left, smiling as she raised her arm in farewell.

ACKNOWLEDGEMENTS

Writing this book has been something that I have been wanting to do for a very long time. The idea was always there, it was just a case of finding the time to do it, and that was where the plan always stalled – finding the time.

As a retired police officer, I stayed away from writing stories about crime and criminals, I didn't want to touch the genre until I had retired, and even then, it took a few years before I eventually got to it.

I am fortunate to have successful writer friends who have encouraged and helped me along the way so far. Two, in particular - Andy Briggs and Tony Lee, have been instrumental in this book coming to life. Andy always badgered me into writing a crime story and Tony Lee who has given guidance and time that I will forever be grateful for. I doubt very much that this book would exist at this time had it not been for my good friends.

I also want to acknowledge the equally important encouragement and support that I have had from my partner, Alison, who made sure that I didn't forget to write even a few words each day, and from my daughter Alexia, whose journey into writing is just beginning and who is far more talented than I am.

My thanks go to Editor Linda Nagle for her excellent contributions, I am thankful to have worked with her and look forward to a long working relationship with her.

I must also give extra thanks go to my partner, Alison, for her help with the cover for this book and for her ongoing support.

Before I sign off, I want you to imagine a room full of police officers who are watching the *'An Eye for an Eye'* movie or TV episode, where at the end they all stand and cheer. That is what I wanted for this series, someone to cheer for the good guys, understanding that real life is tough for them on a daily basis. Something different to what you would normally read in a police procedural crime book. Something that is not overly complicated, fast paced, and at times deliberately tongue-in-cheek.

Finally, thank you reader for taking the time to read my book. I hope that you found it as enjoyable to read as it was for me to write. I look forward to feeding you with many more!

TH

———————

You can reach me at: theo@theoharris.co.uk

———————

ABOUT THE AUTHOR

Theo Harris is an emerging author of crime action novels.

He was born in London, raised in London, and became a cop in London.

Having served as a police officer in the Metropolitan Police service for thirty years, he witnessed and experienced the underbelly of a capital city that you are never supposed to see.

Theo was a specialist officer for twenty-seven of the thirty years and went on to work in departments that dealt with very serious crime of all types. His experience, knowledge and connections within the organisation have helped him with his storytelling, with a style of writing that readers can associate with.

Theo has many stories to tell, starting with the '*Summary Justice*' series featuring DC Kendra March, and will follow with many more innovative, interesting, and fast-paced stories for many years to come.

For more information about upcoming books please visit theoharris.co.uk

Printed in Great Britain
by Amazon

41250426R00159